I Know the Feeling

By Kelli Galyean

For all the women who have poured into my life,
in one way or another over all my years, whether
family, friend, church mother, or teacher.
Your faithful love, presence, friendship, and
courage shaped me, and I am grateful for you.
Let's keep going, all the way Home! ♡

CHAPTER 1

Emotions tend to run high in the ER: Shock. Frustration. Fear. Few people get a heads-up when their life is about to change. But I am not usually the one feeling it all—at least, not in the moment. My role is cleaning up the mess, offering calm reassurance, starting the patient's IV. On that chilly November morning, I was busy doing my job, focused on getting through the day. I happened to be on a break when my phone rang.

Did that just happen? I set my phone in my locker a few minutes later and pushed the cold metal door closed. My brain scrambled to make sense of this new development. *What did I just— How am I going to—Stop.* I inhaled a slow, deep breath and counted the ceiling tiles of the break room.

Unfortunately, I didn't have time to process right then. I was only halfway through my twelve-hour shift in the ER, and I needed to focus on my patients. *What was that breathing thing?* Mia said it helped her when she needed to calm down. *Something about a triangle?* I filled my lungs, held my breath, and exhaled. After a couple of times, it did seem to help.

I inhaled again just as Mia popped her head into the room. "Hey, Maddie! How's it going?" Mia glowed, practically incandescent these days. Even the harsh lights of the hospital could not dim the radiance of a woman in love.

Her boyfriend, Ryan, was the worship minister at our church. They'd been dating a few months now, and it would surprise me if he waited much longer to pop the question. In fact, just last week they'd flown to Atlanta for Thanksgiving with Mia's parents. Mia was almost certain Ryan asked her dad for his blessing while they were there, so it could happen any day now. I was thrilled for my friend, but Mia's glow did nothing to lift my spirits.

One look at my face and she stepped fully through the doorway. "Are you okay?"

So much for the power of deep breathing. It all came out in a rush. "I'm not sure. Melissa Fletcher is having blood pressure issues, so the doctor put her on bed rest. The baby is fine so far, thank goodness. But she's not going to be able to direct the Christmas play at church, like we planned." There. That sounded simple enough. No need to panic. But Mia frowned.

The annual children's Christmas play was a beloved tradition at Dallas Christian Church, and this year, the donations we collected would benefit a local youth outreach program. Like many holiday traditions, the Christmas play started small years ago and then slowly took on a life of its own. Melissa was the children's minister at the church, so directing the play was part of her job description. I'd agreed months ago to be the assistant director—a fun, emotional-support role, requiring very little time or energy. Or so I was told.

Melissa burst into tears when she explained about the bedrest orders. I considered crying myself. Bedrest meant Melissa would have to be seated or lying down twenty-three hours of the day, for the next several weeks. There was no way she could communicate with all the parents and volunteers, lead rehearsals, decorate the sanctuary, organize all the costumes and choreography, and actually direct the Christmas play from her bed.

Of course my heart went out to Melissa. Weeks of unplanned bedrest would be overwhelming news for anyone. We'd been planning for the past month, and rehearsals were set to begin the very next day. There wasn't time to find anyone else.

But the timing could not be worse. I'd recently switched to a new department in the hospital, and I was still learning the ropes. I had no business adding another thing to my plate, much less a time-consuming children's play. I'm not saying the concern on Mia's face wasn't merited, but…

"What else could I do?" I demanded, my shoulders bunched up around my ears. "I lied through my teeth, and told her not to worry about anything." I pressed my fingertips to my temples. Was it just me, or had the walls begun to close in on us? Maybe I was being too dramatic. It wouldn't be the first time. I took another breath, trying to calm down.

"So now you're…" Mia's eyes widened as she realized the scope of my new responsibilities. "That's a lot, Maddie, even for you. I mean, how are you going to do all that, and work full time in the ER, *and* sleep and eat?"

When she put it that way, I saw stars. How was I going to do it all? Was there any hope of doing it well? To say I was practically underwater at work was an understatement. Upstairs on the cardiac floor, I'd been a charge nurse in telemetry for years. Down here, I was a novice all over again.

Nursing was a different enchilada in the ER, from the number of patients to the rapid-fire, focused assessment we used to monitor them. Every day held new challenges and pressure. It was exhilarating, but it was also more difficult than I imagined it would be. I continually had to remind myself I'd wanted a change. I had asked for this, knowing it would take time to learn to think like an ER nurse.

Mia had been a huge help to me through the transition, answering my questions, and sharing all her tips with me. All my life, I'd pushed myself to do things perfectly, to *be* perfect. This season of humbling myself and learning had been good for me, but I was still in it.

Knowing my struggles and limits, taking on the month-long task of directing a children's play at church seemed crazy, at best. But it was too late to find someone else. If I didn't do this, there wouldn't be a Christmas play at all. *Lord, are you sure about this?* I prayed. Mia was still looking at me, waiting for a response.

"I guess the show must go on?" I finally answered. I'd been working and studying a ton, trying to catch up as quickly as possible. This would cramp my schedule even more. *Goodbye, Pilates,* I thought dramatically. *Goodbye to watching TV and taking long walks with Kevin. Goodbye to dinner with friends. Goodbye to everything fun until after Christmas Eve.*

Mia wrapped her arms around me and squeezed. "It will be okay." She was right…probably. "I'm so sorry, I have to go," she said. "I've got to get the meds for room six." She smiled, reassuring me, then she ran down the hallway toward the med room.

I needed to check on my patients too. I turned to head that way, but stopped short when I saw a group of EMTs walking down the hall, away from me. A dark head rose up a little taller than the others. His sturdy gait made him unmistakable: my ex-boyfriend, Cade. I sighed. *The meds can wait another thirty seconds,* I reasoned.

Cade and I broke up a few weeks ago. It wasn't a bad break-up or anything. We only dated for a couple of months. But I still felt bad about it. Cade was great—a wonderful Christian man, confident, sensitive, employed, and extremely attractive. We liked the same things, and we got along well. On paper, he checked every box. The problem was that we always ended up talking about work. Only work.

I tried. I really did. I must have asked myself a hundred times, *what is wrong with me?* Cade was the total package. But I'd been single a long time, and there were a lot of perks. At this point, if I gave up all that goodness and freedom for a man, it would be because I absolutely could not help myself. I probably sounded like a lunatic spinster. Or did I sound like a modern, reasonable Elizabeth Bennet?

"Only the deepest love will persuade me into matrimony..."
Same, girl. Same.

Once the coast was clear, I took off running down the hallway. It was probably smart to get some cardio in wherever I could for the next month.

—

The following evening, I stood beside the front pew in the blue-carpeted sanctuary at church. I held a clipboard in my hand, and a whistle hung from my neck. The whistle belonged to my roommate, Emma. She taught second grade and suggested I bring it along. I felt an extra measure of assurance, knowing it was there if I needed it.

Children ran around, chasing each other and laughing, while parents and volunteers cheerfully visited. The noise in the room was deafening but joyful. I tried to smile and ignore the tightening between my shoulder blades. We had a lot to accomplish in a short time, and my conversation with Melissa earlier that afternoon did nothing to ease my mind.

The church leadership had assigned a staff member to help me: Chris Calvert, AKA Youth Guy Chris. I couldn't hold back a sigh when I found out. As if I needed another kid to manage in this circus.

Chris and I got along fine, for the most part. Everyone at the church adored him. He was confident, outgoing, and funny. As the youth minister, he bore his nickname with humor and grace. He was a talented teacher, and made everyone feel welcome. He worked hard to invite the students into a deeper relationship with God. All that was great.

What *wasn't* great was his tendency to lean a little too hard into pranks. Chris was the kind of guy who thought it was hilarious to switch out your ice cream for mayonnaise when you weren't looking or to push people into the pool— fully-clothed. The man could be straight-up obnoxious.

It wasn't only that. Chris had a history of disappointing me. We went out several years ago. It wasn't serious, only two dates. I thought we had a really good time together, but he never called me again. No explanation, just awkward silence. Over time, I moved past it, and we became friends, more or less.

Then, last summer, I adopted my dog, Kevin. I'd never had a dog before, but Chris grew up with dogs and had a ton of experience. So he came over and worked with me, training Kevin in the house and on the leash—we went on lots of walks there for a week or two. I could feel us growing closer. I was pretty excited about it, until that night at Anna's.

I still couldn't understand what brought it about. One minute, I was laughing with my friends under the patio lights. The next, Chris was shouting about Mia and Ryan sitting in a tree in front of everyone at the party. I will never forget the look on Mia's face. She and Ryan weren't even dating yet! All these months later, thinking about it was still mortifying. I invited Chris that night, so I felt responsible. I liked him a lot. But after that, I was done with him.

It was my own fault. How did the saying go? *Fool me once, shame on you. Fool me twice, shame on me.* I shouldn't have gotten my hopes up. We remained friends, but at this point, I only needed one descriptor for Youth Guy Chris: Absurd Manchild. I'd barely spoken to him since the incident at Anna's, and working with him was not my idea of fun.

I rolled my shoulders, trying to loosen the knot of tension between my shoulder blades. My phone buzzed with the latest text message on the group chat with my friends. I reached out as soon as I got the news earlier.

Me: Y'all. Pray for me. My "staff helper" for the Christmas play is YGC. Noooo!

Anna: Please tell me you are joking! Step 1: Pray. Step 2: Guard your car keys with your life. Remember the fish? #absurdmanchild

Sarah: Oh, Maddie. I'm so sorry! Anna is right. Guard your car! I still have color run powder in the creases of my leather seats from that prank a couple years ago. Do you need protective eyewear for this thing? Thoughts and prayers!

Mia: You can do this, Maddie! I never did get to hide that can of tuna fish in his car. If you get the chance to avenge all of us, take it. I'll pray for you right now.

The latest text brought up even more shenanigans.

Emma: YGC? Do not open ANYTHING he gives you, especially if it looks like candy! It's a trap! That poor lizard is probably still running loose somewhere in the movie theater. Yuck! I'll pray. Keep us posted!

I smiled, grateful for everyone's support and commiseration.

Me: Thanks for praying, y'all. Locking my phone down now so the #absurdmanchild can't send embarrassing texts to anyone when I'm not looking. I'll let you know how rehearsal goes. Wish me luck!

I locked my phone and zipped it inside my purse for good measure. Come to think of it, I hadn't seen Chris in weeks; he'd dropped off the radar lately. I looked around the sanctuary, but he wasn't in the crowd. I checked the time. The pattern of disappointment continued: Youth Guy Chris was officially late.

"Strike one," I grumbled under my breath. During our phone call, Melissa told me Chris's niece and nephew had recently begun coming to the church and would be part of the play. Maybe he was delayed because of them. Just when the idea crossed my mind, the sanctuary door swung open, and the man in question entered the room, holding the hand of a little girl. A little boy wearing a Spiderman sweatshirt barreled in ahead of them and charged down the aisle. He came to a stop with a spin, crouching down, hands splayed outward.

"Uh-oh, don't shoot! Keep your webs under control, Spidey." I held up my hands to show him I was unarmed.

He grinned mischievously, blue eyes flashing. Unruly blond curls escaped from the hood of his sweatshirt, and his round cheeks were pink from the cold outside air. Chris sauntered down the aisle toward me. The little girl looked around as they walked, taking it all in. When they came to a stop, she stayed close to Chris, pressing into his leg. She was similar in height to her brother. Her eyes and face bore an almost identical resemblance to his, but her hair hung in tangled golden ringlets around her face, and past her shoulders. Melissa hadn't mentioned they were twins.

Peeking around her uncle, a shy smile lit the girl's face, and I smiled back. Chris looked down at her and her brother.

"Hannah and Noah, this is my friend Miss Maddie. She's in charge of the play."

I crouched down to meet their eyes, and said, "Hi! I'm glad to meet you both."

Hannah peeked bashfully around Chris.

"How old are you, sweet girl?" I asked.

"Four." Hannah held up four fingers.

"Perfect!" I stood and pointed to a woman with blonde hair in the next section of pews. "Do you see your Sunday school teacher, Miss Lizzy over there? You can sit with her. We'll get started soon."

Noah took off, and Hannah followed. Miss Lizzy beamed and welcomed them with high fives. I arched an eyebrow and looked over at Chris. "Cutting it a little close."

He shrugged. "Dinner took longer than I thought it would. But you do *not* want to see those kids hangry."

Fully looking at him, I paused. Nothing major was out of place, but this typically carefree, energetic man looked tired. Really tired. Dark circles tinged the underside of his eyes, and his hair looked a little long, sticking out from under his ever-present baseball cap. For a man like him, this was an alarming sign. Had he been sick?

"Are you okay?" I asked him quietly.

"Yeah, I'm good," he answered with a pleasant smile. "How are you?"

I ignored his question. "Why do you look…" I searched for a nice way to say it, but couldn't find one. Before I could think of the least-offensive word, he finished the sentence for me.

"Devastatingly handsome?" He supplied, pleased with himself. "Thank you, Maddie, I appreciate it. The answer is clean living and good choices. I'd say genetics, but my brothers are pretty average."

I did not have time for his antics. "Please don't be obnoxious. I'm already overwhelmed as it is."

"Sorry to hear that. But this is as ugly as I get. I toned it down just for you." He tilted his head, his grin impossibly cocky and his eyes twinkling.

A mortifying gasp of laughter bubbled up and escaped. *Where did that come from?* I mentally slapped myself. *No. I am in charge.* I needed to keep the upper hand.

All business, I tersely replied, "Focus. We're running behind as it is."

I pulled his folder from my clipboard and shoved it against his chest. He caught it with a comedic *oof,* as if I'd knocked the breath out of him. I heartlessly ignored him.

"This folder has everything you need: rosters, charts, a map of the stage, and a copy of the script," I explained.

Chris nodded his understanding, and opened the folder to look inside.

"There's no time. You'll have to do that later. Come on," I ordered without waiting for a response. He followed me obediently up the steps to the stage. We stood in the center of the stage, waiting for the chaotic noise to cease. Nothing happened. Chris looked at me expectantly. Did he believe I needed his help? *Think again, buster.* I pulled at the string around my neck.

I assumed Emma was joking when she handed me a whistle. But with all the people in the room, it was the perfect way to get everyone's attention at once. I never fantasized about being a coach or a PE teacher, but I could understand the appeal of wielding this kind of power on a daily basis.

Tweep, tweep! I blew a couple of short bursts on the whistle, and everyone turned to face Chris and me onstage. Chris shifted next to me and concealed his laugh behind a cough. My hand itched to smack him, but this wasn't the time. I'd have to deal with him later.

"Thank you, everyone, for being here tonight. Christmas is in four weeks. We will have rehearsals twice a week for the next four weeks, and then the play will take place on Christmas Eve at 2 pm. Tonight, our goal is for everyone to learn their place on the stage. We'll begin with the angels and go from there."

I waited a beat to make sure no one had questions. The teachers all seemed fine, so I walked toward the steps, ready to go work with one of the groups. But Chris had other plans. Just as I hit the first step, he brought his hands together, clapping enthusiastically. The older children caught on and joined in, which inspired the younger ones. And that is how, on our *first night of rehearsal*, I found myself trapped in a standing ovation. I hadn't been the object of one of Chris's pranks in a while, but the feeling hadn't changed: *Ugh.* The clapping died down quickly. I changed direction, moving toward him. Foolishly unafraid, he winked and smiled broadly.

"Why are you like this?" I asked quietly.

"Couldn't help it. You did such a great job with that whistle," he mocked, laughing to himself. I wanted to give him a piece of my mind, but it would only encourage him. It was probably best to get the first prank out of the way, anyway. I made my tone calm and detached when I spoke to him.

"I need you to work with the angels tonight, please." I didn't wait for Chris to acknowledge my instructions. I stepped down from the stage and made my way to the first graders who would be part of the Nativity scene. *Does the mischievous gleam ever leave his eyes?* I wondered, annoyed. It was distracting.

As a nurse, I was qualified to conduct a totally basic, surface assessment, for reference. Scientifically speaking, Chris was a handsome man with a fantastic smile. He had dark hair and brown eyes full of life, laughter, and mischief. Some might say they sparkled. He was tall, with an athletic build. I could offer God no notes for improving the outside of this man.

But words and actions mattered a lot more than all that. Anytime I was around Chris Calvert, I savagely shut down any and all feelings of attraction as soon as possible. It was easy when I focused on his immature antics. *Absurd Manchild. Absurd Manchild. Absurd Manchild.* I repeated it over and over, as many times as it took.

I wrenched my attention back to the facts: The man was obnoxious, but he was who I had been given for help. I needed him to take this seriously. *Lord, please help me get through the next month,* I prayed.

It took a while, but we got all the children in their places on the stage. After that, Chris and the other volunteers worked with the different groups. We had the Nativity scene, the shepherds, the animals, and a choir of angels and stars all doing different things. It was a rowdy cacophony, but somehow, we made progress.

I had to admit Chris made rehearsal fun for everyone. From time to time, a loud burst of singing would erupt from across the room, and all the children would collapse in laughter. That should probably be my job too, but I was so focused on the details and getting everyone organized. I really didn't have the capacity for being silly. Maybe there was a benefit to having him there after all. The idea was a pleasant surprise, but I kept it to myself.

It wasn't all laughter and games—a few tears mixed into the evening. Little Noah cried because he wanted to be a donkey instead of a sheep. Mia had given me a stash of M&Ms for emergencies. A handful of those and a hug soothed Noah's distress, thank goodness. By the end of rehearsal, he happily *bah-ed* up a storm with the other sheep.

Near the end of our second Nativity scene run-through, a scream of pain caught everyone's attention. I rushed over to the shepherds to see what was wrong. The lead shepherd boy had pulled several little girls' hair.

That sort of thing was not something I was going to put up with, so I immediately switched the role to a different five-year-old whose name tag said Carson. I didn't recognize him; his family must have been new to the church. Carson did great. He was focused, obedient, and non-violent.

The night wasn't free of chaos, but before I knew it, we had made it through our first rehearsal. Once it ended, parents milled around, picking up their children. I stood in the middle of everyone, trying to be visible in case any parents had questions.

"Carson, your parents are here." I looked over to his teacher and gasped. Two familiar faces stood waiting for their son. My fingers clenched around my clipboard, and my chest caved in. *Didn't I specifically request to never see either of them again?* I prayed. I wracked my brain, wishing for an eject button or some other way out of this situation, but nothing presented itself.

CHAPTER 2

I listened as Miss Megan, the teacher, introduced herself to Houston and Heidi Rueland. Suddenly, I was twenty years old again, living in a college dorm and laughing my head off with Heidi every day. Memories flashed through my mind of dance parties, working as camp counselors together, shopping, crying over boys, celebrating together the night I got engaged. Heidi was part of it all. Recalling the pain of that loss felt like a punch to the face, quick and bright. I took a deep breath and tried to center myself. I shoved the memories down, and walked toward them.

"We asked Carson to help out with leading the other shepherds," Miss Megan told them, cheerful as an elf. She was all in on the season, wearing a bright-red sweater with shiny Christmas bows adorning her ears. Houston explained they were new to the church, and Megan welcomed them warmly. She let them know the director could answer any questions they had. She gestured toward me. When our eyes met across the pews, Heidi and Houston both looked as stricken as I felt. I took a deep breath and braced myself for the severe awkwardness ahead. *Calm and collected. Professional. I am in charge!*

I closed the distance between us, and Miss Megan, sweetly oblivious to my silent horror, introduced me. "Heidi and Houston Rueland, this is Maddie Reed, the director of the play. Maddie, the Ruelands are new to Dallas Christian.

Carson goes to preschool with the Fletchers' son. Melissa invited them, isn't that fun?"

I pulled my lips into a tight smile. "Hello, welcome," I said. *Be professional and calm, nothing more.* "Thank you for allowing Carson to be part of the Christmas play."

My former best friend stared at me, transfixed, her pale face turning bright red. She hadn't changed much in nine years, though her hair looked different. It was chocolate brown in college, but now highlights brushed through it, adding a softness. She looked at me, her mouth hanging open, unable to form words. A hand bearing diamond rings rested on the belly protruding under her blouse. My heart clenched a little at the sight. Heidi got to have babies. In that other life, I had dreamed of having babies someday.

Don't go there. I mentally slapped myself. Staying present, professional, and peaceful was imperative to getting through the next thirty seconds. Inhaling a calming breath, I looked at my ex-fiancé. His hands rested on Carson's shoulders. Our eyes met briefly before he looked away. It was only a split second, but it was enough for me to see beyond the moment. He looked exhausted. He and Heidi both did.

"Maddie," Houston greeted me stiffly.

Nope. I told you never to speak to me again, and I meant it. Slimeball.

It was all I could think of to say. But I could hear my mother in my head: *If you can't say something nice...* So I said nothing.

I wanted out of there, away from awkwardness, and loss, and dead dreams. Away from both of them. But I had a job to do. *I'm in charge here. Get through this, and get out.* Barely sparing Houston a glance, I looked down at Carson with my most basic nurse smile. "Are you excited to lead the shepherds in the Nativity play, Carson?"

He smiled up at me, oblivious and undeniably precious. He had green eyes, like his mother. A tiny part of my heart thawed, a cutting ache taking the place of the ice. There was a time when I knew eyes identical to those. Heidi and I had a thousand inside jokes between us back then—a simple look from one of us could make the other collapse into giggles. We'd known each other's hearts, kept each other's secrets.

But I didn't really *know her, or I would have recognized the truth of what was going on behind my back for half my engagement, wouldn't I?* I reminded myself. Carson interrupted the bilious bitterness rising up in me and brought me back to the moment.

"Yes, ma'am," he said earnestly. He was a sweet kid, innocent of the storm blowing through my mind. As he should be. I nodded at him.

"Great! I'll see you Thursday."

Another volunteer waved to me from a few pews away, and I rushed to her side, eager to answer her question.

—

The sanctuary slowly emptied. A few stragglers stayed to chat while their kids climbed the pews, but my work was done for the evening. I sat on the front pew, making notes in my notepad. Four little feet came thundering down the aisle, and Hannah and Noah stopped near me. They looked disheveled and tired, but their little faces practically glowed. Their uncle followed close behind, looking wiped out, but happy. I had to hand it to him—Chris always had a smile handy.

I quirked my head toward the twins. "They have their uncle's energy," I observed.

Chris chuckled. "You have no idea."

Overall, the evening had gone well. We hadn't interacted much, but from what I could tell, he'd done a good job wrangling the children.

"Thank you for being here. One rehearsal down, and it could have gone worse," I told him.

He nodded in agreement. "Good call, switching the shepherds. Evan is a sweet kid, but he's a little unpredictable."

A shrill *ha* flew out of my mouth before I could stop it. *The irony!*

"As unpredictable as, say, a grown adult with a penchant for using the *bullhorn* to wake up everyone at camp at the crack of dawn? Or to interrupt a couple's *first kiss* outside a movie theater?" I asked pointedly.

I shouldn't keep a running list of Youth Guy Chris's sins, but bullhorn sins were loud—very loud. I'd personally experienced Chris's bullhorn greetings on more than one occasion. In fact, I happened to be one half of the kissing couple he snuck up on a few years ago. The moment was lovely, until Chris drove by with the bullhorn. Let's just say the second date turned out to be my last with that guy. I didn't blame him; who could recover from such a jarring experience? To this day, I kept a sharp eye out every time I left the movie theater.

Chris looked pained and lifted his hand to his chest. "The bullhorn broke. May it rest in peace." He briefly bowed his head then lifted it with an unrepentant wink. I shook my head, desperately trying to look unaffected. The last thing I needed was for him to get riled up and start messing with me.

The Bullhorn Bandit interrupted my thoughts. "Okay, you two," he looked at the twins. "It's a long drive home, and we've still got to do baths before bed."

"I'm not tired," Noah warned him, looking mutinous.

"I know." Chris sounded resigned. "But I am, and I'm the one you're going to wake up every couple of hours tonight, so *I* have to go to bed." He stretched and yawned. "Let's go."

I turned to look at him, curious if I'd heard correctly. Why would they wake him up in the night? Were their parents out of town? Could this explain why he looked tired? Our eyes held for a moment, but he didn't answer any of my silent questions.

"I'll see you Thursday, Maddie. Good work tonight."

The kids took their sweatshirts from his outstretched hands and pulled them on over their heads before they turned to walk up the aisle and out the door.

Baffled, I turned to gather my own things and head home. Putting on my jacket, I noticed my shoulders had crept up to rest right below my ears, so I forcefully lowered them. Anxiety wouldn't help anything. I turned my mind to the next task: I still needed to figure out some dinner and walk Kevin.

On the way home, I took the long way so I could enjoy the neighborhood Christmas lights and reflect on the evening. Sure, it was chaotic, but we'd accomplished the goal for the first rehearsal, and I felt good about it. So far, Chris seemed competent. Maybe working with him wouldn't be miserable.

The shock of seeing the Ruelands face to face was wearing off. Goodness, how had it already been nine years since all that? I took a breath and let it out. I was glad seeing them had hit me like a snowball and not a knife. The sting of loss had faded over time. Looking back on that time in my life, I hardly recognized the version of Maddie Reed who wanted to marry Houston Rueland. That insecure, striving, anxious girl had been best friends with Heidi.

Not all the memories were bad ones. I could see now how God had been working in all of it. The day before everything blew up, my mom had left me a little note, as she often did. All her notes to me ended with scripture, and that one was no different. Philippians 1:6: *"I am sure of this, that he who started a good work in you will carry it on to completion until the day of Christ Jesus.* " At the time, I didn't realize God was preparing my heart to trust Him when my life fell apart the next day, but He knew.

Losing my fiancé and best friend in one fell swoop was a horrendous grief, and I certainly didn't handle it well. But God was with me. He saw me through. He'd brought healing and more goodness than I could have asked for or imagined. From that day on, Philippians 1:6 was a special verse in my life, one I looked to for encouragement and steadiness on days when I felt wobbly. *We are all works in progress, and nothing is wasted,* I reminded myself now. *He's been doing good work in me, and He will complete it.*

It was true. God had used that situation then, and He would use this one now. I breathed out a laugh as I prayed. *Not the memory I would have chosen to revisit, but okay, Lord. Help me do this. Give me eyes to see you working here.*

CHAPTER 3

It seemed safe to assume Chris was more accustomed to *being* the life of the party than the one organizing and running it, so we met at a diner Thursday morning to discuss the play.

"What are you going to get to eat?" Chris asked, frowning at the menu. "I can't decide."

I made a face. The struggle was real. "I usually get an omelet, but this holiday menu is really tempting. I don't know what to do."

Chris looked at me. "The holiday pancakes feel like a requirement with the vibe in here."

I looked over at the Christmas tree in the corner. The garland had seen better days, and several of the plastic ornaments had bald spots where the glitter had worn off over time. At the top, the star had colorful, blinking lights at every point. I loved it. To complete the holiday motif, "snow" was sprayed across the diner windows, with a few ornament stickers stuck here and there for good measure. To top it off, Christmas carols played over the speakers. I looked at the menu and read through the seasonal specialties. The holiday pancakes would make Buddy the Elf proud. Doused in eggnog syrup then topped with whipped cream and sprinkles, they looked delicious.

"You think a sugary heart attack on a plate is the way to go?" I asked, trying to talk myself into a healthier option.

Chris shrugged. "We could split the difference and go half and half. It would pay homage to the season, satisfy your raging sweet tooth—"

"*My* sweet tooth?"

"*And* we would both get some protein. I'm in if you are." He closed the menu and set it down on the table. He leaned forward, his smile turned up to at least a level eight. I'd bet money that smile had gotten plenty of people to do his bidding. His voice lowered, a cajoling rumble. "Come on, Reed. You're a health professional. It would be irresponsible of you to allow me to eat a whole plate of pancakes on my own."

I widened my eyes at his attempted guilt trip. "Are you kidding me right now?"

He sat back and dared me with his eyes. "I'm getting them either way. Do you want to participate in the joy or not?"

I sighed. I almost couldn't bear to give him the satisfaction. But the festive picture on the menu practically called my name, and going half and half was the perfect solution. If it were Mia or Emma at the table, I wouldn't hesitate. In fact, I would have suggested it myself. So really, it had nothing to do with him. I nodded.

"Fine. I'm in. Are you okay with the veggie omelet?"

Chris nodded his agreement as the server shuffled up to our table.

"What can I get y'all?" he asked.

Chris looked at me, indicating I should go first. I looked at the server. "I'll have the veggie omelet with fruit, please. And could I also have an extra plate?"

The server nodded as he wrote it down, then looked at Chris.

"I'll do the holiday pancakes, thanks."

The server smiled, looking between us. "Going halfsies! It's the right choice." He winked at Chris, and they shared some sort of bro laugh as the guy took our menus. "I'll be back with more coffee and water," he said, then he walked away.

I shook my head at Chris. "I hope we don't live to regret this."

He scoffed, "No chance. This is going to be the best meal of your life."

———

He wasn't wrong. Everything turned out to be scrumptious. The omelet was perfectly cooked, and the pancakes were a fluffy dream. I wasn't usually one to enjoy sprinkles in anything, but the crunch was very pleasant. I was about halfway finished when Chris set his fork down on a cleaned plate.

"Told ya." He settled back in his chair, satisfied, and sipped his coffee.

I nodded and wiped the sticky syrup off my mouth with my napkin. "It's really good."

We spent the next hour going over the entirety of the play, from our roles and assignments to the songs and costumes. In yet another surprise move, Chris took notes and asked intelligent questions. Eventually, I couldn't hold it in anymore. "You are much more organized than I anticipated," I commented.

He looked up from the note he was writing. "You know I run a whole department, right? The youth group has grown quickly, so we hired Amy a couple of months ago. She's a phenomenal minister in her own right, but up until then, it was me, myself, and I keeping track of all the forms and administrative details and teaching and planning and schedules and games and money and actual youth ministry."

"I hadn't considered all that," I admitted. "Maybe I should have given you more credit."

"Please don't. You'll ruin my reputation." He smiled at my extravagant eye roll. "The fun side of things is the side everyone sees. It's real. I can break dance and paintball with the best of them. But I can do all this too, Maddie. It's a well-kept secret, but I'm not *actually* sixteen. I'm thirty."

I wanted to believe I didn't need the reminder—after all, we had known each other for years. But our relationship had some medium highs and low lows. I hadn't given him much choice but to keep things surface-level. Looking him in the eye, I could practically hear my mother's voice telling me not to be ungracious. I shook my head. "Sorry."

"Sorry for being bossy, or sorry for assuming I am incompetent?" he asked, his eyes crinkling with humor.

He wasn't going to give me an inch, was he? I pressed my lips together, suppressing a sigh. "When you put it that way, sorry for all of it."

"I forgive you. Don't let it happen again," he joked. He looked down at the list. "Alright, next order of business: songs." His face lit with excitement. "Is this our once-in-a-lifetime opportunity to add 'Mary Did You Know?' to the play?"

My jaw dropped, my mouth drooping in distaste. Of course an obnoxious man would like an obnoxious song. *Absurd manchild, indeed.*

"Ugh," I replied. "I hate that song."

"Everyone does. That's why it would be the best prank ever!"

Huh? In tandem, we tilted our heads. Chris scowled with disdain. "Mary, did you know? Of course she knew!"

There was a moment of stunned silence, then we both dissolved into laughter.

"I thought you were serious!" I cried, clutching at my chest. I wanted to lay my head down on the table, I was so relieved.

"What makes you think I wasn't?" He smiled. I met his eyes, confused all over again. "Come on, Maddie. We could literally prank the entire church! A record-breaking prank!"

"Absolutely not!" I shook my head. "I can't even imagine it. It's too horrible!"

"At least consider it." Chris lowered his chin and sang softly into his butter knife, his voice silky and deep, like a boy-band solo. "Mary did you know…"

I cracked up, fighting the temptation to join in.

"That your baby boy…"

He sang louder. He pressed a hand to his chest and furrowed his brow, leaning in. I waved my hands, begging him to quiet down. "Oh my gosh. No!" But I couldn't stop laughing.

"Would one day walk on water…"

A couple of people shot annoyed glances our way. I slouched down in my chair, mortified, but unable to stop shaking with laughter. "Chris!" I squeaked.

"Mary di—I can't." He stopped, cracking up at himself.

This ridiculous man. I couldn't stop laughing enough to focus. *Get it together, Maddie.* I heaved a breath and wiped my eyes, ready to get us back on track.

"Okay, now for the real song list." I straightened in my chair.

Chris got himself under control and made a comically focused face, indicating he was ready. I ignored the face as well as I could.

"They have historically walked in singing 'Silent Night,' but I think 'O Holy Night' would be a good song for the Nativity characters to walk onstage," I suggested.

Over the next few minutes, we made good progress, and we agreed on the real song list surprisingly quickly. I explained the last things on my list: the timeline and order of the performance. Chris paid attention and made reasonable suggestions. He offered to wrangle the shepherds himself for the rest of the month.

That was above and beyond. It made my brain itch with curiosity. Don't get me wrong, I appreciated his attitude, but I hadn't expected him to be this…*helpful*. At all. Something was off, but I couldn't put my finger on it.

We wrapped up talking about the play, and still, it bothered me. I wanted to ask, but how? *No.* It was time to gather my papers into my folder and head home. I ought to let it all go and get out of there. But I couldn't stop wondering about him. There had to be an explanation. Finally, I couldn't hold it in any longer. I put the folder down and leaned forward.

"General behavior aside, you seem…different…somehow." I looked into his eyes. "I haven't seen you around much lately. Did something happen?"

He held my gaze for a few seconds. When he realized I was not going to let it go, he released a long breath, looking down at the table. He nodded.

"A lot happened." Leaving it at that, he closed his folder, preparing to leave.

That's it? Without thinking, I put my hand on his wrist. He could have shaken me off and walked away, but he paused. He looked at me and sighed.

"It's complicated," he warned, as if it would make me want to know any less.

"I can handle complicated. If we're going to put in all this work together, I'd like to know whether or not I'm going to be able to count on you."

He scowled, insulted. "Maddie, you can count on me. I will be at every practice. I take my job seriously. You know that."

It was true. I'd crossed a line. "You're right. I was wrong to say that. I'm sorry."

Mollified, he took a breath.

"Since you want to know so bad, I'll tell you. My sister Chelsea is going through a hard time right now. A few months ago, her husband left her and the twins—decided he wanted to be with someone else. She's getting it together, but it was a big shock, for all of us, and she's still getting back on her feet.

"I'm living with her and the kids, to help out while she works the evening shift at Target. She was a teacher before they had Noah and Hannah, so she's trying to get a job, but it's not a typical time for schools to be hiring. It's been tough to find anything."

Wow. He noted the look on my face and read into it.

"I know. I'm not the best candidate. I'm too immature, too *whatever*. But all my other siblings are married and have children of their own. Everyone lives out in East Texas or in Indiana. My mom still works and takes care of my grandmother. I'm the only one close enough and able to help. So, I'm helping."

I wasn't sure how to respond. All this information was so unexpected. And painful. It was totally uncharacteristic of the fun-loving, playful guy I'd known the last several years. I mentally flipped through my limited bank of Chris knowledge. I remembered a story he told at camp a couple of years ago, about his family.

"There are five of you kids, is that right?" I asked.

He nodded.

"And you're the baby of the family?" I remembered, pointing at him.

He nodded again. "The fun surprise baby. Chelsea is the closest to me in age. She's five years older."

I shook my head. "I'm really sorry that happened, Chris. That's horrible. I'm glad Chelsea and the kids have you."

He shrugged. "Well, you know I'm not worth a whole lot. I am typically pretty self-centered and immature, but I'm a work in progress."

I wasn't prepared for self-awareness. Where had that come from? I cocked my head, perplexed. Questions stacked up in my brain. He read my face.

"Come on, Maddie. Don't give me a hard time. I'm trying here," he pleaded. He ran his hands over his face and adjusted his baseball cap. He took a deep breath and let it out. In all these years, I'd never seen him like this.

I held up my hands. "I'm just taking it all in. Sure, I'm wondering who you are and what you've done with the real Chris. But considering I need this helpful, self-aware version of you in order to pull off the Christmas play, I'm all for it."

His eyes widened, and his eyebrows lifted. His mouth moved into a half-smile. "By all means, don't hold back."

I huffed a little laugh and looked him in the eye.

"When have I ever?" I grinned.

It was his turn to roll his eyes. "Fair point."

We'd known each other for years. We may not have been close, but he knew what he was getting when we started this whole thing. I thought I knew too. But suddenly, the old narrative wasn't quite adding up, and I needed more information.

"That's heavy. But it's not the whole story, is it?" I waved a hand, indicating he had the floor. "If you're comfortable telling me, I'd like to know more. I'm ready to listen." I folded my hands nicely and waited.

Chris sighed and sat back in his chair. He spun his water glass, the leftover ice clinking in the bottom.

"It's been a process," he said slowly.

I tilted my head, encouraging him to keep going. He shrugged, pulled the baseball cap off his head, and ran his hand through his hair, making it stand on end. He turned the cap around and put it on backward.

"Don't get too excited; I have a long way to go." He joked softly. "I've been meeting with Ryan Lyles for accountability every week for the last six months. He's encouraged me to grow up, mature a little bit. 'Leave behind selfishness,' as he calls it. I didn't realize it when we started, but it was actually perfect timing for all this. He's been really supportive and helpful. It's all the Lord—His timing,

His provision, all working together. It's been hard, but it's been good in some ways too."

Again, *wow*. I didn't expect any of that. I probably looked like a fish out of water: wide eyes, mouth hanging open in shock. Mia hadn't mentioned Ryan meeting with Chris. It certainly wasn't my business, but I was fascinated by this new information. Once Chris had opened up about his sister, the seal was broken.

CHAPTER 4

"The whole thing with Chelsea has been pretty rough for my whole family," Chris said. "My dad unexpectedly divorced my mom when I was seventeen, so we're all sorta reeling, re-living that, processing, trying to be there for Chelsea and the kids. We're grieving. No one thought Trent would ever do something like this. Dude kinda went crazy."

He paused and cleared his throat. "The most important thing for all of us is for Noah and Hannah to be okay and have the support and stability they need. The good news is they just turned four last month. They're still so little they may not remember it being any different, which is a huge blessing. But they're struggling. Noah, especially, has regressed a little bit. He's clingy, wants to be held a lot, he's waking up at night. And Hannah has gotten in trouble at preschool a little bit for hitting and arguing with other kids."

"Understandable," I pointed out.

Chris nodded. "Definitely. It will get easier as they adjust and heal, but for now, we're trying to meet them where they are."

"That's all you can do. And you're right; they might not remember. I guess you probably remember a lot from your folks' divorce, being seventeen when it happened," I murmured.

He sighed. "Yeah." He didn't elaborate.

My heart ached for teenage Chris as much as it did for sweet Noah and Hannah. I wanted to ask more questions, but he didn't seem to want to talk about it. I would honor his unspoken boundary…for now.

"It's wonderful that they have you. Fun Uncle Chris!" I pumped my fists in the air.

He smiled. "That's kind. Thanks. I do try to be fun for them, but man. Bedtime."

He rubbed his hands over his face then mimed pulling out his hair. I couldn't help but laugh.

"That bad, huh?" I chuckled.

He blew out a breath. "I don't know how they do it. They seem so tired during dinner. But then they get this second wind during bath time, and they ramp up all over again!"

"I can imagine," I told him.

His eyes lit up, and he said, "The baths and the bedtime stories, and one more glass of water…it's all this crazy gauntlet of survival every night. But then they cuddle up and say their little prayers, and they're so sweet. It's like standing outside in a very confusing hurricane of human emotions, every twenty-four hours or so."

I laughed at his description.

"It sounds like a lot, but you seem like you are actually loving it," I observed.

He nodded, a look of surprise on his face. "I do love being with them. They're so fun. I used to think maybe I wasn't cut out for family life—commitment, parenting, all of it. But they will reel you right in with their bedtime stories, and their jammies, and their little voices. They ask the funniest questions. I have ten other nieces and nephews, and I love them all so much, but I never lived with any of them day in and day out. It's been…an experience."

His smile turned pensive. Then his brow furrowed, and his eyes pierced mine.

"I don't understand how anyone could walk away from that. I was seventeen when my dad left my mom. I was pretty much grown, the last kid left at home, just had to graduate. And even then, it was tough. I couldn't process it for *years*. But Noah and Hannah are still little. They need their dad. You know? Anyway, it's been pretty…transformative."

I nodded, at a loss for words. I couldn't understand it either. I couldn't understand a lot of things. I barely stopped myself from reaching across the table to pat his hand. *Careful*, I warned myself. Some levity was in order.

"That's a big word. I didn't realize you had so many layers," I quipped.

He shrugged. "Everybody's an onion, Reed. I've come a long way since the days of the date limit."

I shook my head, lost. "Date limit? What do you mean?"

"Back in my twenties, I had a relationship that ended badly. After that, I set a two-date limit for myself. No matter how much I liked a girl, it was two dates, and that was it."

A rock dropped into my stomach. "A date limit," I repeated.

Chris took off his baseball cap, scratched his forehead, and settled it on his head again and shrugged. "Yeah. It was a way to stay in the game and not get hurt again—or so I thought at the time." He pulled a self-deprecating half-smile. "Basically, it was the height of your favorite character flaw: my immaturity."

His attempt at humor didn't land. I wanted to swipe the disillusioned smile off his face.

"Is that what you did with me when we first met? We went out twice and hit your *date limit,* so you never called me again?" The pitch of my voice changed, and heat crawled up my chest and neck. It had been years, but I was indignant now, on behalf of myself and anyone else who'd experienced the same treatment. Was he going to try to sugar-coat it somehow?

Chris looked at the table, then up at me, his expression regretful. "Yes." Before I could respond, he said, "But I didn't know you cared. You never said anything."

"What should I have said?" I asked, incensed, then shook my head. I held up a hand. "Don't answer that. A date limit…That would have been nice to know about beforehand," I seethed.

Chris took his time, considering what to say. It had been years. I certainly wasn't crying into my pillow over it, but I remembered well enough what it was like to go out and have a great time with him and think there was something there, then silence. I stared at him, the sharp tension straining between us.

Before I could tell him not to bother, he held up his hands, swallowed, and said, "I'm sorry, Maddie. It wasn't fair to you. Or to anyone else."

I expected him to play it off or make a joke. I wasn't prepared for humility. His simple admission and apology deflated my ire. Suddenly, I didn't fully trust myself not to cry. That wasn't anything new. A big shift in emotions was often a guarantee of tears for me, but I fought them off, nodding acknowledgement of his apology.

"Thank you," I murmured.

I looked at him, processing in the silence. The date limit revelation? Emotional sharing, *plus* a sincere apology? I was perplexed. *How did we get here?* I wondered. It was all so out of place for him. Chris read my mind, or at least he noticed my questioning gaze. He looked down and sighed again, as if all this vulnerability was torture. Or…wait. *Was there more?*

"I've also been going to counseling," he admitted.

My jaw dropped, and I sat back in my chair. *Wow.* I was starting to feel like a human pinball. We'd been all over the place emotionally, and now this? I took a breath. Counseling would explain a lot: the awareness, the emotional connection and sharing. He must be serious about making changes.

My brain had been through a serious workout this morning. This conversation was absolutely fascinating. I had things to do, but I could get back on schedule later. I sat quietly, waiting for whatever else he was going to say.

Chris shrugged. "Ryan sees this great counselor named Brooke. He suggested I talk with her about all the changes and all the feelings this whole thing with Chelsea has brought up. I figured it might be helpful, and the timing is good. So I've been going for a few months now."

I sat very still. This was significant. I was extremely aware of how vulnerable he was being with me, having experienced my own seasons of growth. In the past, Chris would have pulled out a rubber chicken or knocked over my water glass to avoid sharing at all. I didn't want him to overdo it and feel like he couldn't share ever again. I swallowed the rest of my questions and stretched in my seat.

"Thank you for sharing with me. I'm humbled you would trust me," I told him.

He shrugged and cracked a smile. "It's only my life's pain, NBD."

There it was: the joke I'd been waiting for. I chuckled, a little relieved to be back to familiar ground. Chris poured a piece of ice into his mouth and loudly crunched it. He set down the cup and rubbed his hands together.

"Okay," he said seriously. "Your turn. What's the deal with that new family from the other night? You obviously know them—and not in a good way."

I made a face. *Ugh.* I'd hoped we could avoid this subject for all eternity.

"You saw that?" I asked slowly, looking down at the table.

Chris gave me a patient half-smile. "You don't have to share if you don't want to."

First, emotional awareness and humility. Now boundaries? *Who are you?* I wondered, again. But telling him was a reasonable idea. If Houston and Heidi were going to stick around, it would probably come out at some point anyway.

"It's not a big deal. Houston and I were engaged years ago, in college. Heidi was my college roommate and my maid of honor. My best friend. But it didn't work out the way I planned…obviously."

Chris looked me in the eye, his eyes growing wide as he absorbed the meaning behind my words. He let out his breath, a low whistle between his teeth.

"That's messed up," he said. He looked like he wanted to punch something. I'd seen the same look in the mirror a few times. I wrinkled my nose.

"Yeah."

"I'm sorry that happened," Chris said. "It sounds like a *very* big deal to me."

I sighed and shook my head. As much as I appreciated his sympathy, thinking about that time in my life was uncomfortable for a lot of reasons. I shrugged.

"It was for the best. Look at them. They have Carson and another on the way. They're probably blissfully happy."

Chris shook his head. "I'm sorry their happiness came at the expense of yours, though. That sucks."

I agreed. "It did suck. It was a tough time." But I wouldn't let it get me down. I straightened my spine and squared my shoulders. "I was a different person back then. I'm good now," I declared stoutly. It felt good to say the truth and believe it. It had been a long road, but I'd come a long way.

"That's very mature. Also, you get to sleep as much as you want. From where I'm standing, that means you win." Chris pointed it out as if the fact was irrefutable.

I laughed. "I hadn't even considered that."

"Sleep is the new revenge, for sure," he intoned sagely. "I'll never take it for granted again."

"You would know," I said, toasting him with my water glass.

He lifted his glass.

"To sleep." He clinked his glass to mine. It was comfortable, talking with him like this and laughing. But I didn't want to get *too* comfortable.

I looked away, searching for something to do with my hands. My folder sat on the table. I opened it, checking for anything else we may have forgotten to discuss.

"I think we're good for now, but I want to be sure we've covered everything."

Chris put his cup down and gestured to the folder. "It's a long to-do list. Are there any to-don'ts?"

I laughed at his joke, but he stared at the list, all seriousness.

"I've got one." He snapped his fingers.

I looked up at him, bewildered. What had I missed?

He looked me in the eye, positively smoldering, then leaned forward and tapped a finger on the page. "*Don't fall in love with me.*"

I sighed and pinched the bridge of my nose. Just when I thought we were getting somewhere.

"How long, oh Lord?" I shook my head dramatically. "I can guarantee that won't be an issue." After everything, it was an easy promise to make.

Chris smiled, his straight white teeth flashing. Those brown eyes sparkled playfully. He leaned forward in his chair. "Speaking of love, how's it going with Mr. Muscles? Are you still dating him?"

I shook my head. "His name is Cade. And no, we broke up a while ago. You're behind on the gossip."

Chris shrugged. "I've been busy. What happened?" He wrinkled his nose, sympathetic. "His muscles weren't big enough?" He momentarily flexed his shoulders and arms.

Against my own will, I huffed a little laugh at his sarcasm. Cade was a beautiful man, both inside and out. "No! Cade is a great guy, and his muscles are perfectly adequate. He just wasn't the right guy for *me.*"

Chris nodded. "Clear as mud. Glad we got that straight." He checked his watch. "I better get going. I have a meeting at the church in fifteen minutes. Do you have everything you need from me?"

I nodded, my brain swirling. The spectrum of topics we'd covered in the course of this single meeting left me dizzy. I wanted to encourage him. I admired what he was doing for his family, but I wasn't sure how he would perceive it if I told him. He may never open up again. I packed my folder into my large bag, and he gathered his things.

Chris held the door for me as we walked past the shabby white Christmas tree and through the garland-lined entrance together into the mild day.

"Thanks for sharing with me today," I told him. At risk of him turning completely annoying in order to deflect from real emotion, I said the words I'd been thinking since he told me the news about his sister. "For what it's worth, I think what you are doing for your family is admirable."

He pressed his lips together and shrugged. "I'm glad I can be there for them. The only way to the other side is through. You know?"

I nodded. "I do. You'll get through it."

He nodded. "Thank you for listening and for encouraging me. I appreciate it."

"There. Was that so hard?" I asked.

He grinned, full of mischief. I couldn't tell if he was about to burst into song in the middle of the parking lot to embarrass me or walk away quietly. For all I knew, he might have an airhorn hidden in his pocket. I needed to get out of there.

"Have a good day!" I waved and turned to walk to my car.

"Thanks, Maddie. You too," he called and opened his door.

CHAPTER 5

Later that evening, the wind whipped around us as we walked through the parking lot. Rehearsal could have gone better.

"Don't beat yourself up! You couldn't have predicted that Evan would start a game of tag!" I told him.

Chris shook his head. "It was a rookie mistake, leaving one of the kids in charge while I went to find a Band-Aid."

"We're both learning, and we got through it. Next time will go better," I assured him.

Families chatted and loaded up their cars all around us. Chelsea had the night off, so she'd already taken the kids home. Chris's car was parked next to mine, so we walked together. Looking around the parking lot, Chris noted, "Huh. Does Houston always watch you walk to your car?"

"What?" I looked around to where he gestured. Houston stood by his car with the door open, watching us curiously. When our eyes met, he looked away, climbing into the driver's seat. He started up the car and drove away.

"Nah. That's nothing to worry about." I brushed it off.

I expected Chris to move toward his car, but he walked with me to the driver's side of my Camry. I paused, looking up at him.

"What's happening?" I asked, bracing for a prank.

Chris shrugged. "Just making sure you get in okay."

I quickly looked for his hands, making sure he wasn't hiding a can of silly string behind his back. He was still Chris Calvert, after all. I caught sight of his empty hands and relaxed.

"Thanks, but Houston isn't creepy or anything. He's not actually a bad guy. He's just a person from my past who is no longer relevant."

Chris stood facing me and nodded. "Sorry. Chelsea met with the lawyer earlier today, and I feel…a little paranoid. This thing is turning me into a man-hater." He scrubbed his hands over his face.

I laughed at his joke, even as my heart squeezed. "Totally understandable. I'm sorry she's dealing with that. It sounds awful."

He nodded. "It really is."

My heart broke for their family all over again. On impulse, I reached up on my tiptoes, wrapped my arms around him, and hugged him. "It's going to be okay," I murmured, my cheek against his.

Chris hesitated only a second, then he wrapped his arms around me. He squeezed me tight and breathed, relaxing a little bit, then he released me.

"Thanks Maddie. I appreciate you." He gently patted my shoulder and stepped back. "Have a good night," he said, then he turned and walked away.

I could feel myself blushing as I got in my car. I hoped he didn't notice. I'd surprised myself with that impulsive hug. Of course it was the right thing to do. Chris would do the same for me or anyone, but I needed to be careful with my heart. Chris Calvert was good-looking. He was smart and fun, and he loved the Lord. He was funny and charming, and now, *finally*, he'd developed some emotional awareness. All of those things were very attractive to me.

But Chris had had his chance—two of them. I didn't want to go backward. Tonight, he needed a friend, and I was happy to encourage him. But that was *it*, full stop. *Absolutely not*, I reiterated to myself. *Guard. Your. Heart, woman!* I pulled out of the parking spot, and headed home.

On the drive, I forced my mind to think about something else. I hadn't counted my blessings lately. I thanked God for my family. My nephew, Henry, made every family function The Best Yet. I thanked Him for great friends. My longtime roommate, Emma, was a blessing and encouragement.

I thanked God every time I treated someone in the ER who arrived alone, with no family or friends to help them. It didn't happen every shift, but often enough to keep my heart grateful. Where would I be without my people? *Thank you, Lord.* While I was at it, I thanked God for my job and how well it was going, especially since transferring to the ER.

I thanked Him for the chance to serve in my church. Which brought me back to the Christmas play. We still had so much to do with rehearsals, decorating, and distributing the costumes for the performance. There was still a ton of work to be done. But in spite of the stress of unexpectedly taking over as director at the last minute, I liked being part of it. I wouldn't have expected the play to be this enjoyable in such a short time.

I had to admit, Chris was a reliable assistant, and we worked well together. He always brought the fun, wherever he went. He'd sang along to "Joy to the World" with the angel choir earlier tonight and made everyone laugh. He'd acted extra silly, dancing and laughing, trying to help the kids to be less self-conscious.

Did I want to quit my job as a nurse and do children's ministry? Definitely not. I loved working in the ER. But shepherds tag aside, we were on the right track, and I was glad I had said yes.

The next day at work was stressful. The cold front had blown in overnight, and the ER was slammed all day long, with people coughing and struggling to breathe. RSV and flu season was going strong. I finally took my lunch break at three in the afternoon.

While I wolfed down my salad, I checked my phone. Chris had texted.

Chris: Hey, I forgot I have the youth group Christmas party this Tuesday. We scheduled it months ago. I'm going to have to miss practice. Sorry.

I texted him back.

Me: No problem. Enjoy!

I put the phone down and took another bite, my thoughts turning to the lack of Oreos in my lunchbox.

The phone buzzed again.

Chris: Thanks! Hoping I get something good in the white elephant exchange.

Me: You never know.

The dots danced on the screen only a few seconds before his reply came through.

Chris: True. Don't let the shepherds race without me.

Smiling, I sent a gif of a person saluting and then collapsing in a heap.

"Well, well, well, what do we have here?" A voice startled me. I looked up and smiled when I saw Mia.

"Hey girl!" I greeted her. "This day is nuts, huh?"

She sighed, grabbing her lunch from the fridge before she came to sit with me.

"Yup. It's like this every year." She dug into her lunchbox and pulled out a sandwich. She moved her head from side to side and asked, "So, who were you texting, looking so happy? Have you met someone?"

I scowled. "Oh geez, nothing like that. I was texting with Youth Guy Chris. He's going to miss rehearsal on Tuesday. Your M&Ms have come in handy a few times. Thank you for being the fairy godmother of snacks!"

Mia winked at me as she finished chewing her bite and took a drink from her water bottle. "I'm glad to help! How is it going so far? You haven't said much."

"It's going really well, for the most part. It's a lot of kids to keep track of all at once. The shepherds are a whole thing."

"Not the kids, silly!" Mia exclaimed. "Working with Chris! How is it?"

I shrugged. "Oh! It's fine."

"Ryan's been meeting with him on Saturday mornings. He seems to think Chris is maturing and growing a lot. It's actually been really encouraging for Ryan too. I wouldn't have expected it necessarily, but I'll take it."

"What do they do when they meet?" I asked, curious.

Mia shook her head. "I'm not totally sure. Ryan is intentional and organized about it, but it's pretty casual. It would have to be for Chris to do it, right?" She smiled. I nodded in agreement.

"They confess their sins and struggles. They hold each other accountable. They pray. They read scripture together, and they read books about walking with God. Of course they do. If there aren't books involved, Ryan's out," she joked.

I laughed. Ryan did love reading more than anyone I'd ever met.

CHAPTER 6

The next week, on Wednesday afternoon, things were a little slower in the ER. It wouldn't last, but I took the opportunity to enjoy a less-frenzied couple of hours. I picked up the chart for my next patient, a pediatric case named Noah Graham.

"Noah Graham?" I called, walking into the waiting room.

A little voice cried, "Miss Maddie!"

I looked over and recognized Chris's niece, Hannah. She sat next to a woman who could only be Chris's sister. Her face looked thin and drawn from stress, but she had a pleasant demeanor. Noah lay curled up in her lap. Briefly stunned, I stared at the picture they made. Hannah bounced in the plastic chair, excited to see me. I shook myself and hurried over.

"Hi, sweet girl!" I greeted Hannah then looked at her mother. "You must be Chelsea! I'm Maddie Reed. I'm directing the Christmas play at Dallas Christian."

Chelsea's face went blank for a second before she smiled, recognition lighting her face. "Hi! It's nice to meet you. I've heard so much about you!"

"It's great to meet you too! Noah and Hannah are really sweet kids!" I gestured to the big doors that led to the hallway of treatment rooms. Here, y'all can come to room five."

Chelsea moved to stand up, and Noah let out a groan. Poor kid. My heart went out to him. I led them back to the room, and Chelsea laid Noah on the bed. He cradled his arm and cried, "Mama!"

"Shh, buddy. I'm not leaving. Let me help sissy, then I'll be right there." Chelsea handed Hannah her phone and got her settled in a chair, then she climbed up next to Noah on the bed.

"What's going on?" I asked, quickly recording Noah's vitals.

"We were at the zoo. I wanted to go do something fun, lift our spirits. I'm trying to take the kids a few times before our membership expires in a couple months." Her voice grew quieter. "Chris told me he shared with you that we have some new circumstances?"

I nodded sympathetically. "I'm so sorry."

"Thank you." She tried to smile, forcing the tears away. "Anyway, Noah and Hannah were playing chase with some kids in the play area," Chelsea explained. "Noah jumped off the playset, and the little girl who was chasing him grabbed his wrist, trying to catch him. He started screaming and holding his arm. I don't know if it's broken or what." Chelsea was trying very hard to stay calm, but her voice wobbled. "I called the pediatrician, but they were about to close. They said to come to the closest ER."

"Mommy? This isn't working!" Hannah said, her voice shrill.

Chelsea looked over, looking weary. "I'll help you in a minute, baby. Can you wait patiently?"

"I'm so sorry it happened," I said.

Chelsea shook her head. "It's okay. We're okay, just a little…flustered." She looked back and forth between her children and took a deep breath, letting it out slowly.

"I'm happy to help. Let me know if there's anything you need. I could bring the kids a popsicle," I suggested.

Chelsea looked surprised. "Yeah, that would be wonderful. Thank you so much!"

"Of course," I replied. "Can I call someone for you? A family member?"

Chelsea shook her head. "I texted my brother. He should be here soon."

I nodded.

"Mommy? *Mommy*!" Hannah demanded.

Chelsea sighed then spoke calmly. "Hannah, bring it here to me."

Hannah got up and shuffled past me. I smiled at Chelsea. I wanted to encourage her.

"From where I'm standing, you're doing great," I said softly. She visibly relaxed.

"Thank you. I appreciate that," she said, her voice still shaky.

I looked at Noah. "Noah, you're in the right place. We'll help you as quickly as we can." I switched my attention to Chelsea. "I'll get him an ice pack while you wait for the doctor."

I closed the door behind me and ran to get an ice pack and two popsicles. When I got back to the room,

Hannah sat on the foot of the little bed, engrossed with a preschool game on the phone. It was sweet to see them all up there together, a little unit.

"Thank you," Chelsea murmured distractedly when I handed her the ice pack. She immediately placed it on Noah's sore arm and got to work opening the popsicle packaging. "I'm so glad you're our nurse. It's wonderful to put a face with the name."

I smiled. "I've really enjoyed working with Noah and Hannah on the Christmas play so far. They're the best sheep and angel we've got!"

Chelsea beamed. "Thank you! We only started coming to Dallas Christian recently—after everything. I couldn't face..." She paused, wilting a little bit, then shook her head. "Anyway, we've only been going a couple of months, so I haven't met many people yet."

She was about to say more, when the door opened, and Chris swept in.

"Uncle Chris is here!" Hannah announced happily.

"Hey, girl!" He ruffled her hair then looked between Chelsea, Noah, and me. "Hi," he finally settled on a collective greeting. "What happened?" he asked Chelsea. She handed Hannah her popsicle then told him the whole story.

Chris held out his fist and gently bumped Noah's knuckles, his face full of sympathy. Then he turned to look at me. "I thought you worked upstairs."

I nodded. "I used to. I transferred down here in September."

It was clear he had more questions, but now wasn't the time. He accepted my answer with a nod. "Thanks for being here," he said sincerely.

I shrugged. "It was kind of a coincidence, but a happy one for me." I smiled at Chelsea. "The doctor should be in soon," I told them and stepped out, almost colliding with the doctor. While she examined Noah, I checked on my other patients. A little later, the doctor opened the door to Noah's room and flagged me down. I walked in and saw that now Chris sat on the bed next to Noah. Chelsea and Hannah were gone.

"Noah here has nursemaid's elbow, and we need to reduce it. Should only take a second," the doctor told me. "I need you to assist."

I nodded and moved over to the bed. I looked at Chris. "Where's Chelsea?"

"She had to take Hannah to the bathroom. Perfect timing, huh?" he asked humorlessly. He looked a little unsure.

I waited for him to look me in the eye. "Are you okay to do this?"

He nodded. "I can do whatever."

"Just hold him in your lap. It'll be fine," I said.

"Is it going to hurt?" Noah asked tearfully.

I shook my head and winked as I stepped toward him. "We'll be quick, buddy, I promise. Would you like another popsicle?"

"No!" he yelled and flailed, trying to get away. The movement hurt his arm, and he started to cry again. My heart sank. I hated this part.

The doctor nodded. "Let's do this," she muttered.

I looked at Chris. "Hold him still. I'll hold his feet."

Chris wrapped his arms around Noah's torso and held him against him while I moved in and held his kicking feet. It wasn't easy; Noah was strong. At one point, Noah's head connected with Chris's jaw with a crack, but Chris didn't let him go. The doctor carefully extended Noah's injured arm. The joint moved back into place with a *pop*. Noah quieted almost immediately, and the adults breathed a sigh of relief.

I looked over at Chris. "Are you okay?"

He nodded, suspiciously green. Holding a kid down for a procedure was never easy. On top of that, the sound of a joint popping back into place was a guaranteed vomit-inducer for plenty of people. I reached over and pulled an emesis bag from the dispenser and pushed it into Chris's hand.

"Just in case."

The door opened, and Hannah came in, hopping like a bunny rabbit, with Chelsea walking behind her. "We're all done, Mom," I said cheerfully.

Chelsea's eyes widened, and she stepped toward the gurney, reaching for Noah. "Oh! Wow, y'all were fast! I'm sorry I wasn't here to help."

I shook my head. "No worries. Everyone did great," I assured her. Noah curled into his mother's embrace, and

Chris stood. His face was still a little green, his forehead slick with sweat. Chelsea took one look at him and blanched.

"I'll get your discharge paperwork," I told her and hurried out.

When I returned, we discussed the discharge instructions, and I answered Chelsea's questions. Chris gathered the kids' jackets and helped Hannah into hers as Chelsea stood, holding Noah. She wrapped her free arm around me in a hug.

"Thank you for everything," she murmured. "I really appreciate you being so kind to us."

I hugged her back. "Of course! I hope we see each other again soon—hopefully under happy circumstances!"

Chelsea released me and stood back, smiling. "Would you want to meet up for coffee sometime?"

I nodded. "Sure!" I gave Chelsea my number, and she promised to text me soon. With that, the Graham family and Chris walked out of the ER.

A few minutes after they left, my last patient checked out, and I was able to leave a little early. I grabbed my bag and headed out. Hurrying toward the staff parking lot, someone called my name.

"Maddie!" I looked over. Chris waved from several yards away. "Hey!"

I blinked. "Hi! What are you still doing here?"

"Chelsea couldn't remember where she parked. It took forever to find it. Now I'm coming back for my car." He smiled.

I laughed. "It could happen to anybody. The parking garage is *huge*."

"Yeah, especially after all that," he said.

"It was good of you to come help," I told him.

Before he could respond, my stomach released an aggressive goblin growl. Chris's eyebrows went up.

"Hungry?" He smiled.

I huffed a self-conscious laugh. "Sorry. It's been a long day. I'm starving."

"Me too. You want to get some food?" Chris asked.

"Don't you need to get back and help Chelsea?" I asked, surprised he would even consider it.

He shook his head. "She told me to take some time and go get some food. Chelsea hates barf. I think it scared her when I turned a little green. She doesn't need to deal with that on top of everything else."

I considered it. Emma was out tonight. I'd planned to go home and eat a bowl of cereal before collapsing in bed. But some real dinner actually sounded delicious. And Chris was no longer green. "In that case, sure. There's a good burger place nearby."

"Works for me," he said. "I'm parked right there. Want to ride with me, and I can bring you back?"

"Sure," I agreed. We turned to walk side by side to his car. He opened the door for me, and I sat down in the passenger seat. I looked around. It was relatively tidy, but there was evidence of Noah and Hannah. Two booster seats filled the entirety of the back seat with kid-sized water bottles in the cup holders. He opened the driver's side door and got in.

"I like the 'domestic vibe' you've got going on in here," I joked.

He smiled self-deprecatingly and shook his head. "The kids have taken over. I'm sorry if anything is sticky."

"Ew!"

We laughed. Chris shook his head, and held up his hands.

"It is what it is at this point. My dad used to say, if you can't get out of it, get into it. Here I am, definitely in it," he said.

Chris started the car. A radio version of "Rocking Around the Christmas Tree" played softly on the radio. "Okay, where am I going?" he asked.

CHAPTER 7

I directed him to the burger place nearby. We walked inside a few minutes later, past a garishly decorated Christmas tree standing beside the door. Colorful garland glittered along the tops of the walls, the occasional ornament hanging from the center of the unevenly draped loops. Here and there, hospital workers sat in booths, fresh off a shift, like me. I waved at a couple of familiar faces on the way to the booth in the corner. We sat down on the red vinyl benches and looked over the laminated menus.

A middle-aged woman walked up to our table. Small Santa hats dangled from her ears, a tribute to the season. She put napkins and straws on our table. "Welcome, you two. What can I get you to drink?"

"Water for me, thanks," I said.

"Coke," Chris answered.

"Be right back," she said and bustled away.

"Caffeine this late? How will you sleep?" I asked, sounding every bit like the tired woman I was.

Chris waved it off and whistled at the wide-ranging menu. "They've got a variety. What do you like here?"

"I get the goat cheese burger every time," I admitted. "But everyone I work with likes everything here. The vegan burger has even earned Sarah's approval."

Chris nodded. "Awesome. You want to split some fries?"

"Sure," I answered. "It's a huge portion."

"I spend all my time with teenagers, so I eat like a teenager pretty often, but I can't eat as much as they do anymore. I'm getting old," he groaned.

"You look pretty healthy to me," I said, looking him over without thinking.

Chris's eyes lit with mirth. "Was that a *compliment*?"

Instant regret. I closed my eyes and rubbed my temples, trying not to blush. "You have been amazing today. Don't ruin it by being conceited."

"Hey, you said it. I'm just the one receiving your health affirmation. Thank you." He patted his chest. His eyes shone with laughter. He was so ridiculous sometimes. *But he does have the best smile,* I thought accidentally, for the hundredth time. I mentally smacked myself. *Focus!*

"You're welcome, I guess...bro," I deadpanned, shaking my head.

Chris snorted a laugh as the server showed up with our drinks.

"Alright, hon, what can I get you?" She looked at me expectantly.

"I'll have the goat cheese burger with everything, medium well," I told her.

"And you, darlin'?" She turned to Chris.

"The bacon cheeseburger, no onions, and can we split an order of fries too?"

She nodded. "Sure thing."

We thanked her as she walked away.

"So, is it safe to say you're recovered from your adventurous afternoon?" I asked.

He nodded. "Yeah, I'm good."

I saw clergy and ministry staff at the hospital from time to time, but it wasn't consistent. "Do you have to come to the hospital for ministry stuff a lot?" I asked.

Chris shrugged. "I don't spend a ton of time in the ER, but I'm not totally new to it either. Since we're a small staff, we split up the ministry needs. When someone calls, if it's my turn, I go. Youth group kids don't go to the hospital often, but when they do, it's usually sports-related. I try to get there every time, if possible. Of course we've had a couple of kids need stitches when a youth group game got out of hand, but it's rare, thank goodness." He smiled self-deprecatingly.

"Today was different, then?" I asked.

Chris nodded. "I've gone for family before, growing up. But this was the first time I've had to be the adult in the room for one of them. And I've never had to hold a kid down for a procedure before. That part was terrible." He swallowed. "It really helped to have you there. Thank you for the barf bag."

I had to give him credit where it was due. "You did well."

He stretched. "Yeah. 'Cause you were the perfect amount of bossy."

I sat back, feigning offense. Chris didn't back down.

"The *perfect* amount. We make a good team." His eyes sparkled with mischief.

I straightened my shoulders, owning it. "Bossing people around: it's what I do best."

"We all have our gifts, Reed."

I sat there for a second, allowing clarity to set in. For a while now, I'd told myself it didn't matter how charming and fun Chris was; emotional connection wasn't his strong suit. But every week lately, it seemed there was more to Chris Calvert. I couldn't deny it anymore: Chris showed up. He wasn't *acting* selfless and kind. He actually *was* selfless and kind. For months—no, *years*—I'd reduced this man to the sum of my assumptions. Who was I to judge him? Maybe I had some growing of my own to do.

"Chris, I owe you an apology. I haven't been fair to you. You are not who I told myself you were. I was wrong. I'm sorry."

He blinked. "Thanks, Maddie. You don't owe me an apology, though. I've acted like an idiot. A lot."

I fought a smile. "Well, you weren't an idiot this afternoon…or even lately. You've been great, and I appreciate you."

He grinned. "The appreciation is mutual. Three cheers for personal growth!"

I laughed and raised my glass of water. "To sanctification!"

"Amen." Chris clinked his drink to mine and sipped. He set his glass down and met my eyes. "So, tell me about transferring to the ER. Where did you work before?"

"I was in telemetry, on the cardiac floor. It was intense in its own way. Lots of patients, constant, detailed surveillance of their systems and issues, answering calls, cleaning up, wound care, meds. I enjoyed it, but after a few years, I was bored. I didn't want to lose my edge, and I really want to keep loving my job. So, I switched things up."

"Switching to the ER sounds complicated."

I nodded. "It is." He waited to hear more.

I took a sip of my water before I explained. "It has been harder than I thought. There's a lot to learn. Mia has been a god send! I'm good at my job, but everything feels really new.

"The ER requires a different type of surveillance. You have to be able to look for cues and really read people, like a rapid-fire assessment, while you are constantly in motion. Things can change on a dime. It's different from everything we did in telemetry, where you have more time, and you can depend on all the monitors to tell you what the patient's body is doing. Then there's the emotional part. Everyone is escalated in the ER, and I have to really keep my cool. I was a charge nurse upstairs, and this is basically like starting back at square one."

"Cool. I can see how now would be a good time to head up the Christmas play," he teased.

I smiled and shrugged my shoulders. "It's all working out. I have a lot of help." Then I changed the subject. "So how's your week going, other than today?" I asked.

"It's going pretty well. Work is busy but good." He nodded at me. As far as the Christmas play was concerned, it was true. We had come a long way, and we still had a long way to go.

"I know where you'll be on Christmas Eve. What are you doing for Christmas Day?" I asked.

"We're all planning to drive out to my mom's that morning and have Christmas all together. Then the next day the kids will see Trent for the first time since he left in September."

I frowned, surprised. "That's a long time to go without seeing his kids. Why *then*?"

"Trent's family lives nearby, in Tyler. His *parents* want to spend time with the kids," Chris said, incredibly somber.

My heart broke a little bit. "That sucks." I couldn't think of anything else to say.

Chris nodded in agreement. "It really does. But Chelsea is strong. Stronger than she ever thought. I'm really proud of her."

I nodded, still trying to wrap my mind around the situation. Chris went on.

"She got a job at a school, starting in January. She's going to teach second grade." His face perked up as he shared, and his shoulders relaxed.

"I'm so happy for her!" I exclaimed, relieved that something was going right for Chelsea.

"Yeah," he agreed, then he changed the subject. "What about you? What are you doing for Christmas?"

I grimaced, thinking about the answer to his question. "You know what I'm doing on Christmas Eve. Then I'm working seven to seven on Christmas Day."

He sucked in a breath. "No!"

I nodded. "Yeah. It's my year. At least I was able to be off for the Christmas play on Christmas Eve!"

His eyes widened. "Very true."

"You don't want to run the show on your own?" I smiled sweetly, fishing for a compliment of my own. Chris read my face and huffed a laugh. He leaned forward as he gave an exaggerated nod, playing along.

"It would be a disaster without you," he admitted, indulging me. "Is that what you want to hear?"

My cheeks heated at his kind words, but I couldn't take *all* the credit.

"It takes both of us," I offered magnanimously. I held up my plastic water glass, toasting him again. "To partnership." He raised his own glass to meet mine with a *clunk*.

He tilted his head and smirked. "You're something special, Reed."

My heart fizzed a little bit, but I shut it down. *Nope!* I mercilessly steadied myself, ignoring his comment. The food came right then, and we dug in.

I took a big bite of my burger and moaned. The buttery bun was toasted just right, and the tangy goat cheese melted to creamy perfection, a glorious pairing with the meat. The tomato added a freshness, so the burger wasn't too rich. It was so good. I opened my eyes and noticed Chris.

His eyes crinkled, his smile hidden behind his burger. I sheepishly slunk down in my seat.

"Don't hold back on my account. I'm glad you're enjoying your food," he said, reading my mind.

I swallowed and wiped my mouth with my napkin. I shook my head.

"Sorry. I'm starving!"

In response, Chris took his own huge bite and moaned theatrically.

"Ish rea-yee goo," he said with his mouth full.

I couldn't help but laugh. My self-consciousness evaporated, and we both ate our fill in mostly reasonable bites.

I had put away half my burger when Chris wiped his mouth with his napkin and settled back into his seat. His burger was gone. He picked a fry from the overflowing basket and dipped it in ketchup.

"Okay. That was delicious. These fries are perfect too."

I grinned in agreement and nodded. "Yeah, this place is pretty popular with everyone at the hospital. Sometimes the hospital cafeteria is already closed, or you forgot your lunch, and they always come through."

"Are burgers your favorite food?" Chris asked.

I shook my head. "Breakfast, hands down," I declared.

"Ooh, you're speaking my language. Savory or sweet?" he asked.

"Savory. I can't turn down a good skillet or an omelet. But I am still thinking about those pancakes from a couple of weeks ago. What about you?"

He thought about it for a second. "I pretty much love it all. But I probably order pancakes the most. I'm terrible at making pancakes myself."

I sat back. This man was full of surprises. "You cook?"

He shrugged. "Sure. But not pancakes. I destroy them every time. My family won't even let me try anymore. It's pathetic."

Huh. I could boil water for macaroni and cheese, and that was about it.

"So what's your specialty?" Being from East Texas, I expected him to say steak or smoked brisket.

"I make a mean lettuce wrap," he admitted. He read my face and explained. "I'm partial to Asian food."

"Wow, I didn't see that coming from an East Texas boy," I admitted.

"Did you think I'd say smoked brisket?" he asked.

I shrugged. "That or steak."

"Fair guesses." He nodded. "Very typical of my people. But no. I moved out here after college. Once I discovered noodles and sushi and Korean barbecue, I was a goner."

I nodded, appreciating this unexpected side of him.

"What brought you to Dallas?" I asked. I couldn't remember.

"I moved for work," he said. "I was a junior financial analyst for a company downtown. I transferred from Austin. It was boring. You went to SMU, right? Have you always lived in Dallas?" he asked, changing the subject.

I nodded. "I grew up in the 'burbs and then stayed around for college. Then I stayed around for adulthood. Kind of a homebody, I guess."

He smiled. "I planned to go back to East Texas after college. But the Lord had a different path. Some of the youth group kids have been looking at SMU. It's nice. It's close to home. The kids are all talking about rushing. I don't understand all the ins and outs of it. I never did any of that at SFA. I was too busy with baseball and classes. Did you rush?"

I shook my head. "No. I focused on my school work, and I didn't really have the mental space for that kind of pressure. I was hanging on by a thread as it was."

He nodded. "Seriously. It's so crazy what they put those kids through. Kids are under too much pressure already." He ticked items off on his fingers. "School. Sports. Community service hours. Work. Church. Friends. What adult do you know who could do all that perfectly? We had a girl collapse at youth group a few weeks ago. She's been throwing up, starving herself. She needed one thing she could control." He shook his head, gutted, and closed his eyes. "It's so frustrating."

"Oh gosh, that's really tough," I said, my heart squeezing with empathy.

He shook his head. "Sorry. I get worked up about this stuff. Luckily, the parents are supportive and present. They're getting her help, so that's good."

"It's *really* good," I interjected. "Treatment is highly effective. The sooner the better."

"Well, she's getting it, and I'm glad. I guess you have patients suffering from eating disorders in the ER all the time?" he asked.

I nodded. "We do from time to time. There's an outpatient clinic nearby that's helped a lot of people, including me."

He blinked and sat up straighter. "You?"

I nodded. "I had an eating disorder in college."

He blanched. "I'm so sorry, Maddie. I didn't mean to bring up something painful for you."

I shook my head. "It's okay. You're right about the pressure of expectations. In high school and college, my parents had *very* high expectations for me. My dad is in academia; he works at SMU. It wasn't just them. I wanted to be perfect so badly. I worked really hard. I achieved everything they wanted me to do, but I had terrible anxiety, and I never told anyone. In college, I finally found this way to feel more in control, and I took it. It wasn't consistent, but it was part of my life during that time. I started treatment in the summer between undergrad and nursing school. I've been recovered for about six years now."

The compassion in his eyes made my nose tingle, but I refused to cry. I'd come too far.

"That's really hard," he said.

I nodded. "Yeah, it was. It was hard for my parents too. I'd hidden so much from them. They thought they were just pushing me, helping me to do my best. But I'd gone too far. Trying to be perfect had become a destructive thing for me. Anyway, after I told them, they were super supportive. They got me into treatment, and then we *all* did therapy."

"That's really brave," he said, looking impressed. "I wish more parents would go to therapy and handle their stuff."

I nodded my agreement. "It helped a lot."

We fell into silence. Heat crept up my neck as embarrassment settled in. I scolded myself for oversharing. *Why did I tell him all that? It wasn't his business.* But it was too late now. I waited for him to make a joke, but he didn't.

"Thank you for sharing with me. I'm sorry that happened." He paused, thinking. "Hang on. Was that the summer you were going to get married?"

I nodded, a little thrown. "Wow, you paid better attention than I thought. Yes. All the wedding stress made it a lot worse. That was the smallest I ever was. Then everything happened with Heidi and Houston…I was so angry after I found them together. I'd done everything I could to control myself, to be *perfect*. And what did I get? That. So instead of going on my honeymoon, I went to an outpatient clinic. Ha ha," I said sardonically.

Chris shook his head. "I'm not laughing. Is it still a struggle for you?"

I took some time to consider it before I answered. "Not usually. In seasons of stress, I might feel it a little bit, that itch for control. But those scenarios are why treatment is so important. It was really effective for me. Luckily, my case never got severe. My organs hadn't shut down or anything like that. It can do a lot of damage without treatment, so I'm thankful I got help when I did.

"And now I don't have to carry it alone. I can ask for help. My family and friends know about it. They're supportive. And honestly, growing in the Lord has helped a lot, trusting Him with the future. Trusting in His grace, that He was perfect on my behalf. I've been in a good place for a while now."

He nodded. "I'm glad. And I'm here for you too, if you ever need me."

Tears pricked my eyes at his unexpected, simple empathy. He could have said a hundred wrong things, and I wouldn't think twice. Instead, he'd seen and cared for me. I took a deep breath, trying to keep my emotions under control.

"Thank you. I appreciate you saying that. I don't really think about it much anymore. It's not a big deal."

He got a look on his face, his eyes wide, chin down. "You keep saying that, minimizing things you've been through. It's okay to struggle, Maddie. I mean, I'm glad you're doing well. I know you're strong. But it's okay to be a human being."

It was Chris's version of reassurance, and I appreciated it, but I didn't know what to say. Silence stretched as I tried to regroup.

He turned his baseball cap around on his head. "Like I said, it's been a big deal in my world lately. Amy has been a godsend in the youth group. The girls are more comfortable talking with her, and she is fantastic with them. But I'm protective of them. I've learned a lot over the years, but there's always more." He caught himself and sighed. "Sorry. I didn't mean to get preachy."

"I understand." I left it at that and sat back. I appreciated that he cared so much.

He made a face. "Sometimes I can be a little overbearing. At least that's what Ryan and Brooke have told me. I'm working on it."

I held back a snort of laughter. I was tempted to jokingly say, *that's putting it mildly.* But I didn't. I could tell the moment had become a little vulnerable for him too. I decided to ask him something I'd been wondering about.

"Speaking of Ryan, when you and Ryan meet together, what does it look like? What do you do?"

He nodded and chewed another fry. Once he swallowed, he wiped his mouth with a napkin.

"It's basically discipleship. We pray, we study scripture and memorize passages. We hold each other accountable, make sure we're doing our quiet times. We confess our sins, encourage each other."

"Wow," I said. "That sounds like a lot of work."

He shrugged. "It takes discipline, but it's worth it."

"You confess your sins to each other? Isn't that incredibly uncomfortable? I thought men hated vulnerability." And not only men; I really couldn't imagine doing that with anyone.

He barked a laugh. "It took a while, believe me. But it was important to Ryan to create that kind of safe relationship. We worked up to it, and even now, he always goes first. I've never had a chance to walk closely with other men like this. We read books too. That's the easy part. We just finished a book called *Humility*, by this Puritan guy named Andrew Murray. The language is a little dense, but it was really good."

I stared. Once again, the mold I'd constructed around Chris no longer fit. On one hand, I'd never met anyone with as wide an imagination for pranks as Chris Calvert. On the other hand, he was serious about this. Did I believe everyone could benefit from practicing discipleship in community? Absolutely. It sounded great. But it didn't seem realistic. There had to be more to the story.

"So Ryan invited you to do this, out of the blue?" I asked.

"Yeah. He brought it up at camp last summer, told me he'd read about it in a book, and we had our first meeting the following week. He caught me in a weak moment, I guess," he joked. "It's been great though. Ryan has become a really close friend. Kind of a mentor. I feel like I've grown a lot. And now Gage Jones is meeting with us too."

"Wow. How long does all this take?"

"We meet for two hours every Saturday morning," he said. I stared in disbelief.

"Don't be too impressed. We started slow, and we've built in more over time." Chris fiddled with his straw wrapper as he spoke. "I'm always asking the kids to hold each other accountable, to build community together outside of church. If I want them to take me seriously, it's important that I'm living it myself. You know?"

I nodded, hanging on every word as he explained further.

"I'm not only trying to encourage them to make good choices. I want them to really love Jesus and have a strong, growing faith of their own in community with each other. Everyone starts somewhere; why not here?"

"That's a tall order." I raised my eyebrows, still wrapping my mind around it.

He nodded in agreement. "It is. But discipleship is something everyone can do and grow in. I've had to learn discipline. It's not always easy, but it's been really helpful for me. And hopefully, modeling it will make a difference for them too, and they'll see that we can put in effort to do the work, and it's worth it."

He was so passionate. I sat quiet, trying to take it all in, and soaking up the encouragement. Women's Bible study had some similar practices, and this reminded me how much I missed it.

The server approached our table. "Anything else for y'all tonight?"

I shook my head. "May I have a box, please?"

"Sure thing, hon. What about you, darlin'? Can I bring you a slice of apple pie? We make it in-house."

Chris shook his head. "Next time, for sure. We'll have the check for now, please."

"You've got it." She picked up his empty plate and bustled away.

I reached into my purse. "Here, I bet we can split it."

He agreed and pulled out his wallet.

We paid and then headed to the door.

"Remind me, what time do you want me at the church to decorate on the twenty-third?" Chris asked on the way to the car.

I wrinkled my nose. "Is nine a.m. too early?"

He scoffed. "Nine is nothin'. The twins are up by six-thirty, no matter what."

"Great! Then you'll have plenty of time to pick up breakfast for the volunteers on your way?"

I meant it as a joke, but he nodded. "Sure."

As we got in the car, I considered his willingness to go above and beyond. Breakfast was a simple thing, but it made me wonder. Had this servant-hearted side of Chris always existed, or was it new? I didn't have time to formulate a question before we arrived back at the hospital.

"Okay, where are you parked?" Chris asked, squinting out at the parking lot. The lights cast an orangey glow, illuminating the cars.

"You can drop me off at the staff lot entrance. You can't get in there," I told him.

"Will you be safe walking to your car in the dark?" he asked.

"Should be. It's pretty well-lit, and there are usually people around," I assured him.

He nodded. "Okay. I can wait if you want me to."

"That's really sweet, Chris, thanks. But I'll be fine."

I gathered my purse in my hand, and opened the door once the car stopped. "Thanks for the ride!" I said, climbing out. "Give everybody a hug for me."

He nodded. "I will. See you tomorrow," he said, then I shut the door.

I walked to my car, feeling light and pleasantly surprised. It had been a long time since I felt remotely interested in being real friends with Youth Guy Chris.

CHAPTER 8

On Thursday, I was off work, and I had a lot to do. I hurried through the grocery store, my list spinning through my mind. The candy aisle caught my attention. Everyone had worked hard, but they were extra wiggly as Christmas Eve approached. A little candy incentive wouldn't hurt. I picked up a couple of bags and dropped them into my cart.

I stopped by to check in with the printers to make sure they were on track for me to pick up the programs the following day. Once that was done, I headed to the church building. My goal was to get all sixty costumes ready to distribute that evening, and it was going to take a while. A growing pile of props and costume pieces had slowly taken over the back of my car over the last month. It was time to put it all together.

I loaded up all the bags and bundles, carefully balancing the load in my arms as I lugged it to the church office door. My hands were full, so I turned and used my elbow to press the intercom button. A friendly voice greeted me through the weathered speaker, so loud it made me jump. The load in my arms swayed, and I fought for balance.

"Hello?" It was Ms. Rosemary, the spry, sassy church receptionist. Ms. Rosemary was in her late seventies and was equally beloved and feared by everyone at Dallas Christian. She and her best friend, the straight-laced Ms. Alma, headed up a group of older ladies at the church for service projects, get-togethers, and vacations. They called themselves The Merry Widows.

"Hi, Ms. Rosemary. It's Maddie Reed. I'm directing the Christmas play? I've brought so—"

She cut me off, and the crackly speaker blasted for all its worth. "Oh yes! Come right in, dear!"

Something buzzed loud enough to shake the whole building, and I lunged to grab the handle, causing the load to teeter again. I righted myself and observed the doorway. This wasn't going to work. Maybe I should have made two trips. It was too late now. I hoped no one was looking and turned sideways to fit through the doorway. Shuffling like a crab, I moved awkwardly, facing the wall. Something hit the ground beside me with a dull *thud*. Once I was fully inside, I slowly turned and came face to face with Ms. Rosemary, sitting at a large desk. She wasn't alone.

Chris stood next to Ms. Rosemary's desk with the other youth minister, Amy, and his sister, Chelsea. All four of them gaped at the spectacle I made, draped in different fabrics, with shepherd staffs and plastic crowns jutting out from the large bags hanging off my arms. *I should have made two trips*, I admitted to myself. A blinking light on the floor caught my eye. The item that had fallen was Ms. Rosemary's desktop Christmas tree.

"Oh!" I gasped. "I'm so sorry!" I moved to pick it up, and the overflowing bag of wise man props shifted precariously again. I froze. If I bent another degree, everything on my left side would fall, crashing to the ground. I moved slowly back into a balanced position, my face burning with self-consciousness.

I looked up, my eyes landing on Chris first. He pressed his lips together, enjoying this. I could read him well enough to know he was wishing for a camera. But Chelsea's eyes looked like saucers, taking it all in.

I must have looked extra ridiculous. Was I interrupting something important? My face heated. But I didn't have time to wallow in embarrassment. I had a job to do. I straightened my shoulders, lifted my chin the way my mother always did at dinner parties, and made eye contact with Ms. Rosemary. Before I could get a word out, she turned to Chris.

"Don't just stand there. Help this young lady!" she barked.

Chris jumped and scurried over to help me. First, he put the small tree back on Ms. Rosemary's desk, then he turned to help me. He studied the situation for a second then reached out his hands but changed his mind. He stood staring, perturbed and unsure what to try to grab. I sighed and wiggled my left arm. He nodded, and one by one, he pulled the five bags off my arm and set them on the ground then took two more out of my right hand.

"Don't put them *there,* you oaf. Help her take them where they need to go!" Ms. Rosemary's voice cracked like a whip. I almost laughed aloud, watching Chris jump and bend to gather the bags. Everything about this situation was ridiculous, but I kept my mouth shut. I figured it was good for him to problem solve a little bit, and I certainly didn't want Ms. Rosemary to remember I was there and turn her sharp tongue on me.

Chris stood with his arms full and his eyes dancing. He looked at Chelsea. "You can come with us, Chels." Then he turned to me, gesturing with his head. "Lead the way."

Amy stayed behind but waved as we walked through the glass office door into the long corridor leading to the sanctuary. Stained-glass windows lined one side of the wall, and classroom doors dotted the other.

As we walked, Chris gestured as well as he could with his thumb. "Chelsea, you remember Maddie from the hospital?"

I moved my head, trying to move the suffocating brown wool fabric further off my shoulder. Once I could see Chelsea better, I smiled.

"Yes!" Chelsea nodded. "I owe you a text message! That was such a crazy day. Thank you so much for being there for us. You were amazing."

"It's good to see you again. How are you? How are the kids?" I asked, trying not to drop anything and keep up with Chris.

"We're all doing well, thanks for asking! They're at preschool right now." Chelsea reached out with both hands. "What can I carry?"

"I think I've got it. I'm afraid it will all fall if I move anything."

Chelsea nodded. "I understand. I'll keep an eye out. Chris has told me so many wonderful things about you. I've been dying to get to know you a little bit."

"Is that right?" I drawled at Chris, ready for him to make a joke, but he lifted his chin, gesturing.

"Chels, can you open the big wooden door up ahead? It's the storage room."

Chelsea hurried ahead of us and opened the door. We trudged through, both of us having to turn sideways and maneuver our loads through the doorway. Once inside, we crept through the piles of candles and old wedding decor, over to the Christmas play items, and dropped everything on the floor.

"Why do churches always have the creepiest storage rooms?" Chelsea asked, looking around.

Chris gave Chelsea a look. "Remember the puppets?"

"Ick!" Chelsea exclaimed with a shudder. She turned to me and explained.

"When we were kids, our old school Baptist church had Vacation Bible School every summer, and our mom was in charge of the skits. She made these hand puppets, like something you'd see on Sesame Street. They stored them next to the stage curtains on hangers in this crowded, dark room with a single light bulb with a pull chain. It was straight out of a horror film!" Chelsea laughed.

"Are you going to tell Maddie about the time you *created* a horror film?" Chris chimed in, sounding ominous. Chelsea lowered her chin and bit her lips to keep from laughing. Chris looked at me to explain. "The summer I was six, Chelsea and our brother, Chance, played a prank on me with the puppets. I went into the closet to get something for our mom, but they'd snuck in ahead of me. They hid behind the curtain and made the Devil puppet say, "Hey, Christopher, I saw you steal that cookie! You're gonna go to the bad place! Burn, burn, burn!"

"Oh my gosh!" I laughed, equally tickled and horrified. These people were unbelievable. Chris shook his head at Chelsea, but she was laughing too hard to be shamed.

"I'm not proud of it," Chelsea insisted, clutching her chest and laughing. "But I can still see him running from the room, screaming." She doubled over, laughing harder.

Chris shook his head, feigning disgust. He crossed his arms and tried not to laugh too.

Once I collected myself, I responded. "We had VBS puppets too, but I never saw the storage room at my church." I hadn't known to be grateful for that until now. I knelt down as I talked, pulling items from the first bag. "My mom organized the snacks. Much safer!"

Chelsea nodded and walked over to me. "Okay, where do you want to begin?"

"Let's group these items together for now. While you do that, I can count the costumes, and then we can pack them." I turned and saw a stack of bags. "What are those?"

Chris looked over. "Oh. I started on the costumes a few days ago."

I stared at him, unable to hide my shock. "You did?"

He shrugged. "I had an hour between meetings one day. It wasn't a big deal. I may not have done it right, but maybe it will help."

I looked at the pile of large, zip top bags, full of shepherd costumes. "That's great!"

Chris pointed his finger toward the pile. "I set the list over there, so you can check which bag goes where."

I stood and walked over to the packed bags and picked up the clipboard sitting next to them. He'd already counted everything and written down the costumes he'd packed. I looked at him, speechless. Organizing and packing the costumes wasn't hard, but it was time-consuming. Chris had cut the time I would need to be in this creepy closet in half.

He stood by the pile of bags he'd set down, looking around at the shadowed heaps of wedding candelabras from the eighties, tablecloths, discarded vases, and tarnished communion trays. I picked my way over to give him a hug.

"Thank you," I murmured as I squeezed him. "That was extremely helpful."

He patted me on the shoulder and smiled. "I wish I had time to help right now, but I have a meeting in five minutes."

"That was a sweet thing to do," Chelsea commented. *Oh.* I'd completely forgotten about Chelsea for a second, and from the sound of her voice, it showed. I stepped away from Chris, my cheeks feeling hot. I looked over at Chelsea, but I couldn't read her face in the dim light.

"I'll come check on y'all when I'm done," Chris told us and turned to walk out of the room.

Chelsea cleared her throat then arched an eyebrow and pointed an authoritative finger at her brother. "Christopher Blake Calvert, if you lock us in this creepy room or prank us in any way, I will never forgive you, and I will take vengeance for the rest of my days. I know where you sleep."

Whoa. She'd whipped out the middle name and everything. Actually, considering who we were dealing with, it was probably smart to threaten him as thoroughly as possible. Anyone might be tempted by this perfect prank opportunity.

"Good catch," I told her and turned my own stern face at Chris, crossing my arms over my chest. "Same goes for me."

He chuckled as he looked between us. "Noted. It almost feels like a mistake to leave you two alone in here, but I have to go." He gave a small salute and walked out of the room. I turned to Chelsea.

"Thanks for your help. I really appreciate it. Are you sure you don't mind? It's not too late to escape," I joked, stepping over to rummage through the racks of robes and other costumes.

"It's no problem. I'm glad to be able to do something helpful. The kids talk about the play all the time. They feel so big, going to rehearsal with Uncle Chris!" She beamed.

"They're so sweet. It's a madhouse in there half the time; there are so many kids. But it's slowly coming together." I paused to look around. "The shepherds are done. Can you work on the angel robes and the sheep? I'll do the stars and the Nativity people."

Chelsea nodded and moved over to the overstuffed hanging rack. We both got to work.

"So tell me about yourself. We didn't get to talk much at the hospital. I know you're Chris's sister, and that's about it," I said as I grouped some costumes together.

Chelsea looked up from her spot among the robes. "That's pretty much my whole personality these days. Chris's sister. Noah and Hannah's mom." She laughed. "As Chris has told you, I'm going through a divorce. I'm going back to teaching after being home with my kids for the last four years. I'm learning a lot. It's been pretty crazy the last few months." She held up a sheep costume against her chest. "And today I'm in a mystery closet at my new church, organizing and secretly pretending to be a costume designer for a Harry Potter movie."

I cracked up. "Yes! Ha! I love Harry Potter! Great reference. Thank you so much for helping me organize everything. Seriously."

Chelsea checked her watch. "I have to pick up my kids at preschool in an hour, but I'm yours until then."

"That's perfect," I said. "Let's put as many costumes together as we can, and see how far we get."

"Sounds good! Okay, so far, you know about my tragic story and my obsession with Harry Potter," Chelsea pointed out. "Why don't you tell me something about you?"

I made a face. "I'm pretty boring these days. Being promoted from assistant to director of the children's Christmas play is by far the wildest thing that's happened lately. Obviously, I'm a nurse in the ER. I have a roommate named Emma…that's pretty much it."

"That doesn't sound boring to me," Chelsea replied. "The ER? Stressful. Children's play? Stressful. And on top of all that, you're dealing with my brother," she pointed out.

I chuckled. "You have a point there. I guess you've become an expert in stress these past few months."

Chelsea laughed. "That's putting it mildly. I'm ready for a new year, for sure."

I shook my head. "I'm really sorry all that happened."

Chelsea made a face. "Thank you. We're making it through, slowly but surely. God has met us every step of the way. And He gave me a mama who knows the way through. It's a terrible thing to have in common, but I wouldn't trade her for anything."

"What a blessing! I haven't met her, but according to Chris, y'all have a great family."

Chelsea nodded in agreement. "We're blessed, for sure. Chris has been a lifesaver these past few months. I couldn't have done it without him."

"I actually feel the same way. I was really overwhelmed when Melissa went on bed rest. I didn't expect

Chris to be as reliable and encouraging as he's been. He's made this whole experience really great. I'm not sure I could have done it without him." *Stop talking! She already knows how great Chris is. He's her brother,* I warned myself.

Chelsea nodded, smiling. "I hear ya. Okay, enough about the Calverts. Tell me more about you."

"I have a dog, a little gray-and-white maltipoo named Kevin. He's a lot of fun. We go to the dog park and take long walks. Does that count as a hobby?" I asked.

Chelsea nodded. "Definitely. Dogs are the best! We have a big ol' mutt, and we all love her to pieces."

"What's her name?" I asked.

"Edna, of course."

"Oh my goodness, that's fantastic!" I laughed. "I bet Chris loves having her around."

Chelsea nodded. "Yeah, she's great. The kids love her a little too much at times, but she's super patient with them. I think she's drawn the line at dressing up, though. We got her a little Christmas elf hat to wear, but she won't wear it. She pushes it off with her paws every time they put it on her."

"How cute!" I exclaimed. "I have a little Christmas sweater for Kevin. My mom got it for him. Y'all grew up with lots of dogs, right?"

Chelsea nodded. "Yes, we always had dogs growing up. Right now, my mom has two labs, Sam and Elliott. They're named after her celebrity crush."

I cracked up. "Isn't he the guy from *Lonesome Dove*? My mom likes him too. And two labs? That's a lot of dog energy!"

Chelsea laughed. "You have no idea. I'm impressed you recognize *Lonesome Dove*!"

"My grandparents loved the book and the movie. So does my mom. And my dad is an English professor. It was unavoidable, from both sides of my family."

"That's adorable. *Harry Potter* and *Lonesome Dove* in a single afternoon? This is a great day! You should come with us out to East Texas sometime!"

"That would be great," I told her. "A little getaway sounds pretty good right now, once I get through all of this."

"Actually—" Chelsea stopped herself abruptly. I looked up.

"Are you okay?" I asked, a little confused.

Her expression brightened. "Definitely!" She picked up the next costume and folded it to fit its bag.

"Did you grow up around here?" Chelsea asked.

I nodded. "I grew up in the 'burbs, about thirty minutes north, in Richardson." I trailed off, shrugging. "What about you? Did you always live in East Texas?"

Chelsea nodded. "My mom still lives in the house we grew up in. We all grew up running around outside all the time. When Chris came, he was like my very own life-sized baby doll. My mom let me help with him a lot and dress him up. He swears he hated it, but he plays princesses with Hannah all the time now, so..."

We both laughed. I could picture Chris seated in a tiny chair, wearing a tiara and holding a plastic tea cup to his lips. 'Pinkies up!'

"He's really great with kids," I said.

Chelsea nodded. "Oh yeah, he's the dream uncle, for sure. They adore him, and it's very mutual." She paused, then changed the subject. "So, did you grow up playing any sports?"

That was a big shift, but I nodded. "Some. My big sport in high school was track."

Her eyes lit up. "That sounds exciting. What was your event?"

"I ran hurdles mostly."

"Do you still run?"

"Occasionally. I haven't run hurdles since high school, but a leisurely run with a friend? I'm in!"

Chelsea smiled. "That sounds perfect!"

I tilted my head, confused. Perfect for what? "Do you run?" I asked.

"Not really, I'm more of a group fitness girly."

I nodded and looked around, still a little confused. But I shrugged it off. Chelsea zipped the bag on the last costume in her pile. I checked my watch.

"Wow, the time went fast. Thank you so much for your help!" I told Chelsea.

"No problem, it's so nice to get to hang out with you and have adult conversation. I'm up for that anytime!" She looked at her watch. "Okay, I have to go pick up my kids. I'll see you later?"

I nodded. "Thanks again. Bye!"

Chelsea waved and walked out, leaving me with the piles of costumes, all bagged and organized. I checked my list one last time and gathered as many as I could carry. I would have to make multiple trips, for sure, but I was almost done with the creepy closet.

I considered the best way to distribute the costumes. Probably best to set them out on the pews before rehearsal. The bags bulged in my arms so much I couldn't fit through the doorway. I turned to go through sideways and spun a little bit so I could walk backward. Focused on the bags, I gasped when I collided with a tall torso.

"Whoa!" Chris exclaimed and took hold of my shoulders, steadying both of us. I spun around to face him.

"Sorry, I didn't see you there!" I apologized.

"It's okay. How can I help?" he asked.

"Chelsea and I packed all the remaining costumes. Now I have to take them to the sanctuary. Want to help with that?"

Chris nodded and moved past me into the storage room. I walked as carefully as I could to the sanctuary. I could barely see, and I didn't want to run into anyone else. The sanctuary doors stood open, so I walked in and dumped the armload of bags into the first pew.

I was still organizing the piles when Chris walked in a minute later, carrying an even bigger load than I'd brought. "You can put those over there," I directed him, pointing.

"Where?" he asked, unable to see around the load in his arms.

"Oh! Follow the sound of my voice," I said. I jogged to the other side of the pews. "This way."

Chris followed my voice. When he got close, I backed up.

"A little more to the left." I tried to keep the smile out of my voice.

It didn't take Chris long to figure out we were clear on the other side of the sanctuary. He moved his head from behind a bag holding a white robe and halo and laughed.

"Good one," he admitted.

I smirked and put my hand on my hip. "I don't get many opportunities to prank the prankster," I sassed.

"Don't start something you can't finish, Reed," he warned. Laughing, we turned up the aisle and walked over to the pile of costume bags.

He dropped the load and turned to me, laughter in his eyes. "Got any real instructions? I'm all yours."

I pointed as I answered. "We'll put the shepherds in that pew and the angels in this one. The names are written on the bags. Can you organize the costumes in alphabetical order by category?"

He shrugged. "As you wish," he said and got to work. We worked in companionable silence for a while.

It didn't take long with the two of us. When the last costume was placed, I surveyed our work. Four of the back rows of pews held bagged costumes, categorized by group and in alphabetical order. Crowns glinted through the plastic, and the bags bulged with fabric. I shook my head in wonder.

"I can't believe it's time to distribute the costumes," I breathed. "This has gone really fast." Tonight was the last rehearsal with everyone before the big show on Friday.

Chris nodded. "You've done a great job." He held up a hand for a high five.

"It's not done yet," I pointed out. But I raised my hand for a high five anyway. Somewhere along the way, I got distracted by his grin and failed to watch the follow-through. I completely missed his hand.

He shook his head. "Pathetic. Try again."

Why was I the one getting distracted here? *Pull it together!* I held up my hand and tried again. He moved his hand at the last second. I growled in frustration. "You are such a punk!"

Chris laughed at my outburst. "That was a test! You have to watch the follow-through, Reed!"

I made a face at him. Instead of going for the next high five, I poked him in the ribs. His eyes widened, and he reacted immediately, catching my hand. "Foul! Tickling is against the rules, ma'am," he cried, totally failing to hold back his smile. I couldn't help but laugh. But I pulled my hand back before I could do anything more. I didn't want him to think I was flirting with him.

"Okay. I'm going to run home for a bit and let Kevin out, then I'll be back for rehearsal tonight."

He nodded. "I'll be here."

CHAPTER 9

Rehearsal went well that night. The only big issue was the angels. They all started singing at different times, and then they got embarrassed and stopped. So we took some extra time to practice and reminded them (again) to watch the teachers crouching down in front, showing them what to do.

We got it worked out by the time parents arrived for pick-up. I stood with one of the teachers, chatting about the music, when Carson walked up to me, holding Heidi's hand.

"Miss Maddie!"

I bent down to talk with Carson, ignoring his mother for the moment.

"Great job tonight, Carson!"

"I can't wait for the show!" He stepped forward and wrapped his arms around my waist. I hugged him back.

"Me too! I'm excited to see you perform!" I told him. Carson ran off, leaving Heidi and her pregnancy glow. Christmas sweaters are a joke for a reason, yet somehow Heidi looked radiant in a cream knit sweater with tiny, green Christmas trees embroidered all over it. *Of course she did.* Heidi always had great style in college, so why should pregnancy be any different?

I assumed she would follow Carson, but she didn't. *Alright. I'll go,* I thought. I didn't want to talk with Heidi. I turned, about to walk away.

"Maddie?"

My feet paused. My skin felt tight, my heart sinking
as I turned toward her. I'd avoided her and Houston
successfully for weeks, but she'd caught me, fair and square.

"What can I do for you?" I asked, hoping to move
whatever this was along.

Heidi rubbed the side of her protruding belly. "I
just wanted to say thank you. Carson has really enjoyed
being part of the play, and I'm grateful."

Carson was a neutral subject and a pleasant one.
"He's a great kid. We've all enjoyed working with him."

Heidi smiled back at me, her lips tight. She nodded
and looked like she was about to turn away. But she didn't.
She huffed a little breath and dug in.

"Thank you. It's been good to see you again," she
admitted. "I've missed you."

A rock heaved through my stomach, and a hundred
responses filled my mind. What could I say?

I've missed you too?

It would be true. But would it be helpful? We'd said
everything years ago, in the aftermath of my rehearsal
dinner, the night before what was supposed to have been my
wedding. That was a very late night.

Looking at Heidi now, compassion stirred in me.
She looked strained and lonely. Tears brimmed in her eyes
as she held my gaze. What was she asking me for? I couldn't
go there. But it didn't mean I wanted to hurt her. I was free
of that old burden, and I wanted to stay that way.

"Thank you. I wish you all the best. I really do." I mustered a half-smile.

Heidi nodded and blinked away tears, looking over as Houston appeared at her side. His eyes searched her face protectively. He held Carson's hand and clutched the costume bag under his elbow. He looked at me and back at Heidi. He reached for her, placing his other hand on the small of her back. For better or worse, they were a unit.

I remembered praying for Heidi to meet the perfect person to spend her life with. I'd wanted us to live next door to each other and raise our kids together. Had half the dream come true? I brushed the idea away, too tired for math. Heidi's face brightened, looking at Houston.

"Ready to go, Mama?" Houston asked her softly. She nodded.

Carson piped up, "Let's go, Mama!"

"Y'all have a nice evening," I told them and turned to walk away.

Later that night, after Chris, the twins, and I braved the storage closet to make sure all the decorations were ready to be put up on Friday, we walked out the old wooden doors.

"I saw you talking with Heidi earlier. You good?" Chris asked.

I nodded. "Yeah, I am. Thank you." I smiled. "You?"

Chris nodded. "Yup. I'll see you later." He looked back and forth between the twins, plotting. "Okay you two. Ready, set, go!" he yelled and took off, racing the twins to the car. They immediately joined in the fun, their laughter echoing across the empty parking lot.

Smiling, I got in my car and headed home. It was a cold, crisp night. During the drive, passing all the sparkling Christmas light displays, I let myself reflect.

I had forgiven Houston long ago, but seeing him again brought up memories. I could see now that our relationship had been far from perfect, on both sides. In the most painful way possible, he and Heidi actually did me a favor. I hadn't prayed as much back then; self-reliance was a comfortable idol. It still was sometimes. But God had been kinder to me than I could ever deserve. *Thank you, Lord, for your goodness to me*, I prayed.

As easy as it was to see God's kindness in sparing me a miserable marriage, it was hard seeing Heidi. Losing my best friend still stung, even all these years later.

Emma's face crossed my mind, followed by Mia, Anna, and Sarah. My closest friends and safest people. All of them would be in the audience on Saturday, supporting me and cheering on the children. Over the last nine years, I had healed and had been given opportunities for true friendship. Gratitude swelled in my chest, thinking of my friends. Objectively, I could admit one or two dreams had gone unfulfilled, but I truly had everything I needed, in abundance. What a grace it was to have such a fulfilling life.

When I walked into our apartment, Emma sat, curled up on the sofa with Kevin in her lap. They snuggled in the cheerful light of the Christmas tree, eating homemade Muddy Buddies, Em's favorite Christmas delicacy. They both looked up from a Law & Order rerun. A light snow of powdered sugar sprinkled the front of Emma's navy-blue sweatshirt, which meant it was probably in Kevin's fur as well.

"Hey!" I said. Kevin ran over to greet me. I petted his thick coat as he feverishly licked me. Even before the powdered sugar dusting, I really needed to get him groomed. He usually looked like a fluffy little teddy bear, but I'd been so busy lately I hadn't had time to take him to the groomer. Poor Kevin. He was starting to look more like a gray-and-white tumbleweed than a dog.

"I'm sorry, buddy. We'll get you groomed soon," I told him. Unbothered by his extra fur, Kevin flapped his ears and brought me his favorite rope toy, inviting me to play tug-of-war. I pulled on the rope, and he got down to business, growling loudly.

"I saved you some beef stew; it's on the stove," Emma interrupted our game.

"Yum! Thanks!"

I gave the rope one more tug, then released it. Kevin gave the rope a mighty shake, enjoying his victory. I walked to the kitchen and served myself a bowl of the fragrant stew then settled in on the couch with Emma and Kevin in the living room.

"How was rehearsal?" Emma asked.

I wiped my mouth with a napkin before I answered. "It went well. I think we're as ready as we can be."

Emma shook her head. "I can't believe you've actually done it, Mads. I'm so proud of you!"

I stirred my stew. I could hardly believe it either.

"I've had a lot of help," I reminded her. "You've been super supportive, feeding me, and listening to me complain all month!"

Emma got a teasing smile on her face and carefully picked up another bite. Powdered sugar coated her fingertips. "Not to mention the indispensable help of a certain cute youth minister."

I nearly dropped my bowl. "Emma! Where did that come from?" My face heated.

Emma was one of the few people who knew how disappointed I'd been when things didn't work out with Chris—both times. I'd liked him more than I ever let on to anyone else. But that night at Anna's was the final straw. It had to be. I could never be with someone so juvenile.

Emma shook her head and laughed. "I'm joking, Mads. I mean, just because he's obnoxious and immature doesn't mean he can't be cute, right?"

I sighed. "I guess that is true. It's only his face. But it takes more than a pretty face!" I insisted. Emma nodded. I leaned forward to set my empty bowl on the coffee table. I sat back and rested my head on the cushion. I didn't want more teasing, but Emma was my closest confidant.

"I have to admit, something is different—about Chris, I mean. He's been reliable. He's shown up to every rehearsal, and he's actually been really helpful." I thought of how sweet he was with Noah and Hannah. Helping his sister. Giving so much of his evening time for the play. "I'm seeing a side to him that I've never seen before. He's compassionate and selfless. Generous..." I trailed off.

"So, the *opposite* of obnoxious." A questioning smile lit Emma's face.

I shook my head. "Not like that. I'm saying he's grown."

Emma didn't push. "Sounds good to me! I'm glad he's grown. Have you seen Houston again since the first night?"

I nodded, relieved she'd dropped the subject of Chris so easily. "Tonight, actually. Heidi too. That part has been really weird, but their little boy is precious."

"I still think it is amazingly mature of you to let them be part of the play. I could *never*!" She shook her head.

I disagreed. It wasn't maturity. It was survival for my own heart. "You totally could, because unforgiveness would be a prison for *you*, not for them. No man is worth carrying that around." Heidi wasn't worth it either, but letting go of my best friend had been the most difficult part of it, by far.

Emma contemplated the idea. "You might be right. You're like a wise owl, Maddie Reed."

I threw my head back and cackled. "Is that a kind way of calling me old?"

Emma shook her head and laughed too.

"I don't want to be weighed down by a bunch of yuck," I declared.

Emma nodded in agreement. She knew my whole story and how hard I'd worked to get healthy. I sighed.

"Okay, I'm going to walk Kevin right quick, and then I've got to go to bed. I work tomorrow, and then the whole weekend is going to be nuts!"

Emma clapped her hands excitedly. "I can't wait to see the show!"

I smiled. It was going to be great. I told Emma good night and put on my shoes to walk Kevin.

Lying in bed later that night, I considered Emma's words. Forgiving Houston and Heidi was something I had not felt capable of doing for a long time. But now I could see more clearly that it was the right choice back then…and still was. Ryan often reminded us during church that nothing was wasted. Thinking about the women I got to call friends now, I was so glad for the restoration and goodness of God, through every season.

I prayed and thanked God for the work He had done in my life, for all my friends, and a job I loved. I thanked Him for Chris, a man I could never quite forget, who continuously surprised me. *Lord, what's the deal with him?* I prayed. It seemed like Chris was changing before my very eyes.

In what could only be categorized as God's incomprehensible sense of humor, I fell asleep thanking Him for Youth Guy Chris.

CHAPTER 10

"Just a couple more strands to go," Chris coaxed.

He was right. We were so close. He'd gently persuaded me to keep going since I'd hit the wall an hour ago. It was Thursday night, less than twenty-four hours until the big show.

The countdown was officially *on*, and everything was pretty much perfect. The twinkle lights criss-crossing the vaulted ceiling of the sanctuary were the finishing touch. Chris and I were the last two standing. Everyone else had gone home. I'd been on a ladder all afternoon, hooking up long strands of twinkle lights, end to end, to mimic stars. I paused to look around.

"It really does look great, doesn't it?" I smiled.

Chris smiled back at me, his eyes crinkling. "It's awesome, Reed. You did it!"

"*We* did it," I pointed out. "I couldn't pull any of this off without you," I admitted to him, looking down from the ladder. I couldn't hold back the surprise in my voice. "Thank you for staying to help me finish up. You've been a great help."

The last of the strands of lights draped across Chris's outstretched arms, keeping them from becoming tangled. He carefully turned his hand and fanned his face.

"Stop, you're making me blush." He grinned up at me. Then he angled his fingers differently, inviting more. "Actually, keep it coming. I like it."

I giggled helplessly, practically delirious from working all day. I turned to the wall, ready to screw in the hook to anchor the next portion of lights. I twisted the metal hook into its spot, bending my hand weirdly to work around the giant blister on my thumb.

Out of the corner of my eye, a small shadow caught my attention as it emerged from behind a tapestry and skittered along the wall, moving fast. I turned my head and gasped at the huge cockroach headed straight for me.

I shrieked, scrambling to get away from the flicking antennae. In my flurry, the ladder swayed and fell over, dumping me off like a sandbag, right into a pair of strong arms.

"Maddie! Stop! I've got you!" Chris grunted urgently.

Still in the throes of a full-body shudder, my bearings slowly returned. Coming back to my body, I found myself wrapped around Chris, my fingers curled in the soft hair at the nape of his neck. His face was inches away, his friendly eyes open wide. He was as surprised as me.

A second ago, my voice hit a pretty shrill octave, but all I could muster at the moment was a breathless, "Oh." Everything paused—the cockroach, the lights. Breathing. It all faded, and my senses zeroed in on Chris, warm and solid against me. His cologne was mild and sweet-smelling.

From this vantage point, I could see the day's growth shadowing his jaw. That was new; I almost always saw him clean shaven. Curiosity kicked in. Did Chris shave every day? Was he a hairy man? I peeked at the neckline of his t-shirt, looking for evidence of chest hair. *In a very scientific, medical way, of course.* I couldn't tell, even from here.

I had more questions, like how did I fit so perfectly, right here against him? This was, well…a *moment.* My heart sped up in my chest. I looked at his mouth, unable to keep myself from melting a little. When I lifted my gaze, his brown eyes met mine and held. Something in my stomach began to hum. Chris tilted his head and blinked.

"That was close. Are you okay?" His tone, all-business, may as well have been a record scratch, wrenching me back to reality. We were on different wavelengths entirely.

Embarrassment settled into my veins like lead. I pulled my hands back and clasped them on my knees. "I'm fine." My voice sounded strange when I answered. I looked him in the eye again, which was a mistake. He was still holding me. This was way too cozy. Before I could melt all over again, I tore my eyes from his and looked straight ahead. I adjusted my posture as best I could, squaring my shoulders and lifting my chin. There. Much less cozy, totally unaffected, except for some soul-crushing awkwardness. Now I was all business too.

I cleared my throat. "Can you put me down please?" I asked primly.

"Yes, ma'am." His chest rumbled with the words, tempting me to lean into him all over again. *No.* I forced myself to remain straight and rigid.

He set me on my feet and released me as soon as I could stand. No lingering touch, no meaningful eye contact. Nothing. *Which is exactly what* should *happen*, I reminded myself harshly. *Get it together, woman!*

I stepped away from him, unable to look him in the eye. Awkwardness hung in the air. I wasn't sure how to feel or what to say.

"Thank you," I muttered to his scuffed Jordans.

"Anytime." I could hear the grin in his voice, could practically *feel* a joke building in his brain.

I looked around, still getting my bearings. I needed some space, but I couldn't make my feet work.

"The roach is gone. You want to finish these last few lights? I can take a turn on the ladder if you're scared it will come back," he offered.

So, not a joke, a kind word. Feelings went to war inside my head. I wanted to stomp my foot and pout that I couldn't predict him. I wanted to step closer to him and feel his warmth wrapped around me again. I'd almost been tempted to—*nope. The roach.* I wanted to shudder at the mention of that horrible creature!

But I had been a nurse for seven years. I was an expert at putting on a calm demeanor in stressful situations, with the obvious exception of cockroach encounters. I held my ground. "That's very chivalrous of you, but I can do it. Let's get this knocked out, and then we can head home."

He didn't fight me on it but nodded and stepped forward to pick up the ladder. He held it steady for me, and I carefully climbed the rungs. Back where I'd left off, Chris handed me the strand of lights, and we kept going.

It didn't take long. A couple minutes later, the final strand hung on its hook. I stepped down the ladder and landed with a little hop. Chris spun in a slow circle with his hands on his hips, taking it all in.

The twinkle lights brought the whole sanctuary together, lighting it beautifully.

He looked down at me, his brown eyes sparkling. "Well done, Reed."

I smiled sheepishly, trying to keep my jubilation under control, and looked at the floor for a moment. "Back atcha…*bro*."

He snorted a laugh. "Here, I'll put away the ladder. You go on home and get some rest."

"I can help," I insisted.

He leveled a look at me. "Maddie, you're dead on your feet. This will take two minutes, and I'll be right behind you. Go."

With that, he turned and expertly folded the ladder. He picked it up and carried it from the room.

I sighed. He was right. I put on my jacket and grabbed my purse. I reached inside for my phone to check my messages before walking to the car.

My text messages were full of pictures from my department holiday party.

Mia: Wish you were here!

Attached was a picture of Mia and Ryan, both of them decked out in ugly Christmas sweaters. The cardiac floor nurses were celebrating tonight as well. Co-workers from the ER and from my old team had sent similar sentiments and photos, every picture more hilarious than the last. The party was in full swing, and I was missing it. I was tempted to run home, change, and show up late, but my thumbs and lower back were killing me. As much as I enjoyed a good party, it was best to sit this one out. I texted Mia to let her know not to expect me and continued scrolling through the merriment. I reached a message from an unknown number.

Unknown Number: Hi, Maddie! This is Chelsea. Christmas is going to be tough for me this year. Chris told me you have to work on Christmas! Boo! We are planning to redeem a crummy Christmas with a fabulous New Year's the following weekend! Are you off work? I would love for you to come out to East Texas with us! My mom is a great cook, and you can watch our brothers gang up on Chris. It's fun! Please say you will at least think about it!

Wow, that was unexpected. I should definitely say no. I barely knew Chelsea, and I was still recovering from that moment earlier. I didn't need to get any closer with Chris, for my own sanity. *Then again,* a tiny voice argued in my head. *It could be really fun.* It was true. Chelsea and I clicked, and it would be great to get to know her better. And if their brothers were there, I probably wouldn't see Chris much at all, because they'd be off doing man stuff.

Wait. Why was I talking myself into this? *Stop,* I told my brain. I needed some time to think about it, but right now what I needed most was sleep. Footsteps approached behind me.

"I thought you'd be halfway home by now." Chris's voice echoed in the acoustics of the vaulted foyer.

"I'm going, just stopped to check my messages," I told him. I put my phone in my pocket as I walked alongside him out the door and down the steps to the parking lot.

He looked up at the dark sky. "It's later than I thought. Are you okay driving home? Not too tired?"

I nodded, the sting of embarrassment still a little fresh. "I'll be fine."

He gave me an assessing look in the eyes for a second, until he was satisfied. "Okay. Good work today, Reed." He saluted me with a glowing smile and turned toward his car. I watched him walk as I approached my own car. Chelsea's invitation was still rolling around in my brain. On the one hand, it didn't have to be a big deal. Chris and I were friends. We worked well together.

It would be nice to have something to look forward to after all this stress and work, I reasoned. *But it would be weird, wouldn't it?* I flashed back to our moment earlier, and grimaced. I should definitely say no. I pulled my phone out of my pocket before I could change my mind again.

Me: That sounds really fun, but I need to pass this time. Thank you so much for the invitation!

I put away my phone and started the car.

CHAPTER 11

Christmas Eve arrived, cold and clear. I slept in and cuddled Kevin for a bit. It was going to be a long day, so I wanted to take it slow. I bundled up and got Kevin ready to go for a walk. I imagined him rolling his little eyes at me when I pulled his sweater over his head.

"It's chilly, buddy. You'll be glad you have this." He shook his whole body from head to toe with a final, satisfying flap of his ears, and we were off.

The neighborhood was pretty quiet for a morning off, but we encountered several bundled-up runners and fellow dog-walkers along our route. Ryan and Mia caught my eye and waved from a couple of blocks away, before they turned the corner to continue their run. Seeing my friends so happy made me happy, even as it activated a tiny prick of longing in my own heart. Shaking it off, I stopped for a coffee on the way home. I ordered Kevin a puppy cup of whipped cream, and he made quick work of it.

Once we got home, I called my parents. My mom answered on the second ring. "Merry Christmas Eve, Punkin!" I smiled at the nickname.

"Merry Christmas Eve to you! How's it going over there?"

She *tsked*. I could practically hear her looking around, checking to make sure all the presents were in order and ready to go.

"It's looking good! I think Santa's going to come through," she joked. My mom loved playing Santa. "Your dad says I went a little overboard, but it's Henry's first Christmas!"

"I'm sure it will all be perfect. And I'm excited to see everyone at the Christmas play. Thank you for coming!"

"I wouldn't want to be anywhere else, sweetie. Dad and I are so proud of you! I just wish Grandma Lou could be here to see it with us." Her voice trembled. Mom was sensitive this time of year. She'd lost her mother, my Grandma Lou two years before, and her grief sat heavy at Christmas time.

Tears pricked my eyes, missing Grandma Lou with her. I blinked them away.

"Be sure you get there early so you can find good seats. Are Mark and Bree for sure coming?" My brother was a doctor, so he often worked on holidays too.

"Yes, and they're bringing the baby. He's growing so fast, Maddie! You won't recognize him from Thanksgiving!" My mom was absolutely basking in the joy of her first grandchild, and I didn't blame her. My nephew, Henry, was completely adorable. At eight months old, he was super chubby and smiled all the time. I couldn't wait to squeeze him.

I hung up with Mom and jumped in the shower. The clock was ticking, and I wanted to look extra nice for the performance. My phone buzzed as I dabbed on eyeshadow.

Chris: In case I forget to tell you later, you did amazing and I'm so proud of you.

"Aw!" I murmured in surprise. Warmth flooded my chest. I couldn't help but marvel at how far we'd come. The show tonight was going to be a success. I could feel it. I read his text again. Imminent victory was great, but I knew the warmth wasn't only because of that. Over the last month, my friendship with Chris had solidified into something fun and good. Who'd have thought it? I was truly thankful.

Me: Thank you!

Three dots danced beneath my text as he responded. The wait was worth it. I laughed out loud when the words appeared.

Chris: Anything you'd like to say to me?

I laughed, but it was a good reminder: Chris was still Chris. *Take it easy, woman.* If he was that sweet all the time, I might do something incredibly stupid. I typed my reply and hit send before I could overthink it.

Me: How could I forget? ALL GLORY TO GOD!

Chris: Amen. Exactly what I was going for.

I set my phone down. I needed to finish getting ready. But I couldn't let it go. I quickly picked up my phone again and fired off a quick text.

Me: You are a mess.

Chris: You have no idea.

I chuckled and glanced at the clock. I needed to put the phone down and get a move on, if I wanted to curl my hair. *Just one more.*

Me: I have to get ready. See you there.

Chris: I'll be the one in white.

He sent a selfie of him wearing a huge Santa beard. I gasped and laughed so hard Kevin barked. Where had he found *that*? I had to know. I started typing again.

When I arrived at the church (with straight, uncurled hair and later than planned, thanks to Chris), several families were already in the sanctuary. Chelsea walked over to me with an attractive, older woman at her side. The woman was undoubtedly Chelsea and Chris's mother. She was vibrant and warm, and her smile could light up a room. I liked her immediately.

"Hi! Everything looks so great! You look fabulous! I love this sweater!" Chelsea gushed as she hugged me, then she stepped back and gestured between me and the woman next to her. "Maddie Reed, this is my mom, Rhonda Calvert."

"Hi!" I smiled and offered her my hand to shake. "It's wonderful to meet you!"

Rhonda shook my hand. "Likewise, Maddie! I've heard wonderful things about you!"

"I'm so glad you can be here to support everyone!"

"Me too. I wouldn't miss it!"

I appreciated that she'd made the effort to drive in from out of town.

Chelsea turned to Rhonda. "Mom, I've been trying to convince Maddie to join us for New Year's. She has to work Christmas Day, so she needs a redo, too!"

Rhonda lit up at the idea. "Sounds great to me! We'd love to have you anytime, Maddie."

Aw. "Thank you so much! I don't think I'm going to be able to make it work this year, but maybe another time."

Rhonda nodded, understanding.

I wanted to talk more, but I needed to get going. I looked at my watch then reached over to pat Rhonda on her arm. "I have to gather all the children now. Thank you for coming. It was lovely to meet you!"

"Of course! We'll go find seats," Chelsea said.

I turned to walk away and was immediately stopped. Little Carson ran up to me from one direction, Hannah and Noah from another. Hannah wrapped her arms around my knees and fixed her angelic eyes on me.

"Miss Maddie, you look bee-yoo-tee-ful!" She touched the sleeve of my hunter-green sweater dress. "Soft!"

I nodded and hugged her back. "Thank you, sweet girl! You look beautiful too!" She did. Her halo headband pulled her blonde ringlets back, showcasing her rosy cheeks, and her blue eyes were bright with excitement. I looked over at the boys. Noah made an adorable sheep. The twinkle in his eye was far too reminiscent of his uncle, so I made a mental note to check his pockets before the show.

Carson could barely contain himself. "Miss Maddie! Santa's going to come see us tonight after the play!"

He danced with excitement in his shepherd costume. His eyes shone, and his latest missing tooth left a gap in his smile. Every *S* he pronounced had a slight whistle to it.

"How wonderful! Do you think he'll bring you something fun?" I asked.

Carson nodded and said, "Mama says I've been a great helper! She needs help 'cause my sister is coming soon, our sweet Easter baby."

Undone, I pressed a hand to my melting heart. "Well, mamas tell the truth. I'm sure you've been a wonderful helper." I looked across the pews until I found Heidi, standing in the aisle, talking to one of the volunteers. She looked radiant in a red velvet dress, her hand resting protectively on her rounded stomach. It wouldn't be long now, only a few more months. Carson would be a wonderful big brother. I looked away. This wasn't the time to get lost in emotions. I had work to do.

The noise in the room steadily increased, and I saw Evan and some other boys gesturing to the twinkle lights. One of them held a shepherd's staff in both hands above his head. *Surely they wouldn't try to use the light strand as a zip line. Would they? Where is Chris?* I excused myself from the twins and Carson and hurried over to the group of boys.

A few minutes later—zip line crisis averted—I clapped my hands. "Alright, everyone to your rows, and we will get ready for the play!"

While the parents and volunteers got everyone seated and settled, I took a quick look around the room for my assistant. *Where could he be?* The twins were here, so he must be, as well. I checked my watch. I couldn't wait any longer.

I stood at the front and took everyone through the songs for one last rehearsal. Their little voices sounded so sweet as they sang along to the track. My spirits lifted even more as we sang "O Holy Night."

> *Oh holy night, the stars are brightly shining*
> *It is the night of our dear Savior's birth.*
> *Long lay the world in sin and error pining*
> *'Till He appeared and the soul felt its worth*
> *A thrill of hope, the weary world rejoices*
> *For yonder breaks a new and glorious morn'*
> *Fall on your knees*
> *O hear the angel voices*
> *O night divine, O night when Christ was born*

I turned away and surreptitiously wiped my eyes as carefully as I could. When I turned back, I could see I wasn't the only one wiping away tears. Volunteers and parents all around did the same. Who could hold it together, hearing these sweet voices proclaim the goodness and power of Jesus? I took a breath and moved us along to "Joy to the World." The children grew more excited and expressive with every word. I really hoped they would keep this energy and not get nervous in front of the audience. My heart filled with joy, hearing their little voices declare:

We were out of time. The teachers led the children to the fellowship hall to wait for the show to begin. As I followed the last of the angels out, I noticed Chris walking in the main door, across the sanctuary. *Finally.* I turned to walk over to him and stopped in my tracks. Chris wasn't alone. Houston walked with him, deep in conversation. He laughed at something Chris said. A tiny barb of insecurity wiggled under my skin. I shook my head and reminded myself of the truth.

Whatever it was, it was none of my business. I'd let go of Houston, and Heidi, and that part of my story a long time ago. Taking a slow, deep breath, I visualized the barb, its sharp points dulled. Then I imagined it evaporating, ceasing to exist. I felt better. I turned away from the men and walked out the side door to join the children.

CHAPTER 12

The show went great. The children mostly stayed in their spots, and every one of them sang their little hearts out.

At the end, the children sang "Joy to the World" with enthusiasm and confidence, just as we'd rehearsed. But one little voice rose above them all: sweet Carson. Smiling from ear to ear, he sang with all his might. Other kids around him became emboldened by his shouts, and they joined in. Soon, all the children shouted the lyrics instead of singing.

Chris met my eyes from across the pew. *What should we do?* I silently asked him. His eyebrows rose, and he shrugged, lifting his hands as if to say, *If you can't get out of it, get into it.* We nodded at each other and stood, inviting those around us to join in, until the whole crowd stood, singing at the top of their lungs. After the final note, the room erupted in applause.

I looked around, absorbing the moment. The Christmas story would never hit the same way for me after this. *Thank you, Lord,* I prayed, holding back tears. I picked up a microphone the sound person had left for me and climbed the steps to the stage. The clapping died down as I motioned to the children to sit down in their places.

"Praise the Lord, and joy to the world! Because of His great love for us, our Savior has come. He lived a perfect life. He died for our sins and rose again, and I am grateful to celebrate Him with you tonight! Merry Christmas!" The congregation interrupted me with some clapping, so I paused before I went on. "This year we raised money for Youth Engaged for Success. We'll be donating four thousand dollars for their cause. Thank you for your generosity!" Everyone applauded, then I recited my list of thank-yous and highlights. I didn't want to forget any group, so I counted them on my fingers as I went.

As the clapping died down, I considered my next words carefully. If someone had predicted this a month ago, I would have laughed in their face, but here we were.

"One last thing, and then we can go have some cookies and punch in the fellowship hall. When I took over as director, I wasn't sure if I would be able to pull this off. Now I know for a fact I couldn't have done it without the help of Chris Calvert. He has been a fantastic assistant director, showing up faithfully at every rehearsal, seeing to every detail. He's been supportive, encouraging, you name it. Anytime I needed him, he's been there."

Marveling at that truth, I looked down at him from the stage. His brown eyes were full of humility and kindness, but the mischievous twinkle remained. He winked and smiled at me.

"We made a good team. I truly could not imagine a better partner in this endeavor, and I'm glad I got to work with you. Thank you, Chris." I tucked the microphone under my arm and clapped for him. Everyone else joined me.

Chris stood up and walked up the stage steps. When he reached the stage, I realized he was carrying a large bouquet of red roses, tied with a beautiful Christmas bow. *Where did those come from?* I wondered. He took a tiny bow, and then with a huge smile, held out the bouquet to me. I was so touched by the gesture that it took me a second to respond.

He wiggled the bouquet and spoke quietly so only I could hear. "These are for you, Maddie."

Suddenly, my chest grew hot. I could feel my face turning red as I reached out and took the roses, my fingers brushing against Chris's in the process. Ignoring a zing of electricity, I admired the roses. They were even more beautiful up close. Combined with the adrenaline and relief that the play was a success, I wasn't sure I could speak at all, so I silently mouthed *Thank you.*

Moving to stand beside me, Chris took the microphone. "This lady right here is very special. Maddie made this a fun time for everyone, and she was amazing with all the kids—including me." Everyone laughed heartily, right on cue. When the laughter died down, Chris looked at me and said, "I speak for us all when I say thank you, from the bottom of our hearts."

At his words and the ensuing applause, my eyes filled again, and I shook my head, holding back the tears. I reached over, grabbed Chris's hand, and squeezed. He looked at me, his face lit with a smile. Reading my mind again, he squeezed my hand and said to the crowd, "Thank you all for coming! Merry Christmas to all, and to all a good night."

Motion swirled around us as, all at once, the children ran down the steps to their waiting parents. The teachers climbed up to help direct the ones who didn't immediately find their families. I stood with Chris, the two of us stuck in the eye of the storm of people. I sniffed the fragrant roses. They smelled heavenly. I wanted to absorb every detail of the moment and commit it all to memory. What a night!

Chris stirred beside me, looking around at the chaos. He met my eyes, silently asking me a question. Our mind-reading powers must be reserved for very specific scenarios. I couldn't understand him. A hand lightly squeezed mine. I looked down and saw with horror that I was still holding onto Chris! I released him as if his hand was on fire and muttered a quick, "*Sorry.*" He quietly assured me. "It's okay."

Blushing from my faux pas, I looked away. People milled around, but half the crowd had already made their way through the sanctuary doors and to the fellowship hall. Some of the older ladies were kind enough to set up cookies and punch in there, and everyone wanted to get one of Ms. Alma's famous Neiman Marcus bars. They were the very best treat, and she only made them at Christmas.

Chris waited, watching me. He leaned closer. "You okay, Reed?" he asked gently. I nodded at him, drew in a deep breath, and pulled my shoulders back down. I started toward the steps so I could join the crowd. I had certainly earned a cookie. Not only that, my friends and family were waiting for me, and I wanted to see everyone.

Like many of the children, Chris skipped the stairs and jumped off the stage to chat with a group of volunteers. He gestured around the room, and they all nodded. The crew moved into action, wasting no time tearing down the decorations and putting things away. Another group of volunteers was in charge of collecting the costumes. And just like that, my part of the play was finished.

Was I sad it was over? Of course not. The performance had gone well, and now I could get back to my life. The memory of warmth hung on my hand, but I shook it off.

I gathered my purse and my roses and walked up the aisle, smiling and accepting people's comments along the way. Everyone was supportive and kind, and it was wonderful to hear their happy feedback. Another few steps, and the crowd parted to reveal a woman standing several feet in front of me, a festive red velvet dress stretched over her pregnant belly. Heidi made eye contact with me and mouthed, "Thank you."

I met her eyes and inwardly sighed. I couldn't give her what she seemed to want. Our friendship was over long ago. But I could offer her kindness. I nodded and smiled back before I passed her and headed out of the sanctuary. The bright fluorescent lighting of the fellowship hall beckoned from down the hallway.

When I walked in, a squeal was my only warning before I was engulfed in a jumble of arms and sparkly sweaters and hair. Everyone talked at once, squeezing me and jumping up and down. They all backed up, and I looked around at my friends as I tried to catch my breath. Everyone was dressed to the nines and smiling so bright they could supply the sun.

"The kids were so cute!"

"How did you pull all that together?"

"I couldn't stop crying during the songs!"

"You look fabulous! You should always wear this shade of green!"

I took it all in as best I could and let myself take a breath. "Thanks for coming, y'all!"

With a squeal of celebration, we all moved in for another big hug, which turned into a giant group shimmy, which ended when we almost fell over in a laughing heap. Ryan, Gage, and Ben all stood back, indulgent grins on their faces. I thought my heart might burst. The night had been perfect, and now I was with my people. It was the best.

Pam Martin and Stella Lyles joined our little circle, and the conversation took off again.

"Well done, Maddie! That was a well-oiled machine! It must have taken a *lot* of work!" Pam exclaimed. Everyone nodded in agreement.

"Thank you. I had a lot of help," I admitted.

Pam nodded, an understanding smile lighting her face. "Y'all made a great team."

CHAPTER 13

Before I could respond, Anna made a joke. "Youth Guy Chris has to be good for something, right?"

I didn't join in the laughter. Mia met my eyes, a gentle smile on her face. Mia understood needing a chance for redemption and growth. She'd had a winding road herself, and now she wasn't laughing at Anna's joke. She was watching *me*. I knew how it would look if I defended Chris. I certainly used to share the same attitude. But now I knew better, and I wanted to honor the work he had put in. All of it.

"Actually, Chris was great. I couldn't have done it without him." Once I got going, I couldn't seem to stop. "He really cared, and he went above and beyond, every time. I liked working with him."

There. I'd stopped the avalanche of words. *Whew!* I sighed. All my friends' eyes were on me, but no one said anything. I could see them connecting dots that were definitely not connected.

"Don't read into it. I'm as surprised as you are. He was a big help, and he's grown a lot. That's all I'm saying."

Mia spoke up. "I agree with you, Maddie. I've seen a change in Youth Guy Chris. Ryan's been meeting with him, and I think it's been really encouraging for both of them."

"Oh, it's not only me pouring into him." Ryan held up a hand. "Chris is pouring into me and encouraging me too. And now Gage is meeting with us. We can all encourage each other."

Sarah wanted to know more, so Ryan explained about their discipleship meetings, and I inwardly breathed a sigh of relief. I wanted to go home, snuggle Kevin, and go to bed early, but first I needed to find my family. I looked around the room.

Emma interrupted my search. She met my eyes and raised an eyebrow. She'd let it drop, here in front of everyone, but it seemed the Chris conversation wasn't as finished as I would have liked it to be.

Before either of us could say anything else, my parents broke through the crowd. My dad's voice boomed over us. "There's my girl!"

I laughed, ecstatic to see them. "Hi, Dad! Merry Christmas!"

He hugged me back and kissed me on the forehead. "I told your mother, our girl shines so bright! You did a wonderful job! Just wonderful!"

I blushed, my heart soaring. "Thank you, Dad. That means a lot." He released me so my mom could have a turn. She hugged me.

"We are so proud of you!" she exclaimed. "Fantastic job!"

"Thank you, Mom!"

I saw my brother out of the corner of my eye, so I turned to hug him.

"Merry Christmas, Mark! It was so kind of y'all to be here!"

He hugged me back. "We wouldn't miss it!"

My sister-in-law, Bree, stood by his side, baby Henry cuddled in her arms. She smiled shyly and reached for me with one hand.

"Thank you so much for coming!" I hugged her. I stepped out of the hug and looked at precious Henry. He was all drooly smiles, cute as could be. He had his mother's hair in a death grip. Surely it must hurt, but Bree didn't seem bothered.

My heart melted when Henry lifted his arms and reached for me. Bree handed him to me, and he promptly grabbed onto my hair. "An ulterior motive!" I laughed and settled him on my hip. "I'll take it."

Bree apologized. "Sorry, Aunt Maddie!" She carefully extricated my hair from his chubby hand. "He's really taking off, getting into everything." She blew her bangs out of her face. "He started trying to pull up yesterday. I'm not ready!"

"Oh my goodness," I exclaimed. "He's a genius!"

"It runs in the family," my dad bellowed proudly. He held out a finger to Henry, who immediately reached out, took it, and jammed it into his mouth.

"Dad! Germs!" Mark scolded him.

My dad took his hand back, wincing from Henry's sharp tooth. "Sorry."

Bree shook her head. "It's okay. He's teething, so he puts everything in his mouth right now."

Someone tickled the back of my arm, and I turned to see who was messing with me. It was Chris.

"Hey!" I smiled warmly at him and gestured around. "Chris, this is my family. My parents, Bill and Paula, and my brother, Mark, my sister-in-law, Bree, and this is my nephew, Henry."

Henry blew a raspberry in greeting. Chris winked at him and smiled around the circle.

"It's great to meet y'all! Thank you for sharing your Christmas Eve with all of us." He reached out and shook hands with everyone. He smiled at my parents. "I have to say to you both, well done. Your daughter is a wonderful woman."

My parents preened. My neck heated and I looked around for a distraction.

"Is your family here too?" I asked Chris. "I met your mom briefly before the show."

He shook his head. "They were here, but they already left to drive back to East Texas. I'll see them tomorrow."

My mom couldn't help herself. "Would you like to join us for dinner?"

Chris smiled. "Thank you for the invitation, but I already have plans. I wanted to be sure to swing by and meet all of you. Merry Christmas!"

He squeezed my elbow gently, then he turned and walked away into the crowd.

"You can call me Paula!" Mom called. But he was already gone.

I looked around at my family and felt pulled in every direction. My friends. My family. The embarrassingly strong desire to chase Chris down and hug him one more time. *Stop that*, I said to myself.

My mom leaned into me. "Chris seems nice."

I turned to her, inwardly screaming. But I kept it simple. "Ready to go?"

—

Christmas Eve at my parents' house did not disappoint. We spent the evening mostly watching Henry giggle and play in the wrapping paper, until it was time for him to go to bed. We all got in one last snuggle, and my brother and Bree bundled him out the door to go home. We waved goodbye until their car disappeared around the corner, then I turned to my parents.

"I should get home too. Work will start early in the morning." I reached for my jacket. I was so tired I could fall asleep standing there.

"Oh!" my mom protested. "I hate it when everyone leaves!"

She looked up at my dad and leaned against him, her arm wrapping around his waist. His hand grasped her shoulder, the way it often did, and he leaned his head on hers. For a moment, I watched them and thanked God for the bond He had created there. We'd all certainly had our issues, but their connection had held strong for four decades.

It was a comfort to me. Yet, the sweetness didn't erase the tiny sting of a desire unfulfilled. Yes, even I could get a little wistful for a deep, strong love from time to time.

Pushing against the feeling, I summoned a smile. I refused to do the sad-lonely-holiday thing this year. Period. *Lift that gaze, woman!* It was Christmas. I had completed a huge project successfully. I remembered the roses Chris had given me at the play. I'd put them in water here at my parents' house, and now the vase was strapped into the car with a seatbelt and everything. Christmas beauty shone all around me, and I had every reason to be joyful.

I reached out and hugged my parents. My mom rushed to the kitchen and returned with a container of leftovers for me to take home. I'd already taken my Christmas presents to the car.

"Be safe, Punkin!"

"Be sure to lock your doors!"

Smiling and feeling very loved, I walked down the sidewalk and opened my car door.

"Thank you for everything! I love you so much! Merry Christmas!" I called before I sat down and closed the car door. They stood and waved, watching until I turned the corner. I sighed. I had so much to process. I thanked God and praised Him the whole way home.

—

The next morning came early. As usual, I sleepwalked through my routine to get ready for the long day ahead. Holidays were always a little wild in the ER. At six on the dot, I put on my jacket to walk out the door. I paused when my phone buzzed. It was awfully early. Was the sun even up yet? I looked out the window. *Nope. Still dark.*

My mind immediately went to an emergency. My parents. Henry. *Oh no.* I opened my texts and found an unexpected missive from a youth minister I'd figured I was finished with for a while.

Chris: Check your welcome mat before you step outside this morning. Sorry you have to work today. Thank you for serving the community! Merry Christmas!

What in the world?

I walked to the door and quietly opened it, trying not to wake Emma. Looking down, I spied a paper coffee cup sitting on the mat, next to a white bakery bag. A Post-it stuck to the bag, with *Merry Christmas* scrawled in all caps. I sighed. *That man.* Butterflies leapt into my stomach. *No,* I tried to calm myself down. *This is not pursuit. It's an act of kindness. Everyone knows he's an early riser. And now he lives with four-year-old twins. It's Christmas morning. They've probably been up for hours.* As if he'd read my mind, my phone buzzed.

Chris: The twins have been up for two hours already. We needed a field trip.

See? I told myself, the butterflies dying. *Be reasonable!* I picked up the coffee and the bakery bag. How had he found a bakery that was open on Christmas Day? I wondered. Peeking inside, I saw a chocolate croissant. My stomach rumbled. I could ask questions later. For now, it was time to enjoy a wonderful, thoughtful, totally meaningless but delicious breakfast.

Me: Please tell the twins thank you and Merry Christmas!

He sent a thumbs-up emoji, and that was that. My phone was silent.

I turned my phone off during my shift, and I was so busy I couldn't check it until I left the hospital. I turned it on, and it immediately buzzed with wonderful news!

Mia: WE'RE ENGAGED!!!

She'd sent a picture too. She and Ryan held each other close, both of them teary-eyed. Mia held up her left hand, showing off a gorgeous ring. I texted her back immediately.

Me: Finally! PRAISE THE LORD!!!

I walked in the door a few minutes later, excited for my friends, but completely exhausted. Christmas in the ER was a wild mix of flu, random cuts, burns, and meat-related injuries. Not to mention severe food poisoning and one stab wound. (They claimed a family argument got out of hand.) It had been quite the holiday, and now it was time for something normal.

CHAPTER 14

Chelsea and I texted throughout the week between Christmas and New Year's. Trent was a no-show at Christmas. I could only imagine the twins' disappointment and confusion. He insisted something important came up, so they agreed to try again the following weekend. Chelsea handled it, but I could tell it broke her heart.

I had a rough week too. A stressed-out family member in the waiting room exploded at me in front of everyone. I made a mistake, and a doctor in the ER chewed me out, even though I caught it before anything happened. Both times, the circumstances were out of my control. I was just the easy target, but that didn't stop them. Apparently, the holidays brought out something extra special in people, and I'd never seen anything like it in all my years upstairs. Chelsea caught me in a weak moment that Thursday night.

Chelsea: It's not too late. You could still come with us to my mom's house this weekend. After the week you've had, you need some relaxing time away! And I would love to have a friend to hang out with while the kids are with Trent. We're leaving tomorrow morning. Please say you'll come!

I sighed. A relaxing getaway sounded wonderful, and of course I would love to be helpful to Chelsea.

Me: Okay, I'm in. I'll get packed and see you in the morning. Thanks for inviting me!

Chelsea: YAY!!!!!

This may have been a bad idea, I admitted to myself the next morning. A small foot kicked the back of my seat again. Sweet little Noah was stronger than he looked. I shifted, trying to find a more comfortable position in the passenger seat of Chelsea's minivan. The twins rode with their mother in the back, and I sat up front, next to the unusually quiet youth minister in the driver's seat.

The winter sun shone brightly through the windshield. In contrast, tall, dark-green trees densely lined the highway on both sides. So far, East Texas looked vastly different from the concrete jungle of DFW. The occasional road sign brightened the side of the road, and cars sped alongside us. *Veggie Tales* songs played over the speakers and the air smelled strongly of goldfish crackers.

There was good news: the snack situation would make Mia, a certifiable snack queen, proud. Chelsea's *Road Trip Mom Bag* overflowed with enough juice boxes, fruit snacks, apple sauce, pretzels, and goldfish to last a week. It reminded me of Mary Poppins' bottomless carpet bag. She'd even made a little snack basket for Chris and me to share up front. I rifled through it, looking for a piece of consolation chocolate, to cope with the bad news.

It started when I woke up to the sound of Kevin barfing on the carpet next to my bed. Cleaning up put me behind schedule. That was bad. But worse? Chris was surprised to see me—and not in a happy way.

He stood, packing the back of the van, clearly agitated, when I walked up the sidewalk to the driveway. "Help me understand something? This is a weekend trip. Why do we need eighteen bags?" he griped. He stopped and tilted his head, as if realizing I was actually there and not his imagination. "Hi! What are you doing here?" He was kind, but bewildered.

"Chelsea invited me," I explained, suddenly feeling self-conscious and defensive. I ran my fingers down the braid I'd hastily tied my hair into. I hadn't had time to do more after cleaning up Kevin's mess.

His eyebrows pulled together into a frown. "For real?"

I shrugged. "Yeah. It was kind of last minute. She didn't tell you?"

He looked back and forth between the house and me. "I thought she was kidding."

What did *that* mean? We stood, silently staring at one another for a beat. The last time I'd seen Chris, a week ago, we'd been very comfortable with each other. Now, a thick cloud of awkwardness settled between us. Just as the feeling became truly unbearable, Chelsea came running out and threw her arms around me. She must have been watching for me.

"You're here! Yay! Come on inside. We're almost ready to go."

Chelsea didn't wait for an answer; she turned toward the door. I followed, my chest still crushed under the weight of Chris's frown upon seeing me. Was he upset? Annoyed? What just happened?

"Miss Maddie!" Hannah greeted me with a bouncy hug. She stood in the kitchen, dutifully holding the leash attached to a Golden Retriever mix lying next to her on the tile.

"Hi, Hannah! This must be Edna!" Hannah nodded while I leaned down to pet the dog's silky ears. Edna's tail wagged as she sniffed my hand and gave me a lick of welcome.

"If you need to use the restroom before we go, there's a bathroom down the hallway and to the right," Chelsea told me. She gathered up the remaining snacks from the counter and called down the hallway. "Noah! Time to go, bud!"

I hurried toward the bathroom, my mind spinning. *Was this a mistake? It's not too late to leave. But I'm already here. Hannah and Chelsea seemed so excited to see me.* I wasn't sure what to do.

I used the restroom, splashed some cold water on my face, and headed toward the front door. Out the kitchen window, I could see Chelsea and Chris outside, talking. I paused to watch for a few seconds. Chris didn't seem upset, but he didn't seem glad either. He closed the back of the van and walked over to get in the driver's seat. Chelsea headed toward the door, so I met her in the foyer.

"Chelsea, I didn't realize Chris didn't know I was coming. I feel like I made things awkward. Should I stay home? It's not too late," I offered as we moved outside to the front porch.

"What? No, silly! I'm so glad you're here!" Chelsea locked the door as she spoke and spun to walk toward the driveway. She wove her arm through mine and pulled me along. "This is going to be a perfect little getaway for all of us! Do you mind sitting up front? I have to wrangle the kids in the back, and I don't want Chris to be stuck all alone." I followed her then obeyed when she gestured for me to get in the passenger seat.

When I got in the car, Chris smiled at me, much more his usual self.

"Are you ready for this, Reed?" At my shrug, he looked serious. "The first rule of the road trip: I drive, I pick the music. Capiche?"

I was still so thrown from the events of the last ten minutes that I could only nod in agreement and reach for my seatbelt. The awkwardness still pressed on me, but it was starting to dissipate. Maybe it really wasn't a big deal. Chris put the van in gear, and we set off.

An hour later, we were about halfway there. The kids had already watched *Frosty the Snowman,* and now they chomped loudly on goldfish while *Veggie Tales* music played. Edna lay between the kids' seats, catching the occasional fallen bite. I found a Hershey Kiss in the basket and unwrapped it.

"Can I get you anything?" I asked, still trying to make peace.

Chris shifted. "No thanks, I'm good for now." He stayed focused on the road but glanced at me for a second. "How about you? Are you doing okay?"

"Yeah," I answered. I took a sip of water to wash down the chocolate. I hated this feeling that things were off between us. "Sorry again, about you not knowing Chelsea invited me. I didn't know I was coming until last night."

Chris shook his head and adjusted his baseball cap. "It's fine. I was just surprised. You are never the problem, Maddie. You are great."

It wasn't a huge reassurance, but I would take what I could get at this point. I nodded. "I'll try to remember that. Thanks."

"Did Chelsea prepare you to meet the rest of us?"

"What do you mean?" I asked.

"I mean my family is big and loud. We're sarcastic and competitive. Do you have an exit strategy in case you get overwhelmed?"

I scoffed. "I'll be fine. My family can be loud and competitive too."

He grimaced, as if I'd told him I wanted to try professional bull riding. "Maddie. I have four siblings and a dozen nieces and nephews. My two older brothers are *relentless*. I have two older sisters, and you have only met the quieter one. There are kids and dogs everywhere. It's out in the country. It's…a lot."

"Well, thanks for the heads-up, but I'm sure it will be fine," I insisted. "I think Chelsea wants some support, since the kids are seeing Trent this weekend."

"That's not why," Chris stated flatly, a dark look on his face. His eyes flicked to me. "You ran track in high school, right?"

I nodded.

"Secret weapon," he sighed under his breath, shaking his head.

I raised my eyebrows, questioning. He shook his head again. "We have this tradition. We play touch football at New Year's. Besides the fact that Trent won't be there to play, Chelsea's team lost last year, and she has been upset about it ever since. I hate to break it to you, but if you're still remotely fast, she's hoping you will be the source of a different outcome for this year's game."

I couldn't hide my reaction. *What?* I considered everything he'd just said. Chelsea hadn't mentioned anything about playing football. But that wasn't the most important part.

If? My shoulders stiffened, and I sat up taller in my seat. My veins practically hummed with the desire to set him straight, delusional or not. I hadn't raced competitively in years, but I wasn't going to tell him that.

"Of course I can still run fast!" *Probably.*

Chris smirked knowingly. "Great! Good to know."

"I'll be fine," I insisted. "Will I be on your team?"

"No, if you play on Chelsea's team, we'll be rivals."

"Ooh, better watch out, Calvert."

"Noted, Reed. I'm sure you are quite the fierce competitor."

"Obviously."

I picked another Hershey Kiss out of the basket and fiddled with the foil while I chewed. What exactly had I gotten myself into here? My nerves hummed, but I shrugged, nonchalant on the outside. *Cool as a cucumber.*

"It's only been thirteen years since high school, what could go wrong?" I joked.

"Don't be scared, Reed. It should be a pretty quick beat-down. You won't feel a thing." He winked at me. My jaw dropped, and my nostrils flared.

"Well, I wouldn't make assumptions if I were you. You know what *assuming* does."

He barked a laugh. "I do."

I basked in my victory for a moment. Then the reality set in. "You said it's touch football, right? No tackling?"

"Nervous already?" he mocked.

I scoffed. "No, but I want to understand the rules. I mean, if you're the youngest, these people are not exactly spring chickens. I don't want to hurt anyone."

Chris nodded. "Yes, it's touch football. No tackling allowed. And yes, we're all older, so be gentle with us."

I wanted to know more. "Tell me about your siblings. You're the youngest, and you're thirty. What about everyone else?"

Chris took a sip of coffee and adjusted his cap. "Colton is the oldest; he's twelve years older than me. His wife is Heather. Colton coaches football at the local high school. Their oldest is a college freshman. They have three:

Brock is a college freshman, Izzy is sixteen, and Nathaniel is fourteen.

"My other brother is Chance. Chance is seven years older than me. He's married to Stephanie. He's the foreman at a ranch on the other side of town, about an hour away. He's slowed down a little, but he still talks the most trash. They have two daughters and a son. Miles is fifteen, Claire is fourteen, and Ruthie is twelve."

I nodded, lost in all the names. This family was huge! "What about your sisters?"

Chris took a sip from his coffee cup before he answered. He licked his lips as he put the cup back in the cupholder.

"Crystal is between the two brothers. She's nine years older than me, the quintessential oldest daughter. She keeps everyone in line, bosses us around, loves us all like crazy. She's married to Joe, and they have four kids. She was made for big family life. They moved to Indianapolis for Joe's job a couple years ago. They came down for Thanksgiving this year, so they won't be there." He raised his voice so the others could hear. "And you know Chelsea, she's thirty-five. Two kids. Warrior Mom!"

I turned around to look at Chelsea. She blew her bangs out of her eyes, focused on digging for something in her mom bag. She stopped digging and looked at Chris. "What are you saying about me up there? I've got stories too! Maddie, remind me to tell you about Chris's senior prom!"

Chris kept his eyes on the road, but he reached over and turned up the *Veggie Tales*, drowning her out. I laughed and shook my head. "It's all good things!" I yelled to her over the noise.

"Uncle Chris!" Hannah's little voice cut through "The Hairbrush Song," her hands pressed over her ears. "Can you turn it down, please? I can hardly hear myself think!"

Chris immediately acquiesced. I turned and smiled at Hannah. "Are you excited to visit your family?"

Hannah nodded. "Grammy loves us double 'cause we're double precious."

I looked at Noah. He nodded in agreement. "Makes sense to me," I told them.

"For the record," Chris said, "*everyone* thinks Grammy loves them the most—except for me, because I *know* she loves me the most."

Both kids shook their heads extravagantly and gave a thumbs down. This must be a common argument. Noah yelled, "She loves us all the saaaame!"

I looked back at Chelsea. She grinned and shrugged at me. "He only claims that when it's convenient. Otherwise, he insists he's loved equally. Isn't that right, *Baby Christopher?*"

He nodded. "I can tell this weekend is going to be really fun for some people. Maddie, would you like me to drop you off at a hotel, or maybe here on the side of the road, so you can have the *most* fun and avoid witnessing all this?"

I laughed. "Oh, no. I'm dying to see it all for myself!"

He shook his head and sighed. "That's what I was afraid you would say." He signaled and exited the highway. It was almost time to meet the rest of the Calverts. A flicker of nerves fluttered through my chest. I resisted the urge to check my hair in the mirror. I was here as Chelsea's guest, and that was it: the only reason I wanted their family to like me.

Is that really why? my heart whispered treacherously. I tightened my ponytail, straightened my shoulders, slicked on a little lip gloss, and told my heart to shut up.

CHAPTER 15

We drove along a county road for about ten more minutes, passing a couple of small ranches. At one point, I spied a lake, hidden behind the thick forest lining the road. Now and again, the trees opened up to reveal a field or a house or a group of animals. The kids knew this road well. They pointed out all the animals: goats, chickens, alpacas, and some horses and cattle. Chris slowed and turned into a break in the trees, which turned out to be a road. We drove along the paved road for another minute or two before we pulled into a long driveway, where a brick, ranch-style house eventually came into view.

The house wasn't fancy or overly large. It sprawled across the lot, a simple, gray brick with white trim. A wide porch wrapped all the way around it, from what I could tell. Poinsettias sat stationed at intervals along the wooden railing, and small Christmas trees twinkled in the windows. Christmas lights wrapped around every detail of the house, and I knew this would be a sight to behold once the sun set. Chris slowed the car, and Rhonda Calvert opened the screen door and stepped out onto the porch. Once she saw us, she waved and hurried over to greet us with a Labrador on either side of her. One dog was yellow, the other black. I wondered which one was Sam and which was Elliott. They both had graying snouts, but they trotted happily alongside her, their tongues lolling out of their mouths.

Chris's mom opened the sliding door next to Hannah and exclaimed, "There you are, my babies! I'm so happy to see you!"

"Grammy!" Hannah exclaimed. She kicked her little legs excitedly and fiddled with the button to get out of her booster seat. Rhonda pulled Hannah into her arms. Noah flew across the car to his Grammy, ready for a hug. She held on tight for a moment then held each of their hands while they jumped to the ground. She bent down to their level.

"Who's hungry? I made chicken salad!"

"Me!" the kids exclaimed then began talking at once, telling her all their important news.

"I fell down and got a scrape right here."

"Our Christmas teacher, Miss Maddie came with us! She's so pretty."

"Are our cousins here? I want to play!"

"We get to see Daddy while we're here, but we want to stay with you at night, Grammy."

On and on they went. Rhonda listened intently, nodding and smiling. Chris, Chelsea, and I all gathered our things and stepped out of the minivan. Rhonda held up a hand and the twins stopped talking.

"I can't wait to hear more, but let me hug your mama and Uncle Chris right quick."

"Okay!" Noah agreed and took off for the house.

"You can hug Miss Maddie too!" Hannah exclaimed, pointing at me.

I smiled. "Hi, it's wonderful to see you again! Thank you for having me."

"Welcome, Maddie!" Rhonda lifted her arm to hug me. Charmed, I leaned into her for a moment. I could see where Chris and Chelsea both got their outgoing spirits.

Rhonda turned to Chelsea, carefully assessing her daughter. "There's my girl."

Chelsea moved into the embrace, laid her head on her mother's shoulder, drew a breath, and sighed. A tear rolled down her cheek.

"Hi, Mama," she whispered.

Rhonda held on and rubbed her back. "I'm happy to see you, my brave one. It's alright. You're here now, and we'll take good care of you."

Chelsea's shoulders slowly lowered, and she relaxed into her mother, wrapping her arms around Rhonda to hold on. Everything else paused. I watched, fascinated. I could almost physically see the load roll off of Chelsea's back.

What a gift it is, in tough seasons, to be able to come home and feel safe with your mom. Mia's face crossed my mind. Not everyone had that.

My own eyes smarted as my heart swelled with affection for my own parents. They'd expected a lot of me growing up, and it hadn't always been easy. But we'd come a long way. They were supportive and caring. They'd raised me in a household of faith, and I never doubted their love, or the love of God. It took time for me to understand the depth of that blessing, and I was reminded of it again, watching Chelsea lean on Rhonda's shoulder.

A thump sounded from the back of the minivan, distracting me. Chris was already unloading the luggage, stacking the suitcases on the ground. The three dogs circled him, wagging their tails and sniffing each other. He walked over to us carrying a backpack on his back, pillows in the crook of each arm, and an embroidered canvas bag in each hand. His shoulders slumped as he blew out a resigned sigh.

The Calvert women both laughed at him as they released each other. Chelsea wiped her eyes then patted Chris on the shoulder.

"Thanks for driving, little brother, I appreciate it." She took the bags from his hands and herded the twins toward the house.

Chris stepped over and took Rhonda in his arms, a big bear hug. He stood a head taller than her, but she wrapped her arms around him.

"There's my baby boy!" she cried, squeezing him tight. "It's wonderful to see you two weekends in a row like this!"

He stood up, smiling. "Thanks for having us, Mama."

She brushed off his comment. "Oh, you know you're always welcome here. The twins will sleep in the guest bed, so I made up your room for Maddie. Do you mind taking the sofa bed?"

Chris nodded. "That's perfect."

"I can take the sofa bed," I offered.

Chris looked at me like that was the silliest thing he'd ever heard and gave a single shake of his head. "No."

Rhonda backed him up. "No, indeed! You're a guest, and we're glad to have you! Come on in and have some lunch!" It was settled. She turned and headed toward the back of the minivan, taking two bags to carry inside. I hurried to grab my own suitcase then jogged to catch up as they climbed the steps to the porch.

Once the screen door closed behind me, I followed Rhonda down a hallway to the room she'd made up for me. It was a small room with light-gray walls and a double bed. Sports posters and shelves of trophies still covered the walls. A stack of baseball caps sat on the dresser. Everything was clean, and the light coming in from the window bathed the room in a feeling of welcome.

A wooden frame on the nightstand held a picture of a large group of people, all of them smiling. I recognized younger versions of Chris and Chelsea, as well as others who had to be the rest of the Calvert children and their spouses. Goodness, this family. Every one of them was gorgeous!

Chris stood in the middle, wearing a graduation gown and mortar-board. A tall, handsome man—Chris's dad?—stood on one end, his arm around Chelsea. Everyone else held each other close, including Rhonda, who stood on the other end, an older couple standing one on each side of her. They must be Chris's grandparents.

Like the rest of them, Rhonda was smiling, but even after meeting her so briefly, I could see the difference. Hers was a smile made of glass. Her parents seemed to be almost literally holding up her frame. The love was evident, and yet there were obviously a lot of different dynamics represented in this picture. Chris had never shared the details of his parents' split with me. *What was it like when his dad left? How were all the kids now?* So many questions.

CHAPTER 16

A creak in the floor alerted me I wasn't alone. Startled, I looked over, hurriedly setting the picture down. Chris stepped into the doorway. "Hey, you good here?" he asked. I nodded.

"I hope you don't mind sharing the bathroom with me," he said. "It's down the hall. Towels are in the cabinet. Let me know anything else you need."

I nodded. "Okay, thanks."

His gaze shifted to the picture frame on the nightstand. "That was the beginning of my *extra*-good-looking phase."

I couldn't help smiling at his goofiness, but I knew what he was doing: deflecting from deeper questions. This tactic was Youth Guy Chris 101.

"Interesting. When did that end?" After all our trash talk, why not poke the bear a tiny bit more?

His smile widened, his teeth flashing movie star white. "Joke's on you, Reed. You've probably noticed, I'm in my hottest era yet. A 2.0, if you will."

I picked up the frame and squinted, looking between it and him, comparing. "Actually, I'm curious." I held it out to him. Would he open up?

He took hold of the frame and looked at the picture. "You're wondering if I was single back then? Hardly ever." I had my answer: still deflecting. I had to give him credit; he was excellent at this little game. He set the frame on the table.

"Ready for lunch?" he asked, pointing his thumb toward the kitchen.

Six weeks ago, I would have missed his relief. His shoulders lowered by a hair, and his jaw relaxed. He thought the subject was closed, and we were going to move on to simpler topics. *Careful.* I didn't want to push too hard and upset him.

I shrugged and pointed to the frame. "Was this taken before or after your folks divorced?"

His shoulders stiffened, and he looked away before his eyes came back to meet mine. We both stood still for a moment then he gave in with a sigh. "It was about six months later." He looked down at the photograph. "He left the day after Christmas, then he showed up at graduation and acted like he was so proud of me…as if nothing had happened. I barely graduated at all, because I'd gone so buck wild my last semester."

"*Buck* wild?"

He pointed to the center of the photograph. "I am literally hungover in this picture. Grief as a teenager. It wasn't pretty."

I winced in sympathy and looked up at him. "What is it like with your dad now?"

He considered it and finally shrugged. "It's okay." He didn't offer any more.

Chris looked down at the picture again and pointed to the older people. "These are my grandparents, Sushi and

Pop. Pop passed away about four years ago, and Sushi lives here with my mom now."

"Sushi?" I clarified, charmed at her nickname.

He smiled and explained. "Her name is Susan, but Pop always called her Susie. The story goes that Colton overheard it one too many times as a toddler and repeated it with his own spin. No one was going to argue with the first grandbaby."

"That's not a very common grandmother name," I pointed out, loving it.

He nodded. "It's unique, for sure. But it works. She's unique—sharp and sassy, like someone else I know," he said, turning his playful grin on me.

I fixed him with what I hoped was a sharp, sassy look. "I like the sound of that. Which team is she playing for tomorrow?"

He laughed and reached over to give my braid a friendly tug. "She's neutral. Come on, let's eat." He turned and walked out of the room.

Following Chris down the hallway, one wall was stuffed with picture frames. I took my time walking along, fascinated to see the Calvert family through the years—baby pictures, braces, first cars. Chelsea as Homecoming queen. I laughed out loud at one of Chris looking awkward, yet dapper in a suit and tie, dancing with a girl in a dress and white gloves. The wording along the bottom of the photo read *Cotillion Ball*. The pictures continued all the way down the hallway, and the noise of a crowd grew steadily louder with each step.

The kitchen was full of people, all of them seemingly talking at once. The dogs wove around, sniffing and catching whatever bits of food fell. I saw Hannah and Noah sitting at the counter, both of them talking at Chelsea while she sliced a banana onto the plates in front of them. Rhonda stood at the sink, washing plates, while another woman dried. Two men sat at a large round table eating sandwiches. They must be Chris's brothers. A football flew through the air. In a single movement, a young man caught it and walked straight out the screen door. A younger teen boy and two girls followed.

Chris touched my arm and pointed out the plates and food, set out buffet style along the far counter. I walked over and grabbed a plate, suddenly ravenous. The first platter in line was laden with two types of bread and croissants. I took a croissant and spread a spoonful of chicken salad across the bottom half. I served myself some fruit, chips, and some iced tea then made my way over to the table, which had a few seats left.

One of the older men saw me, and his face broke into a smile. "Who do we have here?"

"Hi! I'm Maddie," I introduced myself. "I'm friends with Chelsea and Chris." I set my plate and drink on the table and pulled out a chair.

"I'm Chance," he said. He stood and held out a deeply tanned hand. His arm was covered to the wrist in a sleeve of intricate tattoos. "Maddie, you say? Have we met?"

I shook my head as the other one reached across to shake my hand. "I'm Colton. It's nice to meet you. We've heard good things!"

Chance looked at Colton meaningfully, his eyebrows raised. "So this is *Maddie* Maddie?"

Colton shrugged. "I assume so. How many Maddies could there be?"

A plate clattered to the table next to mine, and Chelsea collapsed into the chair.

"Whew!" she exclaimed. "Have y'all met Maddie?"

Chance nodded at me. "Sure have. Say, Chels, is this Maddie the Maddie I'm thinking of?" He seemed very excited. Chelsea turned her head and gave him a look.

"Maddie directed the Christmas play the twins were in last week. The kids adore her, and we're friends, so I invited her." She stared at Chance.

He nodded slowly. "Got it." I got the distinct impression I was only hearing half the conversation. Maybe the mind-reading thing ran in the family.

On the other side of Chelsea, Chris pulled out a chair. "Hey, Colton, did you tell the kids they could wash your truck?"

Colton sat up straight. "No! The windows are down!"

He stood and shot outside, yelling. Chris lifted his chin toward Chance. "How's work?"

"Work is good," Chance answered. He purposely met Chris's eyes. "I just met *Maddie*."

"Did you ask her about football?" Chris responded.

Chance's eyes lit up. He looked from Chris to Chelsea to me, a whole new calculation going on in his head.

"Maddie, do you play football?" he asked excitedly.

"Not often, but I can. I've played before," I told him.

Chance nodded. "Interesting."

Rhonda called over from the sink, "Y'all don't start going on about football yet. Give everybody time to settle in!"

Chance adjusted his ball cap, turning it backward, and leaned in. "Maddie, I suppose you are aware of the situation?"

I nodded, hoping I looked self-assured and full of knowledge, rather than what I was: vaguely informed, at best. I wasn't even sure whose team was whose. Chelsea cleared her throat and leaned in conspiratorially.

"She's fast. She ran track in high school."

Chance nodded and rubbed his palms together. "We can definitely work with that."

Chris leaned into the circle and shook his head. "I wouldn't count my chicks if I were y'all. Winning is a tradition for Colton and me, and we're going to keep it that way." He looked at each of us and smiled. "See you on the field."

Chris stood and grabbed his already empty plate. Chance looked up at him as he pushed in his chair, his face lit with a confident grin. *Too confident.* Chance pointed his gaze at me.

"You see what we've been dealing with? The bookends think they have the *power of Greyskull,* but they underestimate us, and now *we* have a secret weapon."

I frowned. *Greyskull?* A secret weapon? "Sorry, I'm not familiar. What is *Greyskull?*"

Chance bowed his head and shook it. "Youths! It's from a cartoon back in the good old days called *He-man.*"

I nodded. "Cool."

Chance shook his head again. "We'll have to fix that at some point. But for now your youthfulness will be helpful for our cause."

I laughed. "I wouldn't say I'm *youthful.* I'm thirty-one. You mean the football game?"

Chance nodded.

Chelsea pointed at me. "You're our secret weapon, Maddie."

I shook my head. They nodded, their smiles almost identical. I shook my head more strenuously.

"No way!" I insisted. "Y'all are setting yourselves up for disappointment here."

Chelsea reached over and patted my hand reassuringly. "Don't worry, Maddie. You are the perfect person for this!"

"How? Chris works out all the time. He runs around with teenagers for his job. He's *fast*! I'm okay, but I'm not an athlete anymore!" I explained. I wanted them to have reasonable expectations, not delusional ones.

"You don't have to be faster than Chris," Chelsea assured me. "It's all mental. Chris will be *distracted* by you, and we'll run right past him!"

What? "That doesn't make any sense."

Chance nodded, smiling. "This is going to be fun."

I looked at them, perturbed. The screen door flew open, and Colton walked inside, saving me from having to respond.

"Where's Chris? Nobody was messing with my truck!" he exclaimed, exasperated.

Chance and Chelsea stood and gathered their plates then scattered. What now? I looked around, suddenly feeling a little nervous about tomorrow. Chelsea moved to the counter and began cleaning up after the twins, who were long gone, off playing with cousins. It was only the two of us left in the kitchen. I took my plate to the sink, washed it off, and placed it in the dishwasher. I looked around the suddenly quiet kitchen, bewildered. Chelsea was still there, wiping down the counter.

"Well?" she asked. "What do you think?"

I blew out a breath. "It's a big family."

She chuckled. "Yup. I don't want you to be uneasy about the football game. It's just for fun. But half the glory comes from the trash talk, y'know?"

I shrugged. "It will all work out."

"For sure!" she agreed. "I've got to go make sure the kids aren't setting anything on fire. Are you good here?"

"Yeah. I think I'll go for a walk. It's so pretty here with all the trees."

Chelsea pointed toward what I assumed would be the road. "If you go left, there's a big pond about a mile down the road. It's a nice view."

That sounded good to me. At my nod, she smiled at me. "Thanks for being here, Maddie. I'm so glad you came!"

With those final words and a quick hug, she strolled out of the kitchen in search of her children. I looked around and sighed. I hadn't had much free time lately, so I took a second to absorb the freedom and enjoy it. Then, I went to my room to grab a sweatshirt and headed outside.

Chelsea was right; the pond was huge and really pretty, surrounded by greenery. I saw a couple of deer in the trees. The beauty and peaceful environment gave me space to clear my head and heart.

My walk turned into a little bit of a therapy session between me and God, processing through the last couple of months. I prayed and walked and even cried a little, seeing how God had carried me through. God had met me in the pressure of my job transition, the Christmas play, and seeing Heidi again. It hadn't been easy, but He'd been faithful and good to me.

By the time I got back to the house, I felt lighter but emotionally wrung out. A power nap was definitely in order, because something told me these people would stay up late and do fireworks for New Year's Eve that night. But first, a shower. I'd worked up a bit of a sweat, walking and talking with God.

I went to my room first to grab my toiletries then headed to the bathroom. I undressed, wrapping myself in a towel. Reaching behind the simple white shower curtain, I turned on the faucet. The water was icy cold and needed time to warm up, so I washed my face and brushed my teeth in the sink. Once steam floated up over the top of the shower curtain, I turned and moved it aside to get in. I had one hand on the shower curtain, the other reaching to unwrap my towel when I looked down, and my gaze was met by two beady eyes.

CHAPTER 17

The frog sat in the tub, blinking in the warm spray. Somehow it managed to look simultaneously calm and annoyed. Its speckled green skin was dark against the porcelain bathtub. A bulbous white throat inflated from its deep-green chest, and a croak echoed against the shower walls. It shifted on its squat legs and attempted a small jump on the surface of the tub.

I completely lost it.

Shrieking at the top of my lungs, I jumped away from the shower and fled. Clutching my towel, I scrambled, my fingers flailing against the door. It took me a few tries to grasp the doorknob well enough to turn it. "No, no, no, no, no!"

Finally, I opened the door and ran out of the bathroom, but I didn't get far. A startled yelp escaped me when I collided with a solid, tall, male chest. Chris caught me by my bare shoulders, keeping me upright.

His eyes went wide, full of surprise. "Maddie? You're—"

I cut him off. "There's a frog in the shower!" I yowled hysterically. "Oh my gosh! Yurgh!" Just saying the word *frog* brought on another full-body shudder. "Can you get it out?" I yelled, grabbing the front of his shirt. I pulled on his shirt, practically climbing over him, trying to get away. Chris put his hands on my shoulders again, holding me in place. His face twitched.

"A frog?"

"Yes, a frog!" I repeated shrilly. "*Chris–*"

Something in his expression caught my attention. The frantic words clogged in my throat as the light dawned. He pressed his lips together, looking innocent. Too innocent. In an instant, the truth became crystal clear. A switch flipped, and my freak-out turned to embarrassed fury.

"*You.*"

A laugh choked out of him, and I recoiled, yanking out of his grasp. "A prank. You played a prank on me at your mother's house with a *live frog*?" I yelled in disbelief, each word louder than the last.

He cracked up but quickly held up his hands to ward off my fists. I pounded ineffectually at his chest and shoulders. He held up his hands in defense. "Whoa! Okay! Okay! I'm sorry! I thought you'd see it before you—" He laughed some more, then he yelled, "Maddie, your towel!"

He looked at the ceiling and covered his eyes dramatically.

I paused, looked down to check then back up at him. He'd left his stomach unguarded. I poked him, hard, and he doubled over with a satisfying *oof.* I stepped away from him.

"Ugh!" I growled furiously. I clutched the towel, which was not loose, *thankyouverymuch.* (I'm a nurse. I can straight-up secure a wrap. Any wrap.) He clutched his stomach dramatically, but I pointed my finger in his face.

"Get it out of there right now!" I ordered. "You are the most obnoxious person I have *ever* met!"

He straightened and raised his hands in surrender. Pressing his lips together, his eyes sparkling with mirth, he sidestepped into the bathroom. The sound of water stopped. I tensed at the metallic creak of the shower curtain grommets scraping against the metal rod. In a few seconds, he came back, proudly holding the disgruntled frog up for display. One of its back legs kicked free and paddled at the air beneath Chris's hand.

"Yurgh!" I jumped away, shuddering, and ran to my room, Chris's laughter echoing down the hall as I shut the door behind me. I counted to ten, taking deep breaths. I took the opportunity to make certain my towel was secured while I waited. When I was sure the coast was clear, I poked my head into the hallway and listened carefully.

Finally, I believed the frog (and the prankster) were gone. Sighing with relief, I cautiously emerged and walked to the bathroom. I locked the door and showered as quickly as I could. Changing into the clothes I'd originally brought into the bathroom, I hung up the towel and dabbed moisturizer on my face.

By the time I emerged from the bathroom, I felt better. Calmer. Peaceful. I lay down for a power nap, and when I woke up, it was time to face the rest of the evening. I could hear noise coming from the kitchen, so I headed that way. Walking out of my room, I jumped a mile when a voice startled me.

"Hey!"

Chelsea walked toward me, bundled in a coat and hat and carrying the kids' coats and shoes. "The boys are starting the fire. We're going to roast hot dogs and s'mores for dinner. It's pretty chilly, so you might want to wear a jacket," she told me.

I nodded. "Sounds great!"

Chelsea stopped a couple of feet away. She tilted her head, hopeful. "Are you having a nice time? I hope it's relaxing, even with all these people."

She must not have heard about the recently transpired events. But that wasn't her battle to fight.

I nodded. "Definitely. It's wonderful!" *Frogs and troublemakers aside,* I added silently.

I went to my room and put on an extra pair of socks with my boots. I added another layer under my sweatshirt as well and fixed my hair around a fleece headband to keep my ears warm. I headed to the kitchen to see if Rhonda needed any help.

I found Rhonda and an older woman working together to arrange s'mores fixings on a large tray.

"Are you Sushi?" I smiled at the older woman.

She grinned at me and reached over to wrap my hand in both of hers. She patted my hand, her skin papery and soft. "I sure am. And you must be Maddie. Welcome!" She dropped my hand and reached out for a hug. I wrapped my arms around her carefully, and she patted the small of my back so enthusiastically it stung. "It's about time I got to meet you!"

I smiled at her, then I turned to take a good look at the huge tray on the counter, my jaw dropping in admiration. Graham crackers, marshmallows, chocolate bars, peanut butter cups, and white chocolate bars loaded down the entire surface of the tray. It was impressive, and I told them so.

Rhonda beamed. "It feels good to have the house full. I love it!" Then her countenance changed to one of concern. "Are you okay, hon? I'm sorry about the frog. That boy…" she trailed off, shaking her head. She aimed a helpless shrug at Sushi and sighed.

Sushi huffed a laugh and shook her head. "He really is a sweet boy. But he's always enjoyed a good prank. He learned from the best. My Bobby loved to joke around. I never knew if I was going to find a hairbrush or a rubber snake in my vanity drawer. Used to drive me bananas!"

"I know the feeling," I commiserated.

"We were married sixty-one years, and not a day goes by that I don't miss him," Sushi murmured, her eyes misting over. Rhonda tsk-ed and reached over to pat her mother's hand. Sushi's jaw quivered, even as she smiled. "You don't realize everything you'll miss when they go. I miss it all. But I *had* it all, and that's the sweet part."

My heart hitched a little in my chest at her candid tenderness. What a beautiful gift! But it was quite a pivot. I had assumed we were about to lament the antics of immature men. I wasn't prepared for a conversation about a frog to bring about reminiscence of a life-long love. It poked a little too closely at my own heightening awareness of a certain prankster, and I didn't want anyone getting any ideas— especially me. Rhonda stepped in and saved the moment.

"I'm just about finished here. That'll do it." She laid the final graham cracker and dusted the crumbs off her hands. "Mother, can you hold the door open for us? Maddie, can you carry those chips out to the table, and I'll carry this?"

Sushi nodded and headed toward the door. I turned and saw six bags of chips waiting on the counter. I stuffed my arms full and headed out the door ahead of Rhonda. When we got outside, I realized it was a good thing I'd gone first. I'd need to clear a path for Rhonda and the large tray. The Calverts were scattered around the porch and yard. I noticed several extra teenagers in the mix as well, friends of the nieces and nephews.

We headed down the steps, toward a table out in the grass, already set up with fixings for the hot dogs. Some of the kids played cornhole in the side yard, and dogs laid on the wooden porch slats, on the lookout for scraps and dropped food. The pleasant aroma of woodsmoke filled the air. The sky was dark, but someone had turned the Christmas lights on. As I'd suspected, they draped beautifully, both on the front and back of the house. Strands of patio lights criss crossed above the yard as well. The bulbs twinkled and shone with warm, inviting light.

We slowly made our way to the table closer to the fire pit, a wide, round hole, carved into the ground. Large, uniform bricks of white Austin stone surrounded the dancing flames. Like everything and everyone here, the fire pit was well-loved and beautiful. Chance stood at the fire, already roasting a hot dog on the end of a fancy telescopic stick, complete with a handle.

Rhonda set the tray down and moved over to help me open all the bags of chips and set them up, labels facing upward so the people would see what was what. Once we got everything settled on the table, Rhonda gestured to the crowd, and the kids wasted no time descending on the food. Rhonda and I backed up, out of the way of the stampede. Rhonda wiped her hands on her jeans.

"Thank you, Maddie! I appreciate your help." She drew closer, lowering her voice. "And thank you for coming with my girl. She needs a good friend right now."

I wasn't sure what to say, so I shook my head. "I haven't done anything."

She tilted her head. "You've done more than you know. We're so glad you're here." She put her hand on my arm, stepping closer. "For what it's worth, I really am sorry about the frog. I can't offer you any excuses. We tried everything over the years, but we simply couldn't break him of his love for pranks. Many a frog have found themselves in that shower, through no fault of their own. But only one was ever actually killed, so that's something."

I gasped an awkward laugh. That had turned a little dark.

I waved away her concern. "I can handle Chris's shenanigans. Who knows? I may have a few pranks of my own up my sleeve," I said conspiratorially.

Rhonda laughed, her eyes lighting up. "A woman who can hold her own! I love it! I'll go find us a hot dog. Be right back!"

I nodded in agreement, and she walked away. I looked around, taking in the festive chaos. Over on the porch, Sushi sat on the navy cushions of the wicker sofa. It was warm by the fire, but she was way over there. She had a blanket wrapped over her lap for warmth, and another one across her shoulders. She sat between Chris and his teenage niece, holding each of their hands. The dynamics of this family fascinated me, and I looked around, absorbing all of it.

Chance walked over to stand with me. He held a plate of food, which made my stomach growl. "How's it going, Frog Whisperer?" he asked.

I growled and shook my head. "I'm ready for the football game now. What are the rules about throwing someone in the nearest river?"

He threw his head back and laughed.

"We could probably make an exception, this once. Does Chris play pranks like that on you often?" He asked it conversationally, but I could tell he was fishing for something.

I scowled. "This was a new low, by far. But I'll get him back. Don't worry."

Chance chuckled. "I like your feistiness, Maddie. You fit right in." He finished his hot dog, and walked away to get another one.

I looked around, wondering when Rhonda would return. There were people everywhere, but my eyes swung around to Chris again, like true north. Noah stood at his knee now, engaged in what looked like a very serious chat, man to man.

They might have been talking about the football game. Or maybe Chris was giving his nephew tips on pranking people. I shook my head at the idea, vowing revenge. Noah and Chris exchanged a complicated high five with extra moves. They both did an exploding motion with their hands. Chris started to turn in my direction, and I snapped my eyes back to the fire.

People chatted as they loaded up roasting sticks with hot dogs or marshmallows. Rhonda finally returned, passing me a roasting stick, already loaded, and a plate holding the hot dog bun. We roasted our hot dogs together and chatted.

"Tell me about your family," she said.

"That will take significantly less time than what you are used to," I joked, gesturing to the crowd.

Rhonda smiled, ready to listen.

"I grew up in Richardson. My parents still live in the house I grew up in. They've been married almost forty years. My dad is a college professor at SMU. He taught in the English department for years, but he mostly works with grant writing now."

Rhonda nodded. She fiddled with her plate, grabbing her hot dog bun. As she wrapped the bun around the hot dog, I explained the rest.

When our hot dogs were fixed, Rhonda gestured to an empty love-seat up on the porch. I nodded and followed her. A wicker love-seat with matching cushions sat perpendicular to the couch. Izzy was gone now, but Chris still sat next to Sushi. He met my gaze. Not giving him an inch, I stuck out my tongue at him. He chuckled, looking way too pleased with himself. I silently vowed to get him back later. But for now, I would play nicely. I sat down next to Rhonda and dug into my hot dog.

Sushi smiled at me. "I'm glad you're here, Maddie. You're very beautiful. Are you sure you didn't get a better offer for New Year's Eve than to come out to the country and eat hot dogs?" she asked candidly.

I laughed at her bluntness. "Thank you. I enjoy the occasional sparkly New Year's, but this is nice too." I took a bite of my hot dog.

"My grandson tells me you're a nurse," she said.

I swallowed and nodded. "Yes, ma'am, in the hospital ER."

She looked impressed. "You must be good under pressure."

I shrugged. "I do pretty well…usually."

"That bodes well for tomorrow. It's a high-pressure game when the Calvert children take the field." At my look of surprise, she patted my knee. "Don't beat yourself up if you can't catch little Lightning Britches here. He was born fast, and he kept us all running from the time he took his first steps."

"Oh really?" I looked over at Chris. He'd enlisted his own grandmother for the trash talk? He exuded innocence. "I see how it is," I muttered under my breath. But

I looked at him and spoke louder to clarify something. "Are *you* Lightning Britches?"

He was so confident he didn't even flinch. "Yup. And Patches, because my beard took a while to fill in. Occasionally Baby Christopher, because I'm the baby. I'll answer to most of them, depending on the day and the person."

"Well"—I looked back at Sushi—"No one's ever called me lightning *anything*, but I'll do my best."

"I have no doubt you will. Now come over here; sit and talk with me. Make room, Christopher." She inched away and shooed at him with her hand. He scooted over, and Sushi pulled me over to sit right between them. It was very cozy. The lengths of my arm and leg pressed up against Chris's—a fact I decided to ignore.

Sushi settled in and patted my knee "There. Now, I want to hear about the grossest thing you've ever seen in the ER." She leaned in, eyes bright and eager.

My stomach turned just thinking about the answer to that question. I made a face and set the rest of my hot dog down on the coffee table. "No, you don't. But I'll tell you a different story, if you like."

Sushi looked disappointed, but she nodded, understanding. "As long as it's reasonably gruesome. Okay."

I looked at Chris, checking to be sure. He shrugged and gestured as if to say, *do your worst.*

"Okay. Usually, the grossest things in the ER are gross because they smell bad. Are you familiar with gangrene?"

CHAPTER 18

Later that night, the yard was finally quiet. The men and kids had burned through their stash of fireworks relatively quickly, and at some point, the teenagers had left to spend the rest of the evening elsewhere. I stretched and yawned in my seat by the fire. According to my watch, it wasn't even eleven yet, but I was fading fast. I definitely wasn't going to make it to midnight.

I drained the last few drops of sparkling apple cider from my plastic coupe glass and looked around for Chelsea to tell her good night. I saw her silhouetted against the porch light, darting ahead of a tall, bulky figure. She opened the screen door, and the figure stepped forward into the dim light. It was Chris. He carried the twins, one on each arm, both of them fast asleep on his strong shoulders. Chris moved carefully, carrying them into the house.

Oh my goodness. Attraction burned through me like a lit fuse, and I was pretty sure my ovaries exploded. I sighed, giving myself a break. *Who could see a sight like that and not ovulate a little bit?* I stood there, transfixed, until the door shut. My brain didn't wait for permission. My thoughts took off, blowing right past attraction, headlong into the idea of Chris as a dad. Carrying babies, playing with them, tucking them in…he would be amazing.

The fire cracked loudly, startling me back to cold reality. Glad no one here was a mind-reader, I swallowed and wiped my chin, checking for drool.

"You okay over there, Maddie?" Chance's teasing voice broke into my fantasy.

I turned to Chance. He rocked in a wrought-iron loveseat with his arm around his wife, Stephanie. Knowing smiles spread across their faces. *Oh no. Play it off.* I shrugged.

"Sorry, I'm beat. I'm going to go on to bed."

"Happy New Year," Stephanie said. Had I accidentally said every one of my thoughts aloud? The look on their faces made me paranoid. I needed to get out of there.

"Happy New Year to y'all too. I hope this next one's a really great one."

They both nodded thanks, and I headed inside.

—

The next morning, I woke up early. Looking out the window, the sky was barely light blue. I had tossed and turned most of the night. Burrowing under the warm covers was tempting, but I knew if I went back to sleep I would wake up more tired. I rubbed my hands over my cheeks. I needed to move.

I dressed in leggings then pulled on my sweats over them. The wind chill was in the thirties; I didn't want to freeze. I layered on two shirts and a sweatshirt, pulled my headband over my ears, and walked quietly out of my room. I shuffled through the kitchen and out the door. Out of the corner of my eye, a figure moved on the wicker couch. I jumped, and my heart skipped a beat. It was Chris. *Whew*.

A cup of coffee sat on the side table next to him. He gripped a pen, making a note in the open Bible laying on one half of his lap. Edna's head rested on the other half, her body flopped across the cushions. The yellow Labrador (Sam? Or maybe Elliott? I still didn't know which was which) lay at his feet. It was pretty clear I'd interrupted Chris's quiet time, but I was still a little groggy. I squinted at him.

"Why are you covered in dogs?"

He smiled, the quintessential morning person. He had the grace to ignore my confusion. "Morning! Happy New Year! Just taking some time with the Lord. I'm about to go for a run. Want to sit?" He gestured to the seats around him. The dogs didn't move.

I rubbed sleep from my eyes. "I'd hate to disturb the dogs. They look pretty comfortable."

Chris ruffled Edna's ears. "You sound a little jealous, Reed."

I grunted as I reached for my foot, stretching my quads. "I need coffee before I'm ready for conversation."

Chris nodded his understanding then looked down at the furry head on his lap. "Edna's always ready for conversation. It's one of her best qualities." Hearing him say her name, Edna rolled over on her back, stretching out along the sofa. Chris obliged her with a belly rub. She looked at him adoringly, wagging her tail, tongue lolling.

I shook my head. "Well, there you have it. Edna wants you all to herself, and who am I to interfere with true love?"

Chris chuckled. He looked like he wanted to chat more, but I was already past my pre-coffee word limit.

"I'll leave you two alone. Happy New Year." I said, and went down the steps to start my walk.

When I got back to the house, having worked up a pretty good sweat in spite of the cold January morning, I was fully awake. I stopped to pour a cup of coffee on my way through the kitchen and headed to my room. In the hallway, I passed the closed bathroom door.

The shower curtain grommets scraped along the curtain rod. Chris must have beat me back to the house. I walked into my room and bent down to untie my shoes. I straightened when a terrible idea brewed in my mind. Could this be…an opportunity? Looking around, I considered it for a second. *Could I actually pull it off?*

It was pretty inappropriate. But that made it all the more perfect. *I could be fast*, I reasoned. *He wouldn't even know it was me.* This wasn't the time to be indecisive. Men shower fast. It was now or never.

You like pranks? I thought mischievously. *Two can play that game.*

I didn't give myself time to think it through or change my mind. I kicked off my shoes and padded quietly in my socks to the bathroom door. It might be locked. That would be a sign I shouldn't do this. Only one way to find out. The knob turned silently. *I guess the Lord enjoys the occasional prank,* I smiled to myself.

I opened the door as quietly as I could. Steam rose up from the shower. *It would be a shame if the water turned icy cold.* The opaque shower curtain spanned the entire length of the tub, from one end to the other, so I couldn't see anything. I tiptoed forward, keeping my eyes on the curtain for any sign of movement.

In a few steps, I reached the toilet. Biting my lips together to keep from laughing, I placed my finger on the flush lever. *Whoosh!* The water swirled in the porcelain bowl. Almost immediately, a loud squawk of surprise sounded from inside the curtain. *Success!*

I scurried away, cackling silently with delight. Before I reached the doorway, the shower curtain swished aside. Chris's soapy head and forearm emerged. His eyes popped open wide when he noticed me.

"Maddie?!" His strangled gasp was perfection. He clumsily gathered the shower curtain against his chest, covering up.

Gasping with laughter, I shut the door as silently as I'd opened it. I leaned against the wall to catch my breath and enjoy my moment. What a rush! *No wonder he pranks people all the time.* I never wanted to forget the look of frozen stupefaction on his face. I headed to my room, still chuckling. Somehow, it was extra-satisfying that he knew it was me. But I should probably lock the door every time I showered from here on out.

I went back to my room and checked my phone. Emma had texted me a picture of her and her friends at a party the night before, all decked out in sequins and sparkles. She also sent a picture of Kevin enjoying his first pup cup of the year at the coffee shop. I texted her back, and we chatted for a few minutes.

A short while later, the soft rap of knuckles against the door jamb caught my attention. I looked up, and Chris met my gaze, his brown eyes practically emitting sparks of mischief. His tall frame and broad shoulders filled the doorway. He wore an assessing look on his handsome face.

He'd traded the shower curtain for sweats and a t-shirt, and his hair was still damp. I sat up a little to set my phone on the night stand but remained curled up on the bed.

"Hey there, Mizz Reed," he greeted me casually, his East Texas accent turned up a few notches higher than usual. Goosebumps rose on my arms. He raised his hands to grasp the trim on the top of the door jamb, his biceps and forearms naturally flexing. I wasn't interested in his muscles at all, of course. *But scientifically speaking, if he were a picture in a textbook, a good student would note the symmetrical lines and organic flow of his arms. One couldn't help but notice he was pretty ideally put together. In fact, if a girl was into muscles, his pose would be downright attractive.*

Luckily, I remained unaffected because I am a medical professional, accustomed to the human physique and immune to a wide range of accents. *You can't distract me,* I told him with my mind. It was nice to have the upper hand.

He smiled, cool and calm. I couldn't tell if he'd received the message or not. Maybe he didn't believe me. The silence stretched on. He raised his eyebrows expectantly. Why? *Oh!* He'd spoken to me. I'd forgotten, and now I was being rude.

"Hi!" I replied, full of enthusiastic innocence. "Can I help you?"

He looked down and huffed a tiny laugh. He met my eyes. "Actually, I came by to help *you.*"

"Me?" I asked, wide eyed. My hand fluttered to my chest. *I am so good at this.*

He lowered his chin and oozed male model-esque arrogance. "I wanted to offer a little bit of advice."

"Oh yeah? What's that?" I asked. My fingernails dug into my palm. I forced my hand to relax.

He leaned forward, his smiling eyes locked on mine. "Don't start something you can't finish." The low timbre of his voice rumbled through my entire body, but I refused to flinch.

"Hmm, to my knowledge, I'm not the one who *started* anything," I chirped, perky as a cheerleader at a championship game. *Rah rah ree, kick 'em in the knee!*

Surprise flitted across his face. "Hmm. It's like *that,* huh?"

I shrugged, still feigning innocence.

He pressed his lips together and nodded once. "Okay, then. Good talk." He drummed his fingers on the top of the doorway and winked at me. With that, he turned and disappeared down the hall.

I blew out a breath. *Whew!* I congratulated myself on making it through the conversation without collapsing into a giggling mess. I needed to keep my eyes peeled and ready for a revenge prank, but I wasn't worried. *I can handle Youth Guy Chris,* I assured myself, full of bravado. I checked the clock. It was almost time for the football game.

CHAPTER 19

Most sports movies have that one scene where the team takes the field. They walk shoulder to shoulder in slow motion, looking sharp, put-together, and ready for action. That was how I felt when we walked onto the turf field at the high school out in East Texas. How I *looked* was probably another story. The January wind blew so hard that half my hair came out of my braid before we left the parking lot.

Colton's position as the football coach came with official perks, like year-round access to the football stadium. So we all climbed into the various trucks and minivans and drove fifteen minutes to the other side of town. We drove through a charming square on the way, complete with a historical courthouse. Christmas decorations still hung on every light pole on the main street. Colorful garlands and bright-red Christmas bows and wreaths adorned the doors of different businesses, inviting the whole town into celebration. Sure, Christmas was technically over, but I appreciated the opportunity to savor the season a little longer.

We pulled into the stadium lot and parked. I hopped out of the minivan, and once I got my hair back on better terms with the whipping wind, I looked around in awe. It felt like a scene from Friday Night Lights. I half expected Tim Riggins to be sitting in the bleachers. I said so to Chelsea, and she laughed as Hannah and Noah jumped down from the minivan. Noah reached up and took my hand as if I were part of the family. My heart squeezed at his sweetness.

"Coming here always makes me feel like I'm in high school again." Chelsea smiled, looking at the stadium. She picked up Hannah, whose arms wrapped around her mama without hesitation. The kids had both been clingy all morning, and Chelsea had welcomed them patiently with open arms at every turn. I could tell they were all a little nervous about seeing Trent later. I admired Chelsea's selflessness and energy.

"So," Chelsea began as we walked across the parking lot, "are you feeling fast, like High School Maddie, this morning?"

I laughed. *Not really.* But I didn't want to tell her that. I had a better idea. "Honestly, I only have to think of the frog, and I run a little faster."

Chelsea laughed. "Whatever it takes! I'm not saying I'm glad he played that prank, but I am happy to benefit from the consequences!" She huffed a little bit and shifted Hannah on her hip. "I've got my own share of frog stories to get me fired up. And this is the perfect time to work off some rage."

Colton held the gate open, and we walked through the facility, stopping at the edge of the vibrant green field. The white lines stood out starkly against the uniform turf. Cones marked the fifty-yard line as one of the endzones. That was a relief. The sun shone brightly, but my nose was red from the cold wind. I'd worn layers just in case, though I wasn't sure how long I would need them. Noah let go of my hand and ran over to the bleachers to join the small crowd of friends and family that had gathered. Apparently, Sushi had invited her local domino club, several of whom had brought cowbells.

"Let's go, ladies!" Chance shouted, running past Chelsea and me. Was he actually speaking to Chelsea and me, or was he calling his brothers ladies? Noting the look on his face, I decided to wait on any clarifying questions. I didn't want to start anything. Chris and Colton walked up behind us. They'd swiped eye black onto their faces. I had to admit, it added an extra *zing* to the whole presentation. They wore matching t-shirts emblazoned with "Mustang Pride" and sweatpants with their running shoes.

Some of the locals were joining the game too. I met a couple more cousins and friends out on the field. Chance's son Miles was going to play with us, and Colton's oldest, Brock, was assigned to the other team.

"Aw, that's so sweet! How many boys get to play on the team with their dad and former coach?" I asked, thrilled at the heartwarming development.

Chance snorted derisively and kept moving. He tossed the ball to Miles and took off to catch the return. I looked over at Colton and Chris. They wore similar expressions. Apparently, the trash talk wasn't the only thing that had started early. It was time to focus and put on my game face as best I could.

Cool, cool, cool. Rivalry. Competition. WINNING. Yes.

Chance came back to the group and announced which end zone belonged to which team. He passed the ball to Rhonda, then he and Colton did the coin toss. We got the ball first.

I looked at Chelsea. *Was I ready for this?* We were about to find out.

Rhonda blew her whistle, and I walked forward to take my spot on the line. My job was to rush through the opposition, catch the ball, and run to the end zone as fast as I could. It seemed simple enough.

Cheers emanated from the stands. I was grateful because the sum of it all was a little overwhelming. I had pictured a friendly family game of football. Some banter? Sure. I was all for friendly competition. I could see now that this was a cutthroat, no-holds-barred rivalry that brought out half the town.

It will be fine, I recited to myself, taking a deep, grounding breath. Nurse mode and false bravado for sports were not that different. I needed my mind to settle into that quiet place, and I could do the job. Ignoring my pounding heart, I crouched at the line, listening for them to hike the ball. Chris was playing defense one position over and across from me. His brown eyes held an edge that was more than the eye blacking, but they still sparkled when they met mine.

"You ready for this, Reed?" he asked, wiggling his eyebrows at me.

"Ribbit," I replied, full of attitude, and stuck out my tongue at him. His eyes darted to my mouth then back to mine. The energy between us changed somehow. His smile faded a bit. Chris swallowed.

It was only a look, but the damage was done: his response to the snap was delayed. Luckily, I processed a split second ahead of him. I broke through and turned to catch the football. Once it hit my hands, I cradled it as best I could and ran toward the end zone. I made it about twelve yards before Brock tagged me.

My team congratulated me on twelve yards, but I wasn't satisfied. *No more distractions,* I ordered myself. I needed to keep my head in the game. When I crouched at the line again, I focused all my attention on the task at hand. My eyes did not stray to my left. Chris might have made a similar resolution, because he directed this round's trash talk at Chance, who retorted without missing a beat. We went again and again before Chelsea dropped the ball for a turnover.

Breathing heavily, I headed over to our team huddle, where our team all clapped and high-fived each other. We'd lost the ball this round, but we played pretty well, and I felt great. *I can do this!* I realized.

And I could. As the game wore on, we found our rhythm, and we even scored first. But Colton had the strategic advantage. This field was his house. Additionally, he had some sort of mind meld with his team, and they worked together flawlessly. Before I knew it, they'd pulled ahead of us, and within scoring range again. We agreed beforehand to play to 35, so it was now or never.

"Okay, team, this is it. We can't let them score any more," Chance told us. Our team was all sweaty and disheveled, breathing hard. The sun shone bright and warm, so everyone had taken off any extra layers, down to t-shirts and pants or leggings. Chance looked at me. "Maddie, it's up to you to stop Chris. He's blessed and highly favored today. You've gotta pour it on and keep him from hitting that end zone."

I nodded and clapped my hands, totally in the zone. "Yes!"

Chance instructed everyone else where to run as well to try to stop the ball. We all put our hands in for the big cheer and headed out. I avoided eye contact with Chris, covertly checking when he turned to joke with Colton. He was sweating, but his eye blacking was still intact. I watched him from my periphery as we crouched at the line.

When they snapped the ball, I turned and ran behind my teammates, intent on intercepting Chris. I had a feeling he was going to try to run for it, and I had to stop him. He broke through on the other side of Chance, and I headed to cut him off. His face split into a cocky grin when he saw me. The ball flew into his outstretched hands as if it were magnetic. He pulled it close and ran for the end zone.

I chased him, pushing for all the speed I could muster. As I reached out to tag him, he turned and said, "I don't think so." Then he spun, evading my grasp. The arrogance!

Frustration exploded through me, and my legs found an extra gear. I jumped forward with all my might, my hands outstretched as far as they could go. Tackling was against the rules, but I didn't care. I couldn't let him win! I grabbed his shoulder and held on. He turned, startled. *Ha! That's right, bro!* I wanted to yell.

"Maddie?" he gasped. Then we tripped. It happened in slow motion. The ball fell away, and Chris turned to reach for me. He wrapped his arms around me as we went down. We were going so fast I could see the turf rising up to meet me—hard. But somehow, Chris rolled us. When we came to a stop, he was on the ground, cradling me against him. One hand held the back of my head, and the other wrapped across my hip. I'd instinctively closed my eyes and curled into his neck. I could hear Rhonda blowing the whistle. Everyone was probably running over here. The last three seconds were a blur. I knew I should get up, but my mind and body seemed disconnected somehow. My focus snapped to Chris's voice, rumbling in my ear.

"Maddie! Oh my gosh. Are you okay? Are you hurt?" He sounded far away compared to the adrenaline roaring through my system. I took a deep breath. If I was hurt, I didn't feel it yet. In fact, I was very comfortable. I lifted my head to look at Chris and froze.

We lined up perfectly: eye to eye, nose to nose, our lips barely an inch apart. I'd never been this physically close to Chris Calvert. Awareness zipped through my veins as I dragged my gaze all over his face, taking in his perfect eyebrows; flushed, sandpaper cheeks; his nose, red from the cold. His mouth. I lifted my gaze to his, and I was stuck. I couldn't look away.

Chris blinked, ending our intense staring contest, and began looking me over for injuries. He ran his hands carefully over my hair and shoulders. My brain finally kicked in and told me I should move. I started to shift, but stopped. I wasn't so much curled up against him as I was sprawled across his body in a way that was totally inappropriate at a family football game.

Embarrassment flooded through me. I unclenched my fingers from his shirt and shoved against the turf, trying to lift up off of him as quickly as possible. He sat still and let me, watching me carefully as I awkwardly crawled off of him to the grass. *You know it's bad when Youth Guy Chris isn't smirking.* Pushing through the mortification, I made myself look at him.

"I'm so sorry. I did not think that through at *all*. Are you hurt?"

"I'll live," he grunted, his brow furrowed with concern. "You're bleeding." He gestured to my arm. He started to sit up.

"Careful," I urged, going into nurse mode. I placed a hand on his left shoulder, and he flinched. I needed to assess him, in case he needed medical care.

"I'm fine, Maddie," he muttered, brushing me off. "I'm more worried about you." He pushed himself up to a sitting position and craned his neck to see my arm.

I looked down at the place he'd pointed out. Sure enough, there was a turf burn along my right forearm. It stung, and a little trail of blood ran down my arm. I was relieved to not be badly injured, but it caught my attention.

After a tumble like that, shouldn't I be more beat up? *How did I wind up curled against him like that?* I thought back to thirty seconds ago. I remembered tripping, but everything else had happened so fast. His hands had wrapped around me, pulling me close, as his torso twisted, lifting me up, pushing between me and the ground.

He'd intentionally taken the brunt of the fall.

Stunned at the realization, I looked at him. Something unlocked inside my chest. A wisp of warmth escaped a tiny box I'd shoved it into. Of its own accord, the wisp blossomed and spread all through me. I couldn't speak, but I couldn't stay silent either. I shook my head. "I'll live," I copied his words. "Thanks to you."

CHAPTER 20

An outstretched hand appeared in front of me, interrupting my thoughts. It was Chance.

"Great tackle, Maddie!" he congratulated me. He took my hand and pulled me up to standing. "I love your intensity. But we only play touch football around here, because we're old." He looked back and forth at me and Chris. "Are you both okay?"

Chris nodded, shifting his position on the ground. "Nice hit, Reed." He grinned up at me.

I blushed and had to look away, a confusing mix of pleasure and more embarrassment bubbling up in my heart.

"I'm calling it. Y'all are sitting out the rest of the game. Go on. We'll finish this five on five." Chance looked at me. "You played great, Maddie. Thank you!"

I nodded and smiled wordlessly. Chance pulled Chris up too. He reeled him in for a hug, pounding him on the back. The grimace on Chris's face told me he was feeling the effects of our pile-up much worse than I was.

"I'm really sorry," I told him again.

He shook his head. "I'm fine! Just tweaked my shoulder a little bit." So he *was* hurt!

"Let me take a look at it," I insisted, reaching for him.

He stopped my hands in midair, holding them in his own. He shook his head and spoke quietly. "Not here.

They'll swarm all over me, and I won't have a moment's peace."

At my baffled expression, he sighed. "I'm the baby, Reed. They all love me. A *lot*." He looked over at the bleachers. "We can deal with it at the house. I'll do whatever you want. But for now, let's keep it between us. Please."

I wasn't sure what to make of this. But he'd said he'd let me look at it. Surely we would be back at the house soon. Okay. I nodded, and we walked off the field, side by side. The crowd cheered. Chris carefully hooked his hurt arm around my shoulders and raised his other one to wave at his family. They all cheered loudly, ringing their cowbells.

We'd nearly reached the bleachers when Noah jumped down and ran over to us.

"Nice hit!" he yelled to Chris, relishing the manliness of it all.

Chris didn't miss a beat. He pulled his arm away from me and bent down to Noah's level. "Yeah, bro!" He yelled, and they did a complicated fist-bump-high-five celebration they'd clearly practiced before. I stood watching, the bubbling warmth getting stronger and stronger.

After the last growly *hooah*, Noah leapt forward and wrapped his arms around Chris. Chris caught him with his good arm and squeezed him back. Noah let go and ran ahead of us to the bleachers.

I stood there in awe of all of it: Chris's care for me, his understanding and love for his family, his strength. I still hadn't recovered from my little heart explosion back there. *What's happening?*

Chris lifted his chin at his mother, who'd followed us off the field. "I need to take Maddie home and get her turf burn cleaned up. Can I take your car, and y'all ride home with Chelsea after the hand-off?"

I'd almost forgotten the whole reason I was here: the kids' first visit with Trent this afternoon. But there wasn't time to say anything. Rhonda tossed him her keys. He thanked her then herded me out toward the parking lot.

I finally got my bearings enough to speak. "You don't need to stay and help support Chelsea?"

He shook his head. "I'm pretty sure the entire rest of my family can handle it. Chelsea knows I'm here for her, and so do the kids."

I sighed. "Well, sorry you have to leave because of me."

He shook his head. "It's no problem. It's better that I'm not there to see Trent anyway. If I saw him with both my brothers, we'd probably give each other permission to pound his stupid face into the ground. That wouldn't be good, especially for the kids."

"It's sweet how you all love and support each other."

He smirked. "Well, it's built on a solid foundation of years of fighting over important things, like the last doughnut and calling shotgun, and then being forced to say sorry and hug it out. My mom took a gamble that one day the habit of forced kindness and reconciliation would bear fruit and become actual relationships, and it worked out…mostly."

I laughed. He did too. He shrugged with his uninjured shoulder. "I can't complain. The older ones had it harder than I did because they were closer in age. I was spoiled rotten in comparison. But I idolized them, and they all loved me a lot. We made it through." He smiled.

"I really like your family," I told him as we reached the car.

"Thanks. They like you too. But that's no surprise; they have excellent taste." He pointed his thumb at himself as he opened the passenger door of an older-but-well-kept gray sedan for me. I bit my lip and looked out the window, not wanting to give him the satisfaction of a laugh. He got me settled in the passenger seat then shut my door and ran around to get in himself.

"So, that whole thing back there. I guess the baby is the baby forever, huh?" I asked.

He started the car and put it into gear. "My junior year of high school, I got tackled hard and got the breath knocked out of me. I was fine, but I needed a minute. I lay there with the trainers for a second. I sat up, and here came my family—all of them. They *stormed the field,* Maddie. In front of everyone! It was so embarrassing. Ever since then, if I'm *conscious,* I pop right up."

"Wow!" I exclaimed. "I'm sure they would storm the field for Colton or Chance too, right?"

He leveled a look at me. "They had opportunities. But they never did," he deadpanned. "The depth of my family's crazy wasn't revealed until it was my turn."

I couldn't help but laugh. He shook his head, smiling. "But you're right; it's not only for me. When Chelsea texted on the family text thread and told us Trent was leaving, everybody dropped everything. Looking back, it was probably too much, but we all wanted to help. Everybody drove in and camped out on Chelsea's floor, cooking, cleaning, and playing with the kids. Crying with Chelsea and the kids. It was…well, it was horrible. But none of us were alone in it."

I looked over at him. My heart broke for the whole family, even as it swelled with appreciation for the love they shared. "Well, selfishly, I'm kind of glad we don't have to see him."

Chris chuckled. "Small blessings!" he joked.

We drove up to the house then parked and walked inside together. Chris turned to head toward the bathroom.

"Can you wash it with soap and hot water? I have to get the first aid kit."

"Hold the frogs and other vermin, please," I called, holding up one finger. He laughed.

"I make no promises," he teased.

I tilted my head and stuck my tongue out at him, but he didn't see. I went over to the sink and turned on the warm water. Washing the scrape stung, but I could tell the wound was pretty shallow. *It could be worse*, I thought.

Now that it was clean, I settled into a chair and looked over my scraped-up forearm. I wondered if they had any lidocaine antiseptic spray to ease the stinging pain. I could take a pain reliever too.

Chris walked in holding a basket of supplies. Turning on the overhead light as he passed by it, he walked over and set the basket on the table. I looked at the items he'd brought, impressed.

"I take it this isn't your first rodeo," I told him.

He shook his head. "The youngest of five has *seen some things*," he replied. Standing over me, he considered how the scrape was positioned on my arm. He pulled a chair extra close so he could see and reach more easily then sat down. He dug around in the basket, pulling out different items. He was totally focused on the task at hand.

He sprayed lidocaine spray first, and the coldness of it took my breath away. He fanned the air around it and looked at me, full of compassion.

"Sorry," he murmured. Once the spray dried, he squeezed a thick line of antibiotic ointment along the length of the scrape. Then he gingerly pressed a bandage over it and used strips of tape to secure it. I watched him the whole time, fascinated. He worked carefully and efficiently.

Then he did something so endearing my heart and mind sort of burst into confetti: he kissed my hurt. His lips were warm and dry against the skin beside the bandage. Even with the swipe of eye black still smeared across his cheeks, his eyes were sincere and unassuming. I waited for him to make a joke. Instead an affectionate smile softened his face, full of care and concern.

"All done," he murmured quietly.

"Thank you," I breathed, unable to tear my eyes from his. His thumb brushed across my arm, then he released me. I stayed where I was, trapped in his eyes.

I licked my lips and swallowed. His gaze flicked to my mouth and back to my eyes. The moment pressed in, warming the space between us. I had to squash the impulse to reach up and run my fingers along his jaw to feel his stubble. I hardly ever saw him anything but clean shaven, and my fingers itched with curiosity. My chest ached to lean in closer.

But that would be starting something. Did I want to start something with Chris? Here? Now, in this very kitchen? Would that be wise? Most important of all, would Chris welcome that? It was a lot of questions, all in a row, and zero clarity. Which should definitely make the answer no.

I looked away to collect myself. His sore shoulder was a convenient focal point. I swallowed and took a breath. "Can you take your shirt off?"

CHAPTER 21

Chris's face went blank. His eyes widened, and finally he frowned. "Pardon?"

"I need to take a look at your shoulder. It's easier if your shirt is out of the way. Is that okay?" I asked.

"Um."

Apparently, I wasn't the only one feeling a little dazed. My heart wanted to soar. *Nope, shut that down. Business as usual.*

"Come on," I said, briskly clapping my hands twice as I rose to stand, fully in nurse mode now. "Shirt off, please."

He shrugged. "If you say so, but we should probably have a talk about my purity policy. I am *in* the world, but not *of* it, Reed."

I laughed. Of course he would turn flirty right when I decided to back off—more bad timing. In typical Chris fashion, his joke was just obnoxious enough to strengthen my resolve.

"No, you goof! I need to assess your shoulder. We may need to go have some imaging done!"

He shook his head and rolled his eyes. "Pssh. Maddie, I'm fine."

I looked at him, waiting.

"Fine," he mumbled and pulled at the hem of his shirt. I looked away for a moment. When I looked again, he was sitting obediently, ready to be examined.

In the ER, a basic, textbook notation of a nicely proportioned, shapely torso and shoulders would be understandable for a medical professional such as myself. Just a typical health assessment rating. Textbook, if you will. Overall health: Very good. The question of chest hair was now answered as well: normal and evenly distributed. With that, my medical curiosity was satisfied. But as his friend, I would not be thinking about any of this, so I will stop. Right now. Okay, now. I'm only human. Get it together, woman!

Resolute, I avoided his gaze. Keeping a professional distance, I looked things over carefully. I could tell his shoulder was already sore. But the range of motion was pretty good, and the swelling could be worse. An angry contusion was forming at the point of contact, and his skin was red and inflamed. It looked painful, but his shirt had protected him surprisingly well. *Thank God this isn't worse,* I thought, feeling terrible. Silently, I copied his move, kissing my finger and touching the area near the bruise.

I rested my hand on top of his other shoulder. "I'm so sorry," I said softly.

Chris craned his neck to look at me. "Maddie, I promise, I'm fine. It probably looks worse than it feels." He wrapped his hand around mine and gave me a reassuring squeeze then released me.

I swallowed and switched back to *nurse mode.* "Well"—I stepped away—"I think you got very lucky. Let's ice it for now and see how the symptoms play out. You can put your shirt back on." I moved to look in the freezer for an ice pack.

The sound of footsteps pounding along the porch was our only warning before the screen door opened and Calverts poured into the kitchen.

"What do we have here? Patches! Are you putting the moves on Maddie?" Chance asked.

"Obviously. Get out," Chris ordered, carefully pulling his shirt down over his chest.

I gestured to Chance. "I'm looking for an ice pack for his shoulder. Can you show me where to find one?"

Chance walked over and opened the freezer. "They used to be in the door here."

The stack of blue ice packs sat lined up, ready to go. It helped me settle into nurse mode, calming my heart rate.

"This is perfect," I told Chance.

He opened a drawer and grabbed a thin tea towel, the perfect size to wrap one of the ice packs. He held it out to me. "You can do the honors."

I thanked him and accepted the towel. I walked the few steps over to Chris, wrapping the ice pack in the towel as I went. He stood, hugging Chelsea, encouraging her.

"You're doing it, sis. One day at a time," Chris murmured. Chelsea held onto him, nodding. I stayed back, not wanting to interrupt.

When Chelsea pulled away from Chris, his eyes immediately found mine. He gave a small smile and reached for the ice pack. "Thanks," he said softly.

Chelsea turned to me, so I reached over and hugged her. "Sorry I wasn't there. How are you doing?" I asked.

She sniffed. "I'm okay now. It will get easier. It's only for a couple of hours." She nodded and looked between Chris and me. "Having y'all here really helps. Thank you."

I smiled at her. "Want to go for a walk or something to pass the time?"

"Are you sure you're up for it? That was some tackle," Chelsea answered.

I shook my head. "Oh, I'm fine, thanks to this one." I pointed my thumb in Chris's direction. "You good?" I asked him.

"Yup. I'll sit outside on the couch and ice it for a little bit. Twenty on, twenty off? Is that still right?"

I nodded. "Perfect. I'll check on you after my walk." I turned to Chelsea. "Want to go now?" She shrugged and we turned for the door.

Chelsea and I set out walking along the driveway. She sighed. "Thanks for getting me out of there. My family is great, but when you're sad and they don't know what to do, they sort of *hover*. They hang around you *this close* and attend to every little thing. It's really sweet, but sometimes I need some space. I'm thirty-five years old. I know I can figure out how to make it through this. God has carried me through everything else. But I've got to have space to process. I've got to stay healthy for my kids."

She took a big breath. "I'm sorry. I don't mean to complain. My family is amazing, and I love them. As soon as I needed them, they were there, and I know they always will be. I'm very grateful. But it's hard to think when everyone's up in your grill."

I nodded. "I can imagine. Let it all out, girl."

Chelsea laughed. "Enough about me. How are you doing? Did you enjoy the game?"

I nodded. "Yeah, it was a lot of fun. I still don't know who won, though."

Chelsea shrugged, shaking her head. "Colton is unstoppable. He coached Brock for his whole life. It is what it is at this point. Sorry I put you on the spot and pressured you to be the secret weapon. You are an excellent secret weapon, but it wasn't really fair."

I brushed it off. "Don't worry about it. I'm sorry we didn't win. I really like winning. And I'm sorry I missed the last of the game and dropping off the kids."

"It's all good," she said, huffing a little bit. We reached the road and turned right. We walked at a pretty fast pace along the quiet country road.

"So," Chelsea changed the subject, "are you glad the Christmas play is over?"

I nodded. "Yes and no. It was a lot of fun. I mean, it was chaos, for sure. But I really enjoyed it."

"My kids had a blast," Chelsea said.

"I'm glad. I think everyone did, for the most part." I considered whether or not to share the next part, but I figured Chelsea was safe, and she might want to think about something else. "It was a little weird because I had an unexpected blast from the past. One of the shepherds turned out to be the son of my ex-fiancé and his wife, my ex-best friend."

Chelsea stopped. "What? What do you mean?" She clutched my forearm, her eyes wide. "Oh, I want to hear this story."

I laughed and motioned for her to keep going. "It's been years, so it wasn't a big deal. But it was definitely strange at times. I used to be engaged to this guy, Houston, a long time ago, back in college. I was a very different person back then," I explained. "We started dating my junior year at SMU and got engaged senior year. We were planning to get married that summer, right after graduation. And we almost did, which would have been a disaster."

Chelsea stayed quiet, listening intently.

"It was the kindness of God. We'd finished the rehearsal dinner at this fancy restaurant. Everything was ready for the next day. After the dinner, on the way to my folks' house, I realized I had my purse, but I'd forgotten my wallet at our new apartment. I lived with my parents until the wedding, but Houston was already living there. I figured I'd run by and grab my wallet, no problem. I had my keys, so I let myself in, and he was there—with my best friend and maid of honor."

Chelsea gasped. "Oh my gosh."

I looked down. "Yeah."

Chelsea sighed. "I'm so sorry."

"Thanks," I told her. "At this point, I'm really glad it worked out the way it did. In the long run, Houston and I probably would have been miserable. I don't love the way it happened, but I guess he and Heidi are probably happy together. They have a precious little boy and another baby on the way. And I have a wonderful life, full of community, great friends, and a job I was born to do. I like this much better."

Chelsea agreed. "Yeah, you definitely dodged a bullet there. But still. Your best friend? I can't get over that!"

I shook my head. "Yeah, it was the hardest part by far. She and I were roommates three out of our four years at SMU. We loved each other a lot. Well, *I* loved *her*. She loved me too she just…loved Houston more, I guess." I sighed. "Sorry to talk about something so heavy. I was supposed to lighten the mood!"

Chelsea shook her head. "Not at all! I want to get to know you better and hear more of your story! Man, that really sucks. I'm so sorry. How did they end up doing the Christmas play? Do they go to Dallas Christian?"

"No," I replied. "Or they haven't. Maybe they do now, I don't know. Their son, Carson, goes to school with the children's minister's kid."

"Do you mean Melissa?" Chelsea clarified.

I nodded. "Melissa is wonderful. She was supposed to direct the Christmas play, and I planned to be her assistant, but she had some complications with her pregnancy. She had to go on extended bed rest. Seeing Heidi and Houston was a weird coincidence. Melissa has no clue about my history with them. How could she?"

Chelsea was amazed. "Man, what a small world! Well, thank you for sharing that with me. I'm sorry it happened, but I'm really glad you didn't marry that guy. Being married to a cheater is…well, it's terrible."

"I'm so sorry," I told her.

"It's okay. I'm grateful I have Noah and Hannah, and I wouldn't have them without Trent—and our wonderful fertility doctor, of course."

"I didn't know you went through fertility treatment. Gosh, Chelsea, you're *tough*!" I said.

She laughed. "It was a long road, but it made me stronger. Perseverance and all that." She lifted her hand, literally brushing it off. "Like I said, I can't regret marrying Trent, but it's nice to hear your story and be reminded that good can come out of the things that don't work out the way we planned. Chris and I were actually talking about that the other night, how if he'd never gotten engaged to Becca, he might not be a youth minister now."

I turned to her and gawked. Surely I'd heard wrong. "Sorry." I shook my head. "Did you say Chris was *engaged*?"

Chelsea's eyes grew huge.

CHAPTER 22

"You didn't know that? Are you sure?" Chelsea asked, shocked.

I shook my head and pushed past the awkwardness. "He's never mentioned it."

I kept up with Chelsea's pace, but the shockwave of the news reverberated through my chest cavity. I thought back over the years. After our initial interactions, I'd held Chris at arms' length, much more comfortable with arguing or rolling my eyes at him than anything else. Even last summer, there was never a reason for his past to be my business. So why did I feel…how *did* I feel about the fact that Chris didn't trust me?

On one hand, we hadn't always been close, so it was understandable. But on the other hand, I'd told him about my history with the Ruelands. Maybe there was another explanation, but what could it be?

Chelsea shook her head. "I'm sorry, Maddie. I thought for sure you knew."

I shrugged, not nearly as deeply wounded as I was just plain curious. I needed to access nurse mode in my brain and remove myself a little bit before I embarrassed myself. "I mean, it's his business. I'm sure he has his reasons."

Chelsea shook her head. "I can't imagine what they would be. It's been years. He met Becca his junior year of college. They got engaged their senior year, before they graduated."

College sweethearts. A familiar story. "Go on," I said.

Chelsea shrugged. "Like I said, they were young. Becca was gorgeous on the outside, but once you got to know her, she was your classic spoiled brat. She was a high-maintenance, ungrateful, demanding whiner."

"Whoa," I responded. "I guess she didn't fit in around here?"

Chelsea snorted. "That's an understatement. Anyway, for some reason, Chris was totally blind about her. We all saw her for what she was, but what can you say? You don't get to choose, right? We all love him, so we went along with it and tried to support him the best we could. Back then, Chris was full of 'potential.'" She held up air quotes around the word. "He majored in finance, and he played baseball. He was the big man on campus at SFA. He was *adorable*."

"Said like a true big sister," I joked. She smiled proudly.

"Anyway, he started looking for a job out here for after graduation. He always wanted to live near family and be close with all of us. But Little Miss City insisted on living in Austin. I expected him to stand his ground, but no. He changed course, got an internship in Austin, and moved there right after graduation. He was miserable. He worked long hours and made hardly any money as an intern, but he was on the fast track for advancement.

"It was all for her, you know? But she was never satisfied. They argued all the time. She was manipulative and jealous. She hated that he wanted to see his family or anyone but her on weekends. It was a bad situation in every way.

"Then, one day, she ended it out of the blue. She told him she was bored; she was tired of doing all the work in their relationship; she didn't want to make more money than him. Blah blah blah. She hadn't actually gotten *into* law school yet, mind you. She tore him to shreds, told him they had different dreams, and she couldn't do the *hillbilly lifestyle.* And the cherry on top? She had fallen in love with someone else: an attorney at the firm where she was an intern. And that was that. Oh, *and* she kept the ring."

I stopped, aghast. What could I say to any of that? *Holy cow.* I couldn't help but notice that Chris's experience with Becca sounded like a strong case for a date limit. That would mess up anybody.

"I'm really glad I'm not twenty-two anymore," I mumbled.

Chelsea nodded. "Same, girl! He had to learn a lot—the hard way. All the while, our dad was basically saying the same things as Becca." She lowered her voice. "*Why are you the lowest man on the totem pole? I thought you had potential. Your paycheck should match your worth. Blah, blah, blah.* It all came together, and it really messed with him, torpedoed his confidence."

"Oh my goodness, how could it not?" I asked.

Chelsea agreed.

"He transferred within the company to Dallas to get away, start fresh. He made a lot of changes. Thank goodness he got involved serving with the youth at Dallas Christian. When they needed a new youth minister, they asked him to consider it. He left his job in finance and never looked back."

I took a moment to absorb everything I'd just learned. All I could think was, *wow*. When I met Chris, he was working in the corporate world, but he joined the church staff shortly after. I had no idea his story was so complicated. *An onion, indeed.* Granted, we'd had our two dates, and he'd dropped me. We didn't talk much for a while. Chelsea's voice brought me back to the moment.

"It's crazy how God's plans really are for not only our good but for our best. I have to keep reminding myself…" Chelsea trailed off. Focused on something ahead, she held out a hand and took hold of my elbow, bringing us to a stop. I looked and saw a chicken in the road. We'd gone about a mile or so and were coming up on the driveway for the next property.

The chicken strutted around and pecked at the ground, but something was off. It looked weird and exceptionally tall. But it was still just a chicken. Surely it would leave us alone if we went around it. It flapped its wings a couple times, keeping a stern eye on us.

"We need to turn around," Chelsea said, her voice soft but urgent.

"Why?" I asked, confused. "Are you afraid of chickens?"

"That's not a chicken," she murmured, her eyes glued to the bird in question. "It's a rooster. A mean one.

Walk tall, confident, and turn around slowly. Then we can go back home."

"Okay." I shrugged. It seemed like an overreaction to me, but who was I to judge? I was a guest here, and we didn't get many chickens in the ER. I followed Chelsea's lead, standing tall as we slowly turned and headed back toward the house. Everything seemed fine. We'd walked about ten feet when a strange, squawky growl came from behind us. I looked back. The rooster had followed us. Its red comb wobbled as it stalked closer, the small, sinister eyes staring straight at me. *Great.*

"What's going on?" I asked, dreading the answer.

Chelsea looked behind us and sped up her pace, gesturing at me to do the same. Another squawky growl. I turned to look and gasped. The rooster rushed toward us, flapping its wings. It puffed up its feathers until it looked enormous. Moving surprisingly fast, it sounded off with a loud squawk and leaped into the air. Chelsea and I both screamed and simultaneously broke into a run.

"Look out for its spurs!" Chelsea shouted, waving her arms. *Spurs?* We kept running. Chelsea pulled off her shirt and swung the fabric around like a weapon. It seemed crazy, but I figured I should probably do the same.

The rooster closed in, flapping up to dive bomb me. *How is this reality?* All I could do was try to get away, following Chelsea's lead. I felt the bird flapping by my head right before it pecked viciously at my shoulder.

"Ow!" I cried, jumping away. The bird wasn't even that big; how could it have hit me so hard?

I looked behind me and shrieked. The thing flew at me again, feet fully extended forward. The talons on the backs of its claws were sharpened to deadly points. *Oh, those kinds of spurs!* I did not want to interact with those things. Unsure what else to do, I flung my shirt around my head like a pair of nunchucks. Just when I thought it was going to get me, my shirt made contact. The bird let out a shriek as I knocked it off course, a small explosion of feathers left floating in its wake.

I ran, full out. I could still hear it growling, and I didn't trust that the bird was actually finished with me. Chelsea and I ran, waving our shirts around like human windmills until the squawks and growls faded to silence. We must have reached the end of its territory. *Do birds have territories?* I had no idea. I'd only studied human biology.

I risked slowing down to turn around and check. The rooster had turned and flapped away. It disappeared into the trees, leaving a smattering of feathers behind.

"Welcome to the country," Chelsea panted. I had no words.

We slowed to a walk but kept moving in case it came back. When we reached the Calvert driveway, we were still so freaked out we checked behind us periodically until we reached the house. Edna walked out to greet us, and I finally felt safe.

I couldn't believe I'd just held off a rooster attack, using only my shirt. Sure, I was covered in feathers and potentially bleeding, but I felt like a warrior! Breathing hard, we stopped to rest. I looked over at Chelsea.

"Well, that was new." I shrugged.

"No kidding." Chelsea chuckled mirthlessly as she rubbed behind Edna's ears. She looked over at me and made a face. "You have a—" She broke off and gestured toward my head as a feather fell out of my hair and floated harmlessly to the ground. I grimaced.

"There's probably more where that came from." I shook my head, and sure enough, another one fell.

I watched it land then checked on my bandaged forearm. Running had made it sting again, probably because of the sweat and blood flow.

"The country is a whole other world," I observed.

Chelsea breathed a laugh. "You never know what you're going to get out here, that's for sure." Still catching her breath, she checked her watch. "I'm going to have to go get the kids in a bit."

The wind picked up again. Goosebumps rose on my skin, so I pulled my shirt on over my head as we climbed the steps to the porch. The screen door opened, and Chance walked outside.

"Is *everybody* taking off their shirt here today? Did I miss the memo?" he hollered. He looked to his left, and I noticed Chris sitting on the wicker sofa. He leaned awkwardly against the cushions, so I could tell the ice pack was still there.

"How ya feeling, champ?" I asked, climbing the steps.

He smiled. "Never better." He looked over at Chelsea. "I can come with you to get the kids in a little bit."

She nodded at him then looked at me. "You good?"

I nodded. "I think so." I did a quick spin. "I'm pretty sure it only pecked me; I would have felt those spurs. I'm not bleeding anywhere, am I?" I joked.

"What?" Confused, Chris craned his neck to look at me. "And *yes*." He stood, the ice pack forgotten. "Why are you bleeding through your shirt?" He turned to Chelsea. "Are you bleeding too?"

Chelsea shook her head and walked over to take a look at my back. She pulled at the neckline of my shirt and looked down inside. "It's not deep. But I'd clean it well and put some stuff on it, for sure. Chickens are disgusting." She looked at her brothers. "We had a run-in with the Davises' crazy rooster. It chased us all the way home."

"What?" Chance hurried over, immediately checking Chelsea over. He mumbled some colorful threats of revenge under his breath.

Meanwhile, Chris gently took hold of my shoulders, spinning me so he could see my new wound. I pulled the t-shirt neck aside so he could see. He shook his head in disbelief and spun me back around. "Can't take you anywhere, Reed. Back to the first aid kit, please!" He gestured with his thumb.

We walked along the porch together. "I need to leave in ten minutes to get the kids!" Chelsea called.

Chris held out a thumbs-up as he held the screen door open for me. He didn't stop in the kitchen but headed straight to the hallway, and I followed.

When we walked into the bathroom, he stopped abruptly at the cabinet. I wasn't watching and fully collided with him, bumping my head on his shoulder. I instinctively grabbed his waist for balance. I stepped back and released him, glad I hadn't run into his injured shoulder.

"Sorry," I grimaced.

He shook his head and opened the cabinet to pull out the basket he'd used earlier. Meeting my eyes, he grinned sarcastically and mimicked what I assumed to be my voice. "Shirt off, please."

I looked away and shook my head. "You are so silly."

"Guilty as charged. Come on." He paused and leaned back, a questioning look in his eye. "If you're comfortable, of course."

I smiled. "Thank you for your consideration. I'm fine. I literally ran down the lane, waving my shirt around like a lunatic, trying to get that thing to stop attacking me."

His eyes widened. "That's quite a visual. I'm really sorry it happened, and I'm glad you're okay. But I would pay money to have seen it."

We cracked up all over again. He shook his head and sighed. "Okay. Focus. I've got to hurry."

I complied as quickly as I could in the small space then turned my back toward him. He reached over to turn on the hot water. "I can't believe the Davises still have that rooster. He's always been mean." He tested the water. "We need to get this clean first. In fact, I probably ought to double clean it. Chelsea is right; chickens are nasty." His lip curled at the idea.

He wet a washcloth with steaming hot water and gently cleaned the area with soap. It stung but not as bad as the peroxide. I hissed, breathing through the pain.

"Sorry," he said gently. When he sprayed it down with the lidocaine spray, I flinched at the chill. He winced. "Here's the last little bit. We're almost done."

He expertly spread antibiotic ointment on the scratch and covered it with a Band-Aid. I watched him in the mirror when he bent his head down and kissed my shoulder with a theatrical, "*Mwah!*" His eyes met mine in the mirror, full of laughter. A rush of affection filled my heart at his tenderness and care. *What next?* I wondered silently.

I smiled at his reflection and told him thank you—again. His eyes sparkled at me in that special *Chris* way I had come to almost crave. Then he paused, his eyes turning serious in the mirror. His Adam's apple moved as he swallowed. My cheeks flushed right before Chris lightly took my shoulders and turned me to face him. Everything in me stilled as his hand moved to my face. I instinctively lifted my chin, holding my breath, waiting. Chris reached up and gently plucked a feather out of my hair.

I bit back a groan of frustration. Chris patted me on my uninjured shoulder, oblivious to the chaos he'd unleashed in my lungs. "I've gotta run," he said. "Try to stay out of trouble until I get back."

I nodded, feeling the loss of him immediately. *What was that?* Something was changing here, in my heart and in my mind. Chris was different here. Or was he? Was this the man he had always been? Was the obnoxious thing an act? So many questions. I sighed and focused on checking my hair for more feathers.

CHAPTER 23

I helped Rhonda and Sushi in the kitchen while Chris and Chelsea were gone. Rhonda turned the radio on the oldies station, and we danced around, singing all through making brisket tacos with black-eyed peas and salad for dinner. The tantalizing aromas had my stomach growling.

When the screen door opened, I turned, excited to see Chris, Chelsea, and the kids, but it was just Colton and Heather. They'd gone home to freshen up after the game, and all their kids had plans, so it was just the two of them. Chance was still here, seeing to the brisket on the smoker while we chopped all the veggies and prepared the rest of the food. His wife and daughters had left earlier for a volleyball tournament in New Orleans, and Miles was out with the other kids.

Rhonda had tasked me with chopping the vegetables for a colorful salad. It looked very pretty, if I did say so myself. I stood at the sink, washing the knife, when the screen door clapped again, and two blonde heads tore into the room.

"Grammy!" they shouted. Rhonda knelt down and hugged them both.

"I'm so glad to see you, sweet babies! Did you have fun?" she asked.

The twins nodded. "We ate ice cream!" Hannah exclaimed.

Rhonda nodded. "Oh, that sounds wonderful! Did you save room for brisket tacos?"

They nodded, smiling. Chris came over to see what was on the stove, and Noah followed closely behind him.

"Smells great, Grammy!" He smiled at his mom. He looked to Noah to confirm that it did, in fact, smell great.

Noah nodded enthusiastically. They walked up to me next. "Hmm, salad looks good too."

I smiled proudly. "Thank you. How was the drive?"

"It was fine." He shrugged, unable to say more with Noah right there. I was glad Noah seemed okay, if a little clingy, after seeing his dad. The whole situation made me want to punch Trent a little bit myself. But now wasn't the time to talk. If Chris had pounded Trent into the ground, I would have to wait to hear the details.

Rhonda interrupted my thoughts. "Who's hungry?" she yelled, and everyone crowded into the kitchen to load up their plates.

"Be sure you eat your black-eyed peas for good luck," Sushi reminded everyone.

"I'd rather have ice cream," Hannah declared.

Wouldn't we all?

—

Later, after everyone was full of food and the twins were asleep, the guys built a fire in the fire pit outside. Colton brought out a guitar, and everyone sat around the fire, singing songs and talking. The Calvert children had so many stories, not to mention Sushi and Rhonda. I couldn't stop laughing after Rhonda's story of the time she got a midnight phone call. Chance had been caught swimming in the baptistry at the Church of Christ with a bunch of kids, including the preacher's daughter.

"You've heard of the term 'walk of shame'?" Rhonda asked dryly. "I'll do you one better: I was dragged out of bed at *midnight* to escort my kid and a bunch of other teenagers down the sidewalk in front of the *Lord's house!*" Rhonda said, full of agitation. She shook her head. I laughed, blushing on her behalf. I would have been totally mortified.

Chance laughed. "Nothing happened, I swear! Everyone was fully clothed!"

Chris shook his head. "These stories are a youth minister's nightmare. Don't say any more. You'll only make it worse!"

"I need to defend my virtue!" Chance insisted. We all cracked up. "At least we were Baptist, so Mama could still show her face in the church across town," he reminded everyone. "And after all that, Steph's dad still gave us his blessing when the time came."

"Stephanie was the preacher's daughter?" I asked, eyes wide.

"It doesn't help as much as you think it would," Rhonda sniffed, and everyone cracked up again.

Chance adjusted the baseball cap on his head and smirked. "I got her nice and twitterpated and tricked her into marryin' me before she could change her mind."

"Strike while the iron is hot," Colton agreed, and for some reason, that set us all off again.

When the laughter died down, Chelsea wiped her eyes and groaned, holding her ribs. "It feels good to laugh."

I nodded at her, my sides aching. I was doing my best to ignore the chill creeping through my long-sleeved t-shirt. I put out my hands toward the fire to warm them and rubbed my arms. I wasn't ready to go in yet, but the fire wasn't enough to keep me from shivering.

"Here, Maddie, take this," Chris said, pulling his sweatshirt up and over his head. Moving his sore shoulder carefully, he passed it over to me. The look on his face said he didn't want to argue, so I took it.

"Thanks." I smiled and pulled it on over my head. I sighed in gratitude. The sweatshirt was gloriously warm from his body heat. I burrowed deeper. It smelled like wood smoke and sweet cologne and Chris. *My heavens.* I tried to keep a straight face as I surreptitiously breathed in the smell.

"Warming up nicely, Maddie?" Chance put me on the spot. He was not going to miss a chance to tease. I could feel a blush creeping up my cheeks. Thank goodness it was dark. The only lights were the fire and the twinkling Christmas bulbs hanging on the house.

"It certainly helps. Ooh, it smells nice," I sassed and sniffed it theatrically as I snuggled down deeper into the sweatshirt. Chance and everyone else laughed some more as I pulled the hood up over my head. I yanked at the strings, tightening them until only my nose showed, and tied a little bow.

Chance opened his mouth to make another comment, but Chris beat him to it.

"Chance is just jealous, Maddie. Usually, it's him who needs my sweatshirt."

The laughter started up again, but Chance sighed. He buried his head in his hands dramatically. "It was one time!" he yelled.

"In that case, would you like a quick sniff?" I asked Chance, holding out the sleeve.

Everyone laughed even harder. Chance joined in, his laugh rumbling across the circle. Chance winked at me. "Maddie, you're fun."

I untied the strings and poked my head out, leaving the warm hood on. "Aw. Thanks! Y'all are fun too." I smiled at Chelsea. It didn't seem like a good idea to look at Chris right then. He might read my mind. From what I could tell, he wasn't looking at me either, and the mind-reading channels remained silent. I left it at that and turned my focus on the flames at my feet.

Before Chance could press any further, rescue arrived in the form of sweet Noah. He walked out the screen door and down the porch steps in his footie pajamas.

"Mama?" he called plaintively. "I had a bad dream." He reached Chris first and climbed up into his lap. Chelsea shifted to unfold her legs from beneath her, but Chris waved her off.

"I've got him."

Noah laid his head on his uncle's shoulder, and Chris stood then carried him back inside.

I'd held strong through a lot of things. Chris's kindness and charm, his flirty banter, his cleverness, and even his sweet cologne. But watching him carry that little boy inside, so strong and stable for a hurting kid…that wispy warmth from earlier exploded through my heart. Tears filled my eyes. I could feel myself practically glowing, but I took a breath and forced the tears away.

I looked at the fire, ruthlessly shutting it down. *It's just this place,* I decided and shifted my focus to Chance's next story.

—

Hours later, a sound woke me up. *Boom. Boom.* It was muted, coming from far away. I looked around the dark room, taking a second to remember where I was. Noises were different out here in the country. *Probably more fireworks,* I decided. I rolled over and tried to go back to sleep. But my mouth was dry. I got out of bed and quietly crept from the room and headed to the kitchen to get some water.

Checking the oven clock, I realized I hadn't been asleep long, maybe two hours. The fire pit was dark, and everyone had left or gone to bed. The dogs lay on their big dog beds in the corner of the kitchen. They eyed me, uninterested. I took a glass from the cabinet and filled it with water. I gulped it down and refilled the glass. I turned to go back to my room when a sound startled me. In my stupor, I hadn't noticed the wooden door to the porch was open. Voices mixed with the sounds of the night.

I stood by the fridge and peered through the screen door. In the glow of the Christmas lights, I could barely see Chris and his mom sitting outside on the wicker sofa.

"Thank you for talking with Colton. You helped him gain some perspective about Izzy," Rhonda said.

Chris shrugged and answered, "I'm glad I could help. He's a great dad. That would be a pretty overwhelming situation for anyone. I'm just around it all the time. I talk with parents about that stuff every week."

"You've come a long way, to be the one giving advice now," Rhonda observed. Chris chuckled.

"What is it you always say? Everyone gets their chance to grow up?" I could hear the smile in his voice. "Sorry it took me so long."

Rhonda shook her head. "You grew up in God's timing, like all the rest of us, love. I wouldn't change a thing."

I wondered if the older siblings often asked Chris for advice on dealing with their teenagers, or did they struggle to take him seriously? It was no secret Chris was excellent at relating with students. Surely his family saw that too. I turned away to go back to bed.

"I really like Maddie."

I froze where I stood. Rhonda's words warmed my heart. I really liked her too. But how would Chris respond? My heart beat a little faster. I leaned closer to the door, straining to hear over the rustle of the wind through the trees. It took him a little bit to respond. I was getting pretty antsy when he finally did.

"Yeah, Maddie's great. She's really fun and smart. Super patient and warm. She loves the Lord. She's the real deal."

Wow. That was an extra-kind assessment. I could feel myself blushing in the dark kitchen.

"Have y'all been spending a lot of time together?" Rhonda asked, clearly digging for information. I rolled my eyes. *Classic mom.*

Chris answered her patiently. "For the Christmas play, yes. But that's it."

"Well, a mama can dream," Rhonda said with a sigh. *Aw.* She changed the subject. "It's been a busy couple of days. I can't believe I haven't had a chance to ask you, how are you *really* doing? Are you still seeing the therapist?"

His head bobbed up and down. "Yeah. It's been really good. I wish I'd gone sooner. You were right about that."

Rhonda tsked. "It's best you went in your own time. You seem more at ease, more confident and purposeful."

"I feel like I am. It's hard work, you know that. But I can tell I'm healing. It's helped faster than I expected, after holding it all in all these years. But Brooke said she's not surprised. She says if I'd gone before I was ready, it may not have been as helpful. I guess nothing is wasted, even when we take the long way."

Rhonda didn't say anything but reached over and rubbed his shoulder. *Hmm.* Chris and I hadn't talked much about his therapy. This was interesting. I knew I shouldn't eavesdrop, but Chris went on before I could make myself leave.

"It's strange how stuff stays with you. I thought I was over all that stuff with Becca, but now I see I pushed it all down. I never let myself grieve or even feel all of it."

"Ugh," Rhonda snarled. "That girl did a number on you. I'm still mad she kept the ring," Rhonda grumped, crossing her arms. I wanted to snarl too. I tried to be as pro-woman as possible, but it sounded like a terrible situation.

"Eh, let it go, Mama. *I* certainly don't want it." Chris waved it off and shook his head. "It was tough, but I learned a lot. Talking it through with Brooke, I've realized how Becca rejecting me made Dad's rejection that much more real. Seeing that connection helped me understand a lot of my self-sabotaging tendencies since then. This whole time, I was basically afraid I was unlovable."

I stood there, taking all this in. If by self-sabotaging, he meant all his cockiness, the obnoxious behavior, and that stupid two-date rule, then what? Did it mean all of that was in response to these life-changing rejections? I guessed so. But in spite of those things, Chris had this way about him. He invited people in. Everyone at church adored Youth Guy Chris. I felt dumbfounded by this conversation, even as more puzzle pieces fell into place.

My heart hurt for him, so I was shocked to hear Rhonda burst out laughing. She reached over and patted his knee. "My boy. You are the most lovable person I've ever met!"

"Thank you, Mama," he answered fondly. "But you're my mom. That's what you're supposed to say."

"You don't believe I'm telling you the truth?"

Chris considered for a moment. "I do now. Mostly. I can see now that, for a long time, that fear made it impossible to let anyone in for real. I kept most people at arms' length. It's still not always easy to believe, but I'm better than I was. I think I'm healing to a point where I could believe it fully one day, maybe try for something good with the right person. And that hope is really encouraging."

"So maybe there is some hope for us to get to know Maddie a little better eventually?" Rhonda wheedled.

Chris sighed and shook his head. "Sorry, Mama. I ruined that one a little too thoroughly."

Rhonda remained silent, but it spoke volumes.

Chris explained. "I've made peace with it. I really like being friends with her. Letting go of that side of things has actually been helpful. I'm not nervous around her anymore. I can be myself and not overthink it. I can just…enjoy Maddie from this place of freedom. I think we'll always be friends. But that's all it is, and I am trusting the Lord that it's best."

Rhonda sighed, frustrated.

I felt a little frustrated too. Sure, I'd written Chris off entirely, but I'd liked him a lot back in the day. Even now, I had to fight against my attraction to him. But understanding some of the things that had happened in his life was majorly affecting my perception of our previous interactions.

Had he ruined himself for me forever? I'd certainly thought so at the time. But after hearing all this…I wasn't so sure. And now it sounded like there could be a different obstacle: *he* may have written *me* off.

I frowned in the darkness. *What if?* Rhonda's protest jolted me from my thoughts.

"But I can tell you really like her! And she's the same girl, right? The one from last summer? You've liked her for a long time!"

Wait. *She knew about last summer?!*

This was a big, wide left turn. My neck heated from the memory of that night at Anna's. *Ryan and Mia sitting in a tree….* It soured my stomach to remember it. Chris was right; he *did* ruin that night—thoroughly.

What am I doing? Standing here listening to all this was wrong. It wasn't my business, and it wasn't fair. I turned to head back to bed, but a sound alerted me—a quiet, rhythmic thud. Someone was walking down the hallway. *Oh no.* If they came in here and found me eavesdropping, it would be awful. I looked around, searching for a place to hide. The steps grew closer. I dove behind the table and crouched down behind a chair. As long as they didn't turn on the lights, I should be okay. I took a deep breath, trying to slow my breathing so they wouldn't hear.

I peered through the jumble of wooden table and chair legs, breathing a sigh of relief that I'd hidden in time. Chelsea emerged from the hallway and walked to the cabinet for a glass. She filled it at the sink and leaned over to see outside. I hoped she couldn't hear my heart pounding. She drank her water sip by sip, shamelessly eavesdropping on the conversation outside. Chris and Rhonda had continued talking while I searched for a hiding place, and now Chris's exasperation carried through the screen door.

"I never should have told y'all about her."

"Your siblings love you. They want good things for you. So do I," Rhonda reminded him.

Chris sighed. "I know. Last summer was just…bad timing. I wasn't ready, but I liked her too much to care, which was selfish. Then that phone call with Dad set me off. I don't know why. It wasn't anything new. He was only being himself. *'Why didn't you take that job my friend offered you? Don't you want me to be proud of you? You're wasting a perfectly good degree on ministry.'* On and on. I couldn't handle it. I freaked out, and I was too embarrassed to tell her the truth, so I just…ruined it."

I put my hand over my mouth, staggered. I had no idea.

"I'm so sorry that happened. Doug Calvert's impeccable timing, as usual." Rhonda's tone made it easy to picture her face. Then her voice softened. "You know, he could never please his own father. No matter how hard he worked, he was always inadequate in some way. He's spent his life looking for a way to overcome that pain. And then he followed in his father's footsteps. I'm so sorry."

I admired Rhonda's capacity for compassion, especially for a man who had left her. But frustration welled up in me. *How dare he?* My heart broke for Chris and for the effect his dad's wounds had had on him. Rhonda's voice continued, full of strength.

"But sweetheart, you *can* overcome it. By God's grace, you *are*! You have worked hard and come so far. I can see it. Don't let him hold you back. If you want something, go for it."

Chris sighed, frustrated. "I'm trying, Mama."

"Tell me more," Rhonda replied.

Chris paused for a second, then he spoke. "I'm in a good place. I'm maybe the healthiest I've ever been. I've learned a lot this year and found a lot of healing. I've grieved a failed engagement from years ago. I've grieved a difficult dad. I've put up boundaries with him for the first time ever. I've stood by my sister through unimaginable pain. And I *still* have a lot of work to do. If I started a relationship with someone right now, I have no clue how it would go."

"Probably have to take it one day at a time, like everyone else," Rhonda said mildly.

Chris chuckled. "Wise words. You're probably right."

"So are you telling me you're not *ready* for a relationship? Or you don't *want* a relationship?" Rhonda asked, getting serious again. Chris didn't respond right away.

"Look at me, Christopher," she said. I heard him shift on the cushions. Rhonda's voice was low and firm, calm. "You know there's no such thing as a perfect person or a perfect relationship, right?" she asked kindly.

"Yes, I know that," he mumbled.

"You are not your father. You are not *like* your father. You are totally capable of a loving, healthy relationship if you choose to have one."

"I know," he insisted then paused. "In my *mind*, I know it. But in my heart, it feels…like I need to be careful."

I missed what Rhonda said next because Chelsea had heard enough. She turned and padded out of the kitchen and down the hallway to go back to bed. I ought to follow suit. I gave her a second to get back to her room before I stood, ready to go.

But as soon as I got upright, a different person cleared their throat in the hallway. *Are you kidding me?* Resigned, I sat down behind the chair, this time in a more comfortable position. Sushi shuffled into the kitchen and proceeded to get a glass. This was getting ridiculous. If we were all this parched, Chance must have oversalted the brisket. Taking her sweet time, Sushi drank her fill and moved carefully over to the screen door to see what was going on outside.

"I'm not saying it will always be like this," Chris assured Rhonda. "I'm going to keep working at it. I'm growing a lot, in my faith and in my life. But the fear is still there. And everything with Chelsea has made it harder, seeing how hurt she and the kids have been by that jackwagon Trent. Some days, I feel like I would rather be alone forever than open myself up to that kind of pain."

It took everything I had to stay behind the chair. I wanted to run out to the porch and tell Chris all the good I'd seen in him over the last month and a half. To reassure him. But I didn't need to.

"Well, I can understand that." Rhonda took a deep breath and continued. "Everyone takes a risk when they give their heart to another human being. No one can predict how life is going to go, how they will handle grief or disappointment, or reconnecting with an old flame on the internet, as your dad did. We cannot control any of it, and we cannot let fear control *us*. All we can do is show up, one day at a time, and trust God to be with us through whatever comes. It sounds cliche, but it's true. You *are* in a good place, I can tell. I wonder what it might be like if you let yourself dream a little, maybe let yourself try."

Chris didn't respond aloud, but Rhonda was on a role.

"You said yourself you've been growing a lot. How are you going to *apply* it?" she prompted, her voice gentle.

He sighed. "I see what you're saying, but wanting something and taking hold of it are two different things."

"Sweetheart, we all have good and bad in us. But we choose, every day. By His grace, we choose Jesus. Jesus is the only thing that doesn't change. Jesus has to be the source of your identity, or you will not be able to overcome the lies of the enemy. You cannot let fear keep you from living your life. From love! It is for *freedom* that Christ has set you free!"

I was glad I'd stayed hidden. Rhonda had said it all better than I could have.

Chris replied, his voice gritty, "I know."

"You could always ask Maddie what she thinks," Rhonda suggested. I had to hand it to her, she did not give up easily.

Chris snorted. "I can see it now: 'Hey, Maddie, sorry I threw away the *second* chance you gave me because of a phone call with my dad. It wasn't you; it was me. How would you feel about giving me a *third* chance?' That's ridiculous. I'm sorry, Mama, but it's not going to happen. I'm not going to throw away my friendship with her, on top of everything else."

More silence. Rhonda must be patiently staring him down.

He sighed. "I don't want you to worry about me. I have a great life. I'm happy. I am walking with faithful guys who hold me accountable and hold themselves to the standard. I love my job and my friends. I love my church. The timing with Maddie was wrong, and I'm really grateful to be friends with her. It's enough, Mama."

"Well, are you going to date anyone else?" Rhonda asked matter-of-factly.

I could imagine him throwing up his hands in helpless frustration. "I don't know. Someday, I probably will. I can't worry about it right now, living with Chelsea and the kids. I need to get through one thing at a time."

"Well, I guess that is true. But don't take too long. I'm not getting any younger."

I couldn't see what Chris was doing, but it took him a second to say, "I'll keep that in mind."

"I appreciate you, you know? You're a good man, and you have a proud mama."

"Thank you, Mama. I appreciate you too. Now, is it finally my turn to ask a question?" She must have nodded. "Sushi told me the sheriff has been coming over for dinner every week for a month. What's going on with *that*?"

They shared a laugh before Rhonda answered. "It's probably nothing. At my age, it would be too weird."

"Yeah, right. I don't believe that for a second. Do we need to sit him down and have a talk about his intentions?" I could tell he was teasing her, but I wouldn't put it past the Calvert boys.

Rhonda scolded him. "Don't you dare!"

Sushi huffed a quiet laugh in tandem with Chris. "It's not very fun when the tables turn, is it?" he joked.

I could imagine the look on Rhonda's face when she replied. "Nothing has happened. He's only kissed me one time."

Chris reacted exactly as she intended him to.

"Rhonda Calvert! Gross!" It sounded like he slapped his hands over his ears. "*Please* never talk to me about kissing again!"

Oh please, I thought. But I had to cut him some slack. No one wants to hear about that from their parents.

"Don't ask questions you don't want answers to, son." I silently giggled at Rhonda's sass.

There was a pause, then they both cracked up laughing again. When they calmed down, Chris's voice had grown gritty with exhaustion. "On that terrible note, I have to go to bed."

Oh no. Sushi was still in the kitchen. I was trapped. If Chris caught me here, he'd never forgive me. How was I going to get out of there before they found me? I could see their silhouettes on the curtains above me. Their shadows rose from the sofas.

Sushi turned and high-tailed it down the hallway. I breathed a sigh of relief when the two shadows melted together into a hug. *A nice, long hug*, I prayed. Half-panicked, I stood and scurried across the kitchen floor to the hallway. I crouched there in the shadows, waiting for Sushi's door to close.

Rhonda's encouragement, "I'm going to keep praying," faded into incomprehensible murmuring as I slunk down the dark hallway to my room. I slid beneath the covers, my mind spinning like a carnival ride. I held my breath until footsteps ambled past my room, and then I took a huge, slow breath. *Okay.* I needed to have a serious conversation with myself.

Two things seemed certain: One, Chris had decided I was a lost cause and moved on. This was understandable, especially after last summer. Unfortunately, this revelation did nothing to hinder my attraction to him. If anything, after everything I'd heard and seen this weekend, my attraction to the man had exponentially grown.

But it takes more than attraction. Chris had said it himself. *Timing is everything—the right person at the wrong time is still the wrong person. Ugh.* Disappointment sat heavy on my heart, crushing my lungs. But I had a choice in this.

I'd been single for a long time, and had years of experience with dating. I'd been disappointed before. I reminded myself that it was okay for this to hurt. But if I let myself obsess over it, I would never get to sleep. I needed to lift my gaze and rest in the unchanging love of God. I'd memorized Psalm 23 years ago, and the Lord brought it to mind.

The Lord is my shepherd, I shall not want.

He makes me lie down in green pastures, he leads me beside quiet waters.

He restores my soul; he leads me in paths of righteousness for his name's sake.

Even though I walk through the valley of the shadow of death, I will fear no evil,

For you are with me; your rod and your staff, they comfort me.

You prepare a table before me in the presence of my enemies;

you anoint my head with oil, my cup runneth over.

Surely goodness and mercy shall follow me all the days of my life,

and I will dwell in the house of the Lord forever.

I prayed the promise again: *Surely goodness and mercy shall follow me all the days of my life.*

Oh Lord, let that be true. I don't know what you are doing, but I know you are good. As I prayed, the truth grounded me. *God is good. He* does *good and has a good plan for my life.* I had seen it again and again. I remembered my verse from Philippians. God had done good work in my life and He was still at it. He wasn't going to let me go.

If Chris is not the guy for me, I'll be okay. It would take time, but I could accept it and move on. After all, nothing had really changed. My lungs felt lighter and my body began to relax. I took a slow, deep breath.

The other certainty was this: Chris Calvert had earned my respect and friendship. He'd worked hard to grow, to be a healthy man of God. I wanted to honor that, even if it meant letting go of the possibility for more.

Lord, I need your wisdom. I need to keep the main thing the main thing. Help me to be faithful and to trust you, I prayed and closed my eyes.

CHAPTER 24

Sunday morning came early. I stretched and sat up in bed. Chelsea, Chris and I had agreed we would head home that morning. I didn't like missing church, but we all needed to get back. I was scheduled to work Monday, and my to-do list spun through my mind like a hamster wheel. I had a lot to accomplish for the day, but first I needed to pee.

When I shuffled out of the bathroom, still groggy, Chris was walking up the hallway, already bright-eyed. Knowing him, he'd probably been awake for a while. He wore the sweatshirt I'd returned to him after the fire last night. Everything from the night before came back, and heat raced up my neck. I had no doubt he would read my mind and know I'd listened in on his and Rhonda's conversation. Feelings and words welled up within me. *Where to begin?* I wanted to say everything and nothing, all at once. But no words reached the surface; it all stayed a jumbled mess in my uncaffeinated brain. I settled for basic manners.

"Morning." I yawned.

"Good morning. There's coffee in the kitchen. Did you sleep well?" he asked.

I nodded, about to walk past him. But something stopped me. No matter how wonderful he was, he was still Chris Calvert. And he was *awfully* close to my bedroom. All those oniony layers…an alarm went off in my head, and I froze, mere feet away from him.

Squinting up at him, I held up a halting hand. "Where are you coming from?"

He gestured with his thumb. "The kids' room. They're getting dressed, then they're going to help me make breakfast."

I straightened my spine. This wasn't the time to lose myself in how great of an uncle he was. This was the time for vigilance. I looked him in the eye, mentally fluffing up like the rooster from yesterday. I pointed a finger at him.

"If I go into my room, and there's a frog in the bed, I'm going to kill you," I said evenly.

He smiled and shook his head. "There's no frog in your bed, Reed—at least not from me. Scout's honor." He held up three fingers.

Before I could respond, the kids came bounding down the hallway. "Uncle Chris, can we make pancakes?" Hannah implored, her blue eyes huge.

Chris shook his head. "You know the rules, ma'am. I'm not allowed. How about some breakfast tacos instead?"

Noah nodded and looked at Hannah. "Mommy can make pancakes when she wakes up," he offered. Hannah nodded, satisfied for the moment. She ran over to take Chris's hand in hers, and they all strolled past me, headed to the kitchen together.

I walked into my room to get ready. I needed to pack too. I rummaged through my suitcase and changed quickly into fleece-lined leggings and a comfy, long-sleeved t-shirt. I folded my pajamas, packing as I went. I looked around for my shoes, and something caught my eye.

It sat on the nightstand, leaning against the alarm clock. Pink hearts replaced the pupils of the comically bulbous eyes, on top of a big green smile. A white belly sloped down between the green legs, ending at green, speckled, webbed feet. A little cheer rose up in me before I could stop it. The watercolor frog on the sticker was much cuter than the real thing, and the perfect souvenir from the weekend. He must have cut it out of one of the kids' art books or something. *Or maybe it wasn't him,* I reasoned. It easily could have been Hannah or Noah.

Whoever had left it, I loved it, and I would keep it. I carefully zipped it into the pocket of my suitcase, finished putting on my shoes, and headed out to start the day.

—

After the best breakfast tacos of my life (Chris really could cook!), we packed the car then took turns hugging Sushi and Rhonda goodbye.

"Thank you for coming, Maddie," Rhonda said, squeezing me tight. "It was wonderful to have you here and get to know you a little bit."

I hugged her back. "Thank you for everything. I had the best time."

"Come back soon!" she murmured.

"Edna! Not again!" Hannah's voice rang out, distracting everyone. We turned to look. The minivan's sliding doors sat open, and Edna must be ready to go. She'd climbed up to sit in the driver's seat, one paw on the steering wheel.

Charmed, all the adults laughed. Chris opened the driver's door. "Edna, we've been through this. You can't drive," he said.

"Edna has no thumbs," Noah looked solemn as he spoke to Rhonda and me. "Otherwise, she *could* drive."

"Has this happened before?" I guessed, fighting to keep a straight face and match his sincerity.

He nodded. "Every time." He heaved a long-suffering sigh and climbed up in the car to help Chris get Edna where she needed to be.

I cracked up as quietly as I could and took a moment to catch my breath before I opened the door to sit down in the passenger seat.

Chelsea hugged Rhonda one more time then hopped into the minivan, ready to go. The kids insisted we wave and blow kisses until their Grammy was out of sight.

—

Chris seemed lost in thought, navigating the Sunday traffic on I-20. Noah and Hannah munched happily on pretzels while listening to an audiobook with Chelsea in the back.

"I had a great time on the trip. It was exactly what I needed," I told Chris.

He perked up and adjusted his ball cap. "You needed to be attacked by a killer rooster?"

I wrinkled my nose. "Well, maybe not that part."

"Sorry it happened—again," Chris said.

I shrugged it off. "I'm good, so long as I have an expert in first aid nearby."

He grinned. "Happy to help."

"Thanks," I said, thinking of my next question. I considered talking about a different subject, but I was curious, and I might not get another chance. "Can I ask you about something a little more personal?"

"More personal than flushing the toilet while I was in the shower?" His eyes went wide but playful. I bit my lip. He shook his head. "That was pretty scandalous, Reed. I didn't know you had it in you!"

"It served you right, after the frog!" I insisted, laughing. He grinned mischievously. "But it's nothing like that," I assured him, trying not to blush. "Chelsea told me you were engaged…before."

His face fell, his mood instantly less jovial. He sighed.

"Why didn't you ever mention it? I told you about Houston," I said.

Different expressions crossed his face, but he looked ahead, watching the road. "It's not a secret or anything. It was a long time ago, and I generally try not to think about it."

"I can understand that," I said.

He looked at me and nodded. "It was a bad experience, but Chelsea especially hated her, so in the interest of fairness, I should tell you that it wasn't only Becca who was the problem. I was far from my best and just as culpable. It was a really unhealthy relationship at a really unhealthy time in my life…foolishness ruled me in every way back then. I made a lot of stupid decisions, set a bad example for my nephews and nieces…I was not wise, in any of it."

"You set a bad example? Isn't that a little harsh?" I asked.

He licked his lips. "Becca and I lived together in Austin after we graduated."

I couldn't hide my surprise before he looked over at my face, anticipating my reaction.

"I know. It was a huge point of contention. My mom did not raise us to live that way, and it was a big deal to my whole family—as it should have been. It was wrong. I was drunk on love and pride, and I thought I had everything figured out. I used every reason I could think of to justify it. We were engaged. It was cheaper for her to live with me in corporate housing. We could save money for the wedding. On and on."

He shook his head. I said nothing, and he kept going. "Everyone was really disappointed in me, but Colton was the worst. He got upset, said it was a bad example for the kids. It was a whole thing. We'd had ups and downs after my dad left and throughout my college years. He and

Chance both tried hard to encourage me, rein me in, and I just wouldn't. I did what I wanted to do.

"Graduation weekend, right before I moved to Austin, my brothers sat me down and held me accountable. They were kind about it, but they didn't hold back. They said it was time to decide what kind of man I was going to be. I mean, we all grew up in church. They knew I knew what was right, but I wasn't living it. They'd tried before.

"They probably figured they didn't get through to me that time either, but it was rolling around in the back of my mind the whole summer. Then Becca dumped me, and I moved to Dallas. I was really broken, but I knew what I needed to do. I finally turned to the Lord for real, laid it all down, and He was there."

I wasn't sure what to say. I didn't want to say the wrong thing, and I didn't want to start crying and make it awkward. In all these years, Chris had never shared any of this with me. I didn't want him to stop.

"You seem to have a strong relationship with Colton and Chance now," I observed.

He nodded. "Yeah, we're really close. We stayed close through my time at college too. It was tense sometimes, but they never gave up on me. I always knew they were there if I needed them. They were glad when I moved to Dallas and started to wake up out of that foolishness."

What to say next? I settled for a little levity. "I bet that story was fun to share in the youth minister interview," I joked.

He released a choked laugh and looked over, giving me the side-eye. "That's one way of looking at it." He looked back at the road. "By the time I interviewed, that whole thing had been over and done for a few years. God had done a lot of work, changing my heart, changing my ways. I mean, the elders know about it. I shared it with the interview committee. I told them my whole testimony. And the topic of cohabitation was a portion of the theology inventory."

"Glad they're thorough," I remarked.

"Yeah. It's not something I am proud of, at all, and I don't share it widely. I don't want the youth group kids to think I would condone that or that they could use me as an excuse to do it themselves. But the Lord met me where I was. He's used it and done a lot of healing. Ryan always reminds me, nothing is wasted. And now, living God's way is important to me because I love Him. I'm grateful for that. But it was a tough lesson."

I nodded. "It's hard to be wise when you're twenty-two."

"That's putting it mildly." He wrinkled his nose. "I still don't like to think about it."

I nodded. "Thanks for telling me. I'm sorry it went so badly. That loss is tough to walk through."

He smiled a little half-smile. "Thanks. I look back at that college kid and wonder, *what was I thinking?* But sometimes you just…can't see. You know?"

I nodded. I definitely knew. Time was a good gift.

"I felt a lot of shame for a long time," Chris admitted. "Brooke has helped me with that too."

I smiled. "Brooke. Thank goodness for that woman! She's helped so many people. Mia has shared Brooke's wisdom with the rest of us many times. We all joke that we should contribute to the co-pay, because Brooke is really doing group therapy for all of us," I said, smiling.

Chris chuckled. "I'm not surprised. She's got a lot of wisdom. We're all going to have to name our first child Brooke to make it up to her."

I laughed, but I didn't want to change the subject yet. "So, are you past the whole Becca thing now? Or still working through it?" I asked.

"Like, am I over her?" he asked, looking at me. "Yes. I have been over her for a very long time." He paused. "Have I grieved it in a healthy way and moved past it? Yes. Finally."

"Good for you," I said.

He nodded. "Yeah. Counseling really is helpful. Who knew?"

"A lot of people," I replied. We both laughed. "I'm glad you're free of it," I said.

He nodded. "Me too. A little freedom goes a long way."

"Can't argue with that," I agreed. Then it hit me. I turned to him.

"So was the date limit in response to everything that happened with Becca?"

He made a face. "Pretty much. We broke up in August, and I applied to transfer to the Dallas office as soon as I could. I moved in September and basically started over.

I kept in touch with a couple of old teammates, but everyone else was too close with Becca, or they were living the way I didn't want to live anymore. I wanted friends and a social life, but I was done partying all the time. It was a lot of change all at once, and I was messed up and sad, and scared to get hurt again."

He'd never shared any of this with me in all these years. I'd never given him the opportunity. My mind whirled, trying to keep up.

"I wanted to move on, but I couldn't figure out how to heal. I didn't trust myself to know what to look for in a woman. Colton and Chance told me to date casually, take my time. So I took their advice, but I added some *very strict parameters* for myself. Self-reliance at its finest." He shook his head. I said nothing, waiting for him to continue.

"It wasn't healthy, but it was all I could do at the time. I did other, healthier things too. I joined a gym, made some friends, found a church home, made friends there. And eventually, I had a whole new life." He shrugged.

"Thank you for telling me," I said.

"You're friends with an onion, Reed. I hope you don't mind."

"Not at all," I said. "It would be pretty hypocritical if I did mind. You're not the only one who had some growing up to do."

"Oh? You got some layers of your own?" His voice held a teasing lilt.

I cleared my throat and looked at my knees. "Well, I haven't lived with anyone, but I obviously have a past. I made mistakes and choices along the way that I also do not like to think about."

Chris's face stretched into a grimace, probably thinking about Houston. He drew a breath to speak. I pointed a finger at him, cutting off whatever he was about to say. "Nope. Do not make a joke right now. I don't want to *think* about it, much less talk about it."

For a second, he looked stuck, as if the joke was clogged in his mouth. Then he pressed his lips into a half-smile and shrugged. "Well, I'm sorry you went through that, and I'm glad we both dodged some bullets." He held up his hand for a high five.

I swatted his hand and huffed a relieved laugh. "Thank you." I left it at that, still feeling a little awkward. Like Chris said, I tried not to focus on that time in my life.

My brain was practically on fire, trying to process all the new information. The date limit still seemed ridiculous to me, but I understood more now. Anorexia had shown me over and over how easy it was to overcorrect into self-destructive choices in the name of control and perfection. My past with Houston, and even other guys I'd dated, had taught me a lot too. I wasn't sure where I would be if any of those situations had gone differently, but I felt very grateful to be right here. *God's plan really is best*, I admitted, observing Chris's profile out of the corner of my eye. My heart settled, resting in that truth.

We sat quietly for a few minutes, watching the trees go by. I turned to the back of the car. Chelsea was up to her elbows in her bag of snacks, getting ready for the next round.

"When do you officially start in the classroom, Chelsea?" I asked.

"Thursday," she answered. "I set up the classroom right before Christmas, so it's ready to go. I have meetings Monday through Wednesday this week, and then it's off to the races!"

She seemed genuinely excited. I smiled, glad to see everything was finally working out.

"We need to celebrate ASAP!" I told her. She held up a thumbs-up and turned to answer a question for Hannah.

I plopped back down in my seat and reached into my bag. I had a box of Hot Tamales candy in there. Mia had rubbed off on me.

"Want some Hot Tamales?" I asked, holding out the box. Eyes on the road, Chris wordlessly held out his hand, and I poured a few into his palm.

"So, did you pound anyone's face into the ground yesterday?" I asked quietly so the kids wouldn't hear.

He snorted and shook his head. "Tempting, but no. *Someone* has to set a good example."

"That's too bad," I commiserated.

He nodded. "Actually, there was a breakthrough of another kind. On the way there, Chelsea told me she's ready. She wants me to move out."

CHAPTER 25

My eyebrows shot up. That might have been the most shocking statement of this whole car ride. "*Now?*"

He made a face and shrugged. "I wasn't expecting it either. I mean, it's fine, of course. I'll do it. But I didn't see it coming."

He wasn't the only one. I sat there, gaping at him. This seemed out of nowhere. He reached out for more Hot Tamales, and I obliged.

"I thought she'd want me to help during the transition to the new job," he said. "But she said they've got to figure it out together, the three of them."

He paused.

"How do *you* feel about this?" I asked. He loved those kids so much.

He shrugged. "I'm okay. I mean, moving in with them turned things upside down for me in a lot of ways, so it will be nice to have my own routine again. The commute to work will be a lot shorter. And I'll still go over there all the time. It's sooner than I expected, but Chelsea's right: she's got to figure it out."

He popped a piece of candy in his mouth. "But I'm gonna miss them." He said it calmly, but I could tell it was emotional for him. I didn't know what to say. My heart went out to all of them. It was a lot of change all at once. I reached out and gently squeezed his forearm, careful not to disturb his hold on the wheel. He placed his other hand over mine and gave me a grateful smile. He patted my hand a couple times and shifted away to change lanes.

"Thanks for being there this weekend. You helped her see that she really can do it." He spoke quietly so no one else could hear.

"I had a great time, but I don't think I did much, if anything," I told him.

He shook his head. "No, you did. Friends are different from family. Hanging out with you boosted her confidence. She needed that. So thank you." He took his eyes off the road to look at me fully. His eyes, usually so sparkly, radiated a deep sincerity that captured me and held on. One second turned into two before he turned back to the road. My lungs released. As bad as the timing was, it was hard to shut down my feelings, but it was more important than ever that I do exactly that. I swallowed past the intensity and forced myself back to the surface.

"Well, I loved being there," I admitted then gave him the side-eye. "Just when you thought you were rid of me!"

He laughed and joined in on the joke. "It was a struggle at times, but we made it through."

"Mama, I need to go potty," Noah announced, tearing any remaining tension to shreds.

Chris sighed and signaled for the next exit.

—

We made good time and arrived home by noon. I hugged everyone goodbye and headed to my apartment.

Kevin met me at the door, jumping up to smother me in doggy kisses as I put my bag down.

"Hi, buddy!" I picked him up and kissed his little teddy bear face. He'd finally visited the groomer last week, and it was nice to be able to see his eyes again. I held him close as I walked to the kitchen and found Emma in there, making a sandwich.

"Hey, frog warrior! How was it?" she asked, cutting her masterpiece in half.

I shrugged. "It was great! Everyone was really nice. But it's good to be home."

She walked over and curled up on the couch with her plate. "I want to hear everything. What's the family like? How was it with Chris?"

I sat on the opposite end of the couch. I thought back to leaving him just a few minutes ago. Chris's hug had been friendly but brief. I refused to overthink it—or any of our interactions over the weekend, for that matter. We were friends, full stop.

"I really enjoyed myself. Their mom is wonderful, so comfortable in her own skin, and super welcoming. All the siblings are hilarious together; they mess with each other constantly. But they are protective too." I told her about how supportive they all were to Chelsea.

Emma would not be dissuaded. "Okay, but how was it with *Chris*?"

"It was fine," I told her.

Emma dug in. "Did anything happen?" she asked with a sly smile.

"Of course not!"

Emma looked frustrated. "You expect me to believe that after the frog thing?"

I shrugged. "You know how sometimes it's hard to tell if Chris is just having a good time or if he's actually flirting? I'm pretty sure it was the former," I admitted.

Our conversation in the car left me more resolved than ever to ignore my little crush. Chris had been through a lot, and he needed my friendship more than anything else right now. It was enough.

I looked around and considered everything I needed to accomplish today. "Okay, now I need to do some laundry and run to get some groceries for the week," I told her. "Do you want to come with me?"

She nodded. "Sure. Could we stop by the mall too? I'm still looking for a pair of shoes to go with my dress for Sarah's wedding."

I sat up. "Oh yeah! It's only two weeks away!"

"I want to look really good." She raised her eyebrows. "I asked Luke to be my date."

I clapped my hands. "That's an exciting update! When did this happen?"

Emma smiled. "He was at the New Year's Eve party I went to, so we talked for a while. I asked him, and he said yes."

"Ooh! That's worth celebrating!" I held up my hand for a high five. "I'm so proud of you for putting yourself out there!"

Emma nodded as she bent down to pick up Kevin. "I'm pretty proud of myself. The moment hit, and I figured, it's now or never. So I jumped."

"I get that. Well done," I said. Timing was a whole thing these days. I changed the subject before my heart could sink. "Thanks for reminding me I need to pick up my bridesmaid dress."

In all the madness of the Christmas play and traveling over New Year's, I completely zoned out about Sarah's upcoming bachelorette party and wedding. I felt a little bad. I still needed to buy them a wedding gift too. I turned to go start the laundry, my head already filled with mental notes.

Emma cleared her throat. "Ahem." She looked at me expectantly. I stopped.

"What?" Was I missing another detail? An event of some kind? I wracked my brain. Nothing surfaced.

She gave me a pointed look. "Don't *you* have a plus-one spot to fill as well?"

"Oh. I completely forgot that part," I groaned. I'd been so focused on everything else, it truly hadn't occurred to me. I looked around, checking the kitchen floor for date options. None popped up. I knew what Emma was *not* saying, but I wasn't sure I was ready to go there.

Emma, however, went straight there. "Don't you think you and Chris would have a lot of fun together?" she prodded.

I licked my lips, feeling the weight of the question. As of now—and possibly forever—Chris and I were friends. I wanted to be a good friend to him, no matter how attractive he looked, kissing my hurts, carrying children, and being generally amazing.

"I don't know," I answered her honestly.

Emma looked confused. She knew me well, so she usually knew when to push and when to back off. But I wasn't ready to talk about it. There was too much to process. I assumed she would read me and back off, but instead, she doubled down.

"I say this out of love, Mads: Don't wait around. Ask Chris to be your wedding date. Then marry him and have lots of babies."

I looked away from her, blushing. "Emma! That's a lot of life stages for one sentence."

She laughed. "Would you rather go for it or waste another five years having fun?"

I sighed. "We're friends. What's wrong with having fun?"

"Nothing," she declared. "Unless you want more. You need to be honest with yourself. You like him. A lot. You've learned some things over these last several weeks. I'm not trying to tell you what to do, but I think you know you have some stuff to figure out."

I groaned and covered my face. She didn't know the half of it. "I have to figure it out *now*? I just got home."

She laughed. "Not right this second, Whiny McGee, but yes. You need to figure it out. I've had my opinions of Youth Guy Chris in the past. We all have. But things change. I'm all for it, and I'll support you regardless, but I am protective of you. You are amazing, Maddie. If he wants to be with you, he needs to man up. Don't go backward."

CHAPTER 26

Chelsea and I checked in periodically through the week, texting about this and that. When she invited me to dinner at her house Friday night, I said yes, assuming it would be me, her, and the kids. Surely Chris had youth group duties or other plans. *That doesn't matter anyway,* I reminded myself. *I am excited to see my friend and hear about her new job.*

I arrived at Chelsea's, carrying a package of Hawaiian rolls. I was looking forward to a low-key night to start off a busy weekend. Chelsea and Edna met me at the door.

"Thanks for coming." Chelsea hugged me, and talked a mile a minute. "Here, I'll take these. Dinner's almost ready. Do you want something to drink? I'm having a glass of wine. I earned it," she laughed.

I nodded and scratched Edna behind the ears. "That sounds great, thanks! What can I do to help?"

Chelsea gestured to the living room. "Make yourself at home."

I followed her into the kitchen. "So, how's it going so far?" I asked.

She smiled, reaching into a cabinet for a wine glass. "It's really good! I love the class; they are super sweet. My team is great. I love the principal. It's tiring, but I think we'll adjust pretty well." She practically glowed with energy.

"That's amazing! I'm so glad!" I told her.

Chelsea smiled. "How about you? How was your week?"

"I can't complain," I admitted. Working in the ER was finally starting to feel normal. I had finally made it through the week without making any mistakes.

"No rooster attacks?" Chelsea joked. I laughed and shook my head.

"No rooster attacks. But we treated one pretty nasty dog bite." I accepted the glass of red wine she held out to me and took a sip. It was nice and smooth.

Chelsea walked over to a crockpot and stirred the contents. "Can I do anything to help?" I asked.

She shook her head. "No. We're almost ready. Can you go back to the kids' room and let them know dinner's ready?" She pointed toward the hallway that led to the bedrooms.

I nodded and headed that direction, with Edna at my heels. The sound of laughter carried down the hallway, and my heart lifted. Chris was here.

I poked my head into the doorway with the light on. The room was painted white with two twin beds sticking out from the far wall, underneath a window. One had a frilly pink bedspread, and a purple canopy hung from a tiara-shaped ring suspended from the ceiling above it. The other bed had a green-and-blue comforter with dogs on it.

A shelf full of books and bins sat along the other wall, under a window. Hannah and Chris sat in tiny chairs at a kid-sized table in the corner, having a tea party. They hadn't heard me approaching.

Hannah wore an elaborate blue princess gown with a plastic tiara atop her golden ringlets and pink evening gloves. She smiled and giggled with her guest. Wearing his own version of princess garb, Chris looked comical in the undersized chair. His denim-clad knees rose up past the top of the table. A tiara sat askew on his head, and a pair of enormous plastic jewel earrings clung to his ears. A feather boa spread across his shoulders and looped around his neck. He held a tea-cup, pinky extended, fully in character as he toasted Hannah.

"To you, dah-ling. You're a kind friend. I'm proud of you for playing nicely with Taylor at school today."

Hannah nodded and raised her own cup. "To you, too, dah-ling. You're nice."

Chris thanked her. They clinked their plastic tea-cups together then pretended to sip. Enchanted, I let myself enjoy the show for a few seconds before I took a breath and cleared my throat. They turned to look. Hannah's face lit up.

"Miss Maddie! You're here! Want to play with us?"

"Hi, sweet girl! I'd love to play, but it's dinner time." I looked at Chris and complimented him. "Nice earrings, Miss Calvert."

He chuckled and looked down, collecting himself. His eyes sparkled when they met mine. "It's *Lady* Calvert. And thank you. They match my tiara," he explained, straightening it on his head.

I nodded, loving it all more and more. I looked between them. "Like I said, dinner's ready, you two."

Chris looked at Hannah. "Shall we pause our tea party to eat dinner, Princess Elsa?"

Hannah nodded. "Okay."

They stood up from the table. I walked into the room and asked Chris, "How is your shoulder feeling?"

He rolled it back and forth. "Good as new."

"Glad to hear it," I said. I turned and walked down the hallway. Hannah ran past me, her blonde ringlets bouncing as we arrived in the kitchen. Chris came in after us with Noah, ear lobes unadorned. He must have left all the jewelry in Hannah's room.

"Thank you for that, Chels," he said pointedly.

I wasn't sure what he meant until Chelsea looked over at him, an impish smile on her face. "You're welcome, Lady Calvert." She looked at the kids. "Let's all wash our hands, please."

Ah, the Embarrass Chris Game was still afoot? Was it for *my* benefit? I wondered. He must not have confided in Chelsea yet. I felt a little bad for him, but not really. He was the king of pranks, after all.

Once everyone was clean and ready, we sat down to a delicious dinner of barbecue chicken sliders.

"How was work this week?" I asked Chris, right as he took a bite.

He nodded, swallowing. "Mostly meetings. Amy and I are planning the spring retreat, gathering ideas for summer, those kinds of things. Two of the high school senior boys want to start a Bible study, so I met with them. All good stuff. The church is growing fast right now, so we're kinda sharing the load a little more so the bulk of ministry doesn't fall on one or two people. We're taking turns with visiting people in the hospital, regardless of their age."

"Interesting," I remarked. "So you're ministering to adults now too?"

He nodded. "It's already been in motion, but now it's more official."

Chelsea seemed concerned. "Do you have time to do that? You're a pretty busy guy already."

Chris shrugged. "It will all work out."

Chelsea looked at me, shaking her head. "All these people who think youth ministers only exist to keep kids entertained. I don't know anyone who works harder, or puts in more time, or more prayer."

Chris slumped and looked at the ceiling. "Chelsea."

She shrugged. "I'm just sayin'."

"Thank you for seeing me," Chris told her, then he changed the subject. "Okay, time to spill. Who's the worst kid in your class?"

Chelsea laughed. "There isn't a worst kid! I told you, they're all really sweet so far!"

I tilted my head. "Oh, come on. It's been two whole days, surely you've got a story or two. My roommate teaches second grade, and she adores those kids, but she *always* has a new story. Kids are hilarious!"

Chris tilted his head and looked at her expectantly. She looked right back, bouncing her gaze between us. "I'm serious!"

"Okay," he said, smiling. He looked at me. "Chelsea was a talker in school, so I'm assuming she's going to get her comeuppance."

Chelsea laughed. "Oh, *I* was the talker? Am I the one who got detention for singing over the school intercom when I was *supposedly* supposed to be in the nurse's office?" She broke into a chorus:

Love me, love me
Say that you love me
Fool me, fool me
Go on and fool me

I hadn't heard "Love Fool" by The Cardigans in years. I laughed out loud and shook my head at Chris. He looked at me, wide-eyed, innocent. I tilted my head, waiting for it.

"I was fourteen," he conceded with a shrug. "Very young and impressionable."

"*Fourteen?*" I gasped. "Old enough to know better!"

Chelsea nodded. "That's what Mama said. He was grounded for a *month*!"

Chris held up his hands. "In my defense, I had to do it! Jessica Atchley said she'd go out with me if I did. She was the hottest girl in ninth grade!"

We all cracked up. I couldn't wait to hear the rest. "Well? Did you get the girl?"

"*Pfft!*" He smirked. "Of course! For one glorious week. Then she broke up with me to go out with Shane Legler."

Chelsea was theatrically sympathetic. "Bless your heart."

"I'll get over it…eventually," he joked.

"Mama, can I have dessert?" Noah asked.

Chelsea nodded. "Yup, as soon as you eat all your green beans."

Noah's head rolled back dramatically. "Not the green beans!"

Chelsea winced at him, full of empathy. "I know, it's tough. But if you are still hungry, we shouldn't waste the food on your plate."

Once upon a time, I, too, did not enjoy green beans. I sat between Noah and Chris. I could be helpful here, but I would have to go about it carefully.

"Whoa, what's that?" I asked, pointing out the window. Noah and Hannah jumped down from their chairs to look outside. While everyone's back was turned, I took all but one of his green beans on my fork and quickly dropped them on my own plate.

"I don't see anything," Hannah declared.

"Oh, it's gone now. It was a cardinal flying around outside," I told them.

Chris looked at me keenly. "Do cardinals fly at night?"

I shut him up with a look. As everyone else righted themselves, I loaded up my fork and ate the evidence.

CHAPTER 27

After we all enjoyed a delicious dessert of brownie sundaes, I helped Chelsea clear the table while Chris herded the kids to get ready for bed.

"Can I have bubbles in my bath?" Hannah begged as she bounced down the hallway.

Chris laughed. "Sure."

They left the room together, leaving me with Chelsea. "They are too sweet, Chelsea," I told her.

She smiled. "Thanks. I love them a lot. Chris has been the most amazing gift these last several months. I don't know what we would have done without him."

I rinsed off the dishes and put them in the dishwasher while she put the leftovers in containers.

"I think he's enjoyed it," I told her. "You're all very lovable."

Chelsea laughed. "Thank you. We feel the same way about you."

We finished up the dishes and headed into the living room. Edna lay sprawled on her dog bed in the corner. She gave a single wag of her tail and continued her nap. I could hear shrieks of laughter coming from the hallway as Chris played and read bedtime stories with the kids. We sat on the sofa, and a few minutes later, Chris came in. He collapsed in the leather recliner and lifted the footrest.

"Those kids are wild tonight," he declared. "Noah must not have eaten enough green beans." He gave me a look.

I looked away, feigning innocence.

"I'll go snuggle them." Chelsea stood up.

I roused myself. "I should probably go. It's getting late, and I'm sure you're tired from your first week of teaching. I'll get out of your hair."

"No! You should stay and hang out," Chelsea insisted.

I shook my head. "Thank you, but I have a bachelorette party to go to tomorrow night. It's going to be a late night. I need to sleep to get ready for that."

"Sarah's?" Chris asked. I nodded. "That'll be fun," he said. "I'll walk you out while Chelsea gets the kids down."

I hugged Chelsea goodbye and promised to come back soon, then I walked to the door and gathered my purse and jacket. Chris opened the door for me. "Here, I'll walk you to your car. It's dark out there."

"Thanks," I agreed. Butterflies took off, flapping around in my stomach. But why? I had grown so comfortable with Chris, I wouldn't expect to be nervous. Or was I curious? Excited? I couldn't tell.

"You didn't put a frog out here, did you?" I asked, trying to get out of my own head.

He laughed. "When would I have had time?"

"That's not a no!" I pointed an accusing finger at him, but he just shook his head. I watched him out of the corner of my eye as we walked along the dark sidewalk. I didn't see any frogs. "You *were* pretty immersed in the princess tea party. I guess that took most of your focus."

"I can't pretend to understand the rules of the princess tea party. I only know I'm great at it," he bragged, stuffing his hands in his pockets.

"I could tell. You filled out the feather boa very well. It was your color and everything!" I smiled up at him.

"Don't feed my ego, Reed. I'll be out of control," he warned as we reached my car.

I chuckled. "I think we're probably past the point of no return on that." He huffed a laugh, and I met his eyes. "Thank you for having me. I had a great time."

Chris reached out and gave me a quick hug. "Come back anytime. But it's a bring-your-own-princess-attire establishment, in case you couldn't tell."

He released me, and I took a step back from him.

"Oh, I forgot to ask. Have you figured out what you're going to do, as far as moving out?" I asked.

He nodded. "I found an apartment yesterday, close to the church. It will be easy. I'll move in in a couple weeks."

I nodded. "That will be great! I'm glad it's working out."

He agreed. "Yeah, I've loved being here, but they're ready. I'm ready. It's time."

"For what it's worth, what you've done here is incredibly selfless and kind. You're a good man."

"Well, thank you. That's high praise coming from you."

"Don't let it go to your head."

"It's already done. You can't take it back. My ego is inflating even more as we speak!" He taunted me.

This happened every time. I got so sucked into playing with him. Pressure built in my chest as I considered asking for something I was scared to want. Maybe he couldn't give me exactly what I'd begun to wish for, but at least we were friends. It was enough. *Stop overthinking.*

"Do you have plans next Saturday?" I blurted as nonchalantly as possible.

He thought about it, squinting. "Isn't that the night of Sarah and Ben's wedding?"

I swallowed. "Yes. I'm a bridesmaid, so I have to do the whole shebang. There's a wedding party dance, which means I need a date for the reception. I actually kind of forgot about it. I've been so busy and—" *Stop rambling!*

We stood there for a beat. Finally, he raised his eyebrows, laughter in his eyes.

"*This* is how you're asking me to be your date to Sarah's wedding?" he deadpanned.

I sighed, pinching the bridge of my nose. "Please don't mess with me right now. Asking someone is embarrassing!"

He snorted. "How do you think it feels for literally everyone else?"

I tilted my head. "Chris! Come on. You know you want to go to this wedding. It's going to be so fun! Please?"

"It *is* going to be fun. I actually received an invitation, complete with a plus-one option of my own."

My heart sank. "Have you already asked someone else?"

"No," he answered mildly.

I huffed, indignant. "Then why not?"

"You didn't ask me very nicely, for one," he pointed out.

Flaring my nostrils, in the flattest voice I could muster, I spoke. "Chris, will you please go to the wedding with me?"

"I'll think about it."

I stomped my foot. "You know what? Forget it. You'd probably bring a frog and let it loose on the dance floor or something, and I don't want to deal with that."

"What an inspirational idea! You really are the best, Reed." He smiled down at me. The sparkle in his eyes shifted as we stared at each other. The air changed, and my frustration mellowed down to a glowing ember.

"Why me?" he asked sincerely. "You could have anyone."

I smiled at the compliment. "Thank you. But no one else has pictorial evidence that they did the cotillion on the wall at their mother's house."

He blew out a breath and dropped his head with a soft laugh. I took his hands in my own and danced to an imaginary beat. "I bet you can *dance*," I said, sing-song style.

He nodded, an indulgent smile on his face. "I can."

I shimmied my shoulders side to side. "We would have fun," I wheedled, picking up the beat a little bit.

He looked into my eyes. He swallowed. "We would."

He stood there, still as a statue, in spite of my excellent moves. An idea hit me that had my humor sinking like a lead balloon. *He doesn't want to hurt my feelings.* I stopped dancing and took a step back, preemptively mortified.

"I thought you were messing with me. But I just realized you may *actually* not want to go, or you might have someone else in mind." Now I couldn't stop babbling. "It's okay. You won't hurt my feelings—" I broke off when he squeezed my hands.

He shook his head. "No. I'll go with you." He squeezed my hands again, summoning my eyes back to his. "I'd love to go with you."

I believed him. Relief flooded my chest. My heart secretly went off like a Roman candle. *Boom, boom, boom.* It was good he couldn't see how outrageously happy it made me. Chris stood, patiently waiting for me to speak.

"You had me worried there for a second," I admitted.

He smirked. "Just playing a little hard to get."

I leveled my eyes at him. "Annnd we're back," I declared, trying to act unimpressed.

He smiled at me and released my hands. "Be safe driving home, Reed. See you at church on Sunday."

"I'll be there," I waved and got in the car. I turned the key in the ignition and watched him walking away in the rearview mirror. My heart turned over in my chest. *He said yes!* Technically, nothing had changed. I should probably calm down, but I couldn't help myself. I squealed, a fizzy sphere of relief and excitement effervescing in my heart.

CHAPTER 28

"Please remind me to tell Sarah she wins the award for Best Bachelorette Bash," sighed Anna, snuggling down in the chaise lounge next to mine. I nodded in agreement. Having finished our facial treatments, we relaxed, tucked in among the cushions, wearing soft white robes and matching slippers. Massages were up next. We sipped champagne out of plastic flutes next to the cold plunge pool. It was official: The Clayborn Luxury Spa was the most wonderful place I'd ever been.

"I wonder if I could move in here," I speculated, examining the cucumber slices the attendant had given me to put over my eyes. I carefully balanced one then the other on my closed eyelids. *I could get used to this.*

"So, did you decide on a date to bring to the wedding?" Anna asked.

I nodded, and one of the cucumbers slid down to my chin. I took a sip of champagne and carefully put the cucumber slices back in place. "Yup, Chris Calvert."

Anna's gaze cut through the cucumbers and bore a hole in my head. I kept my eyes firmly closed.

"Seriously?"

"Yeah. It will be easy. He already knows everyone who will be there, *and* he can dance."

"Is that all it is?"

"Yes, Mother Hen." I smiled at Anna's protective nosiness. I cautiously peeked from behind one of the cucumbers.

She leaned her head back and placed her own cucumber slices over her eyes. "Gage told me he thinks Chris has changed, maturity-wise."

Playing it cool, I nodded. "I could see that."

"A man of character, *and* he can cut a rug? That seems like it could be good," Anna pointed out shrewdly.

I remained silent, eyes closed. It meant a lot to me that Anna would give Chris the benefit of the doubt, but I didn't know what to say. A thousand words popped into my head, the product of a day spent obsessing over a situation I could not control. Ugh. *Get ahold of yourself, woman!* I shrugged nonchalantly. "We'll see."

Someone plopped down next to me, jostling my champagne. I turned, and both cucumber slices slid onto the neck of my robe. I set them aside, giving up. The plopper was Mia. She sipped from her own flute of champagne and sighed happily.

"That massage was the best thing I've ever experienced. This is where I belong!" She let her head fall back onto the cushion, enraptured. Sarah emerged from the treatment rooms, a similar stupefied grin on her lips.

"Here comes the bride," Anna sang, holding Sarah's glass out to her. She took it and settled onto the foot of Anna's chair.

"Thanks for being here, ladies," she said, smiling at each of us.

"We wouldn't want to be anywhere else," Mia assured her. Anna and I nodded our agreement.

After our next round of treatments, we all headed over to Mia's apartment to do mani/pedis and watch *Father of the Bride.* We each ordered our favorite takeout and gathered in Mia's living room. Sarah was a good sport, wearing a tasteful 'Bachelorette' sash over her comfiest jammies.

"It has to be said, Sarah. This is the best bachelorette party I've ever attended!" I told her. Everyone agreed.

Sarah smiled excitedly. "Thanks! It's my dream party! My best girls doing some of my favorite things." She threw her arms in the air, and the whole group of us did a little shimmy. She sighed. "It's a little untraditional, but I'm so tired from the holidays and all the wedding stress. I wanted to keep it simple and relax with y'all."

We could all understand that. "It's a little untraditional," Anna smiled, "but I'd like to pray over you *tonight*, so we don't all ruin our makeup next week."

Sarah bit her lips, tearing up already. "That sounds great. Thank you."

We huddled up and prayed for our friend, that God would bless her new life with Ben. After the prayer, I looked around, reflecting on the women around me. Anna was married, Sarah was about to be, and now Mia was freshly engaged. As happy as I was for them, the stark difference of my life dulled my joy just a tiny bit as I ate my gyro bowl.

I knew I shouldn't compare myself to my friends. I loved my life. Marriage to the wrong person would have been miserable, and I knew God had rescued me. Looking back, if I'd gotten married when I planned to, I would have missed out on a lot of goodness.

My mind sneakily jumped to a certain pair of kind, sparkly brown eyes. Chris embodied qualities that I really wanted to look for in a man. He loved to be silly and laugh, and he followed the truth and God's way. He held himself to a standard, and he valued others. I was grateful for him.

What in the world? If someone had told me at Thanksgiving that I would be secretly thinking about Chris Calvert in a moment of longing, I probably would have punched them in the face. Yet, here I was. I marveled at my own heart and mind. *How did I get here? And what would my friends think if they knew?*

"Earth to Maddie," Sarah teased. "Ten bucks says she's thinking about Youth Guy Chris."

Maybe not so secretly. A rush of giggles set off around me as the scarlet blush ran up my cheeks. The next thing I knew, my friends were teasing me (in the most supportive way) about an idea that I once believed I would never want to consider again. All the feelings duked it out in my head and my heart.

"Nothing's happened, y'all. I don't know if anything will," I admitted. I told them the gist of what I'd overheard that night at Rhonda's house. "I think it's too late. He's moved on."

They all shook their heads.

"I don't believe it. I've seen the way he looks at you!" Mia insisted. She tilted her head. "And for what it's worth, he really has changed. I don't say that lightly. I've known some disappointing guys. But when I look at his growth and attitude and the choices he's made over the last six months, I'm not just supporting you, Maddie. I *want* you to go for it. I think you could be really great together."

Sarah nodded. "I second everything Mia said. Chris has never been a bad guy. He just needed a little longer to cook. He's perfect for you, Maddie! He can keep up with your energy and match your playfulness. He will keep you laughing, but he can be serious too." She gave me a look. "He's strong enough to stand up to you and work together when you're feeling stubborn. That partnership is really valuable. After seeing y'all together at the Christmas play, I think he cares for you. I really do."

These affirmations were a comfort to me. I wasn't the only one who'd seen the changes in Chris. An ember of hope in the bottom of my stomach flickered into a flame.

Anna was the last to speak. She had one eyebrow raised. "You know I have a sense about these things. A year ago, I would have told you he was a waste of your time and beauty. But I can't help but agree. Gage says Chris is different. Ryan says Chris is different. These men are walking with him in his life, and I believe them. *You* say he is different. I believe *you*, Maddie. And whatever happens, time is your best friend. You don't have to do anything permanent right now. You can take it slow and see what happens."

I nodded. "He's going through a lot of stuff with his family right now. I don't know if the timing is right. And he may not like me like that anymore."

Sarah and Mia both leveled their eyes at me. *Don't make me say it again,* they seemed to say.

"You'll know," Anna assured me, solid as a rock. Mia and Sarah nodded along with her, all of them sharing that air of women who have experienced *The Knowing*, for real. These women were trustworthy. They knew me, and they cared for me. I trusted their opinions. I sighed, my heart full of gratitude for my friends.

"Okay, enough about my boy drama," I said. "We have a movie to watch!"

—

I got home the next morning with barely enough time to get ready for church. My back was a little stiff from sleeping on Mia's living room floor, and I could have used a few more hours of sleep. Yawning, I noticed a paper cup of coffee waiting on the welcome mat, bearing a frog sticker. The frog winked with one eye. The coffee had grown lukewarm, but undeniable warmth seared through my whole self. Maybe my friends were right after all. Or maybe it happened to be on his way to the church, and he was trying to be nice. I was too tired to overthink it. I smiled, grateful for coffee, and walked into my apartment.

—

Later that night, I got home after spending the afternoon with my family. Mark, Bree, and Henry had come over for a while, which was always fun. I made a mental note to go through the pictures I'd taken on my phone and decide which ones to keep. I probably only needed a few pictures of Henry drooling on Kevin, as opposed to the one hundred I had taken. Henry was at a really cute age. His big blue eyes reminded me of Noah and Hannah.

I hadn't seen or heard from Chris, and he'd been mysteriously absent from church. Before I could overthink it, I opened my text messages and texted him.

Me: Hey! I didn't see you at all today, but someone left a frog on my welcome mat. Made me think of you.

I waited a few seconds to see if he would write back. The reply dots appeared, and my stomach tightened, dancing along.

Chris: Hi, Chelsea got sick, so I came home to help. Pretty sure it was food poisoning. She's much better now.

Me: I'm sorry that happened. Glad she's feeling better!

Chris: Thanks, me too.

I couldn't help but notice he didn't say a word about the frog. My heart dipped a little bit. Maybe the coffee had been dropped off by mistake, and I had drunk a gift meant for one of my neighbors. *Nope, stop right there.* Speculating wasn't going to lead to anything, and I had a ton of things to get done before the week took off. *Get to it, woman!*

—

Work that week was absolutely crazy. Flu season was raging and the ER was slammed from the time I clocked in, all the way to clocking out.

I did get to sit down and eat lunch with Mia one day, which was a blessing. We sat down in the cafeteria, slathering our hands with hand sanitizer before we ate.

"So, have you talked to Chris?" Mia asked.

"Not much," I answered.

"Not even about the wedding?" she asked.

I shrugged at her wide eyes. "I've been busy! I'm sure he has too. Chelsea got food poisoning over the weekend."

Mia sat back as if the words themselves were contagious. "Ew."

I nodded, agreeing. We saw the most brutal effects of food poisoning in the ER. I wouldn't wish salmonella on my worst enemy.

"Have y'all talked on the phone at least?" Mia pressed on. I shook my head, and she frowned, frustrated. "I assumed he'd at least call you by now."

I shrugged. "Nothing." I wanted to leave it at that, but Mia raised an eyebrow, insistent. I shrugged. "It's entirely possible he really isn't into me anymore, and his whole goal is friendship. It wouldn't be the end of the world."

Mia shook her head and took a breath to respond, but I held up a hand, stopping her.

"He's been through a lot, Mia. I didn't understand how much until that trip. I really want to honor where he is and what he wants. And I sure don't want someone who doesn't want me. What else can I do but wait and see?"

It surprised me how passionately I felt about this. I probably needed to calm down. I'd been praying about it a lot, and it felt more important than ever for me to be open-handed and trust God with this situation. Chris was in a time of transition in his life. I didn't want to rush anything, and I didn't want to force something and ruin it because of bad timing. I liked him a lot, but Chris was more important to me than the gratification of changing our relationship status.

I had to keep reminding myself of these things, because I really did miss him. It got worse with each passing day. I'd gotten spoiled by seeing him multiple times a week, and now I'd basically gone cold turkey. I didn't like it. I was lost in thought when Mia asked a question I hadn't considered.

"Maddie, does Chris *know* you like him?"

I paused. "What do you mean?"

She shrugged her shoulders. "I mean, I wonder how he would feel if he knew he had a real chance with you. Y'all are both flirty, fun people who don't take things too seriously. Does he realize things have changed for you? Have y'all talked about it?"

I frowned. "Well, no. But I asked him to be my wedding date. *I* put myself out there and asked *him*. It's not a huge declaration, but it's pretty significant. Do you think I should stand beneath his window and serenade him in the moonlight or something?" I asked, clutching my chest dramatically.

Mia giggled at the idea. "I agree you should have boundaries. The wedding date thing is a great start! But it's important that he understands what you want. Clarity is kindness, right? When you asked, did you ask him as a friend or as a *date*? You know how guys can be. Sometimes they're a little…obtuse. You have to spell it out. Ryan can be that way sometimes. Even the most secure people in the world need a little nudge of encouragement now and then."

"Speaking of Ryan…" I shifted in my chair, gladly changing the subject. "Have y'all set a date?"

Mia's eyes lit up, sparkling. "May first!" She took hold of my hand, and we both squealed, bouncing in our chairs. It was easy to celebrate this milestone for my friend. I sat back, looked at my watch, and saw that my lunch break was over. I had to get back. I stood and leaned over Mia for a hug.

"I'm so happy for you, friend. You deserve all the joy!" I told her. Mia's eyes filled with tears.

"I still can hardly believe it sometimes. Is anything too hard for the Lord?" she beamed.

Her words encouraged me. It was a beautiful reminder that God is good all the time, and He always has a plan. His sovereignty and goodness were much better things to think about than anything else. We gathered our lunchboxes and headed back to the locker room. Mia waved and took off, her shoes squeaking on the floor. I was putting my stuff back in my locker, thinking about our conversation, when my phone buzzed with a text message. My heart skipped a beat when I saw who it was from.

Chris: Are we still on for the wedding this weekend?

Me: Yes! Can I meet you at the reception? We're assigned to a table with Mia, Ryan, Anna, and Gage, so you'll know most of the people.

Chris: Sounds good. My suit is black. Is that okay?

Me: Definitely. You'll blend right in with the black bridesmaid dresses! I'm planning to get a spray tan tomorrow after work so I don't look ghostly pale.

Chris: Me too.

The text cracked me up right as I was taking a drink from my water bottle. I choked and sputtered, water dripping from my nose. *Very attractive, Maddie.* Good thing this was over text; he didn't need to see my mess. I grabbed a tissue and wiped my face dry.

Me: I figured you wouldn't need a spray tan to look good.

Chris: Fair point. I haven't had a spray tan before. My only point of reference is that episode of *Friends*. Do you have to count Mississippily?

I gasped another laugh, glad I'd set the water bottle down.

Me: I love that episode. It's been a while, so I'm actually not sure. If I end up at a level 8, like Ross, will you still dance with me?

Chris: Of course.

Me: I'd understand if you didn't.

Chris: Stop fishing, Reed.

A small flock of butterflies had been zooming around in my stomach since this conversation began. I took a deep breath, trying to calm them. I checked the time.

Me: Got to get back to work. See you Saturday.

Chris responded with a thumbs-up. I put my phone in my locker and headed out to see my patients.

—

I spent Friday preparing for the wedding. After an uneventful spray tan, I got my nails done and ran errands the rest of the day.

The rehearsal dinner went off without a hitch. Sarah and Ben made the whole night fun and endearing for everyone. It was sweet to watch their families celebrate—both sides were very supportive of them. I'd forgotten how close Sarah was with her extended family, and there were a *lot* of people there. Mia, Anna, and I were all bridesmaids, plus her sister, who would be her maid of honor, and her college roommate. I'd met them both before, so it was great to see them, like a mini-reunion. After the meal and speeches, Sarah's dad prayed over her and Ben's life together, and there wasn't a dry eye in the house.

I woke up Saturday and immediately jumped into action. Kevin and I went for a long walk. Emma was invited to the wedding, but she wasn't part of the wedding party, so she would be home with Kevin for most of the day. I wanted to make him as easy for her as possible, so we walked, and I made sure he had food and fresh water. I packed everything in a duffel bag so I didn't forget anything. I'd made a list earlier in the week, and I checked the items off scrupulously.

Getting dressed for the bridal luncheon, I found myself looking back on all the fun we'd had over the years. Camps and camping trips, Bible study and movie nights, and so much coffee. Remembering all of it had me turning mushy. Sarah and I had been close for ages. We met while serving together at church.

When I invited Mia to Bible study several years ago, I didn't know much about her. We were good friends at work, and sometimes she joined in when we did things as a big group. We grew closer as she got to know the Lord and shared more over time. Eventually, Anna came along with Mia and fit in perfectly. Emma had her own group of friends, but she fit in well with mine, and we had grown very close. Over the years, God had solidified us into a sturdy, faithful unit. I did not take it for granted. Not everyone had friends they could count on, who felt like family.

Thinking of family reminded me of my parents. I probably needed to check in soon and touch base with them. I made a mental note to call them tomorrow. At the moment, I needed to focus on making my eyebrows even. *Sisters, not twins,* I reminded myself, to take the pressure off. Once I finished getting ready, I checked my list one more time then threw my bag and my plastic-covered bridesmaid dress into the car and took off.

During the bachelorette party, Sarah had asked me to pray and say a few words at the bridal luncheon. Unsure where to begin, I prayed about it for a few days. Eventually, I remembered a passage in Romans that had struck me a few years before in Bible study. When I went back to read it, I knew it was exactly what my hope for Sarah and Ben—and really any marriage—would be, so I wrote it down to share.

Romans 15:5-7 *May the God of endurance and encouragement grant you to live in such harmony with one another, in accord with Christ Jesus, that together you may with one voice glorify the God and Father of our Lord Jesus Christ. Therefore welcome one another as Christ has welcomed you, for the glory of God.*

I couldn't imagine trying to build a life without the Lord. I was so grateful to have Him. I teared up a little bit, reading it. I looked over at Mia, who sat at the table, fully crying. At least I wasn't alone.

When I finished reading, Sarah stood up, wiping her eyes, and hugged me. My eyes overflowed too. I walked over to sit down, and Mia reached over and squeezed my hand. Whatever happened, I knew these friends would have my back and be there for me.

CHAPTER 29

Later that afternoon, all of the food had been eaten, and the blessings were said. We'd changed into our dresses, taken pictures, and Sarah had come back from the first look with Ben. It was almost time for our friends to get married. All of us girls crowded around the big mirror in the little bridal room at the church, touching up our lipstick and straightening our jewelry one last time. Sarah looked exquisite in her classic A-line white dress and veil, completely beside herself with joy—not a nerve in sight.

The wedding coordinator knocked on the door: it was time. We gathered our flowers and lined up in the foyer, ready to walk down the aisle. Sarah's dad met us by the sanctuary doors, tears rolling down his red cheeks. He wiped his face with a handkerchief and hugged his daughters. The photographer snapped the candid moment quickly then stepped into place. The doors opened, and the music carried out to the foyer. Ryan played the guitar and sang.

Great is Thy faithfulness, O God my Father
There is no shadow of turning with Thee
Thou changest not Thy compassions they fail not
As Thou hast been Thou forever will be
Great is Thy faithfulness
Great is Thy faithfulness
Morning by morning, new mercies I see
All I have needed Thy hand hath provided

I took a second to make eye contact with Sarah. She blinked the tears from her eyes and whispered, "Love you."

I winked. "Love you too," I said, and turned forward. Anna went next.

Pardon for sin and a peace that endureth
Thine own dear Presence to cheer and to guide
Strength for today and bright hope for tomorrow
Blessings all mine, with ten thousand beside
Great is Thy faithfulness
Great is Thy faithfulness
Morning by morning new mercies I see
All I have needed Thy hand hath provided
Great is Thy faithfulness, Lord unto me

Once Anna made it halfway down the aisle, Mia stepped through the doorway into the sanctuary. Out of nowhere, the guitar hit a dissonant *twang*. Mia jumped, along with the rest of us. Everyone looked over at Ryan. Had he broken a string? His jaw hung open, staring at Mia.

When he realized what happened, he startled and cleared his throat, his face turning red. An indulgent laugh carried softly through the room. No one could blame him. Mia looked gorgeous in the strapless black dress Sarah had chosen for us, even blushing bright red as she was now. I cracked up and lightly clapped with the crowd as Ryan collected himself and kept going. I looked at Anna, and it was easy to see she was already brainstorming a new nickname for Ryan after his adorable faux pas.

A few beats later, it was my turn. I took a breath, straightened my shoulders, and stepped into the aisle, Ryan's golden voice leading my pace. A few steps in, my eyes found Chris. He looked so handsome in his dark suit that my knees wobbled, but I kept going. For a split second, he looked stunned, as if he'd been punched in the face, but he recovered quickly. He blinked, and his joyful smile was back.

Are you okay? I asked him silently, but nothing came back. Our mind-reading capability must be off that day. I hoped he was all right. I took my place on the steps, turning to face the audience. Following the bridesmaid rules, I squared my shoulders, standing tall on the step, one knee slightly bent, and made sure my flowers were centered. Sarah's sister reached the top step, ready to do her maid of honor duties. The doors closed, and Ryan invited everyone to stand and join him in the chorus. We all turned to see as the doors opened. Sarah floated down the aisle on her dad's arm as we all sang together:

> *Great is Thy faithfulness*
> *Great is Thy faithfulness*
> *Morning by morning, new mercies I see*
> *All I have needed Thy hand hath provided*
> *Great is Thy faithfulness, Lord unto me*

I'd done so well holding it together most of the weekend, but happy tears filled my eyes and fell. I looked over at Ben. He stood tall, his face dry, eyes shining, full of certainty and joy. An enraptured smile filled his face. Sarah reached his side, and they only had eyes for one another. It was such a perfect picture it almost hurt. The minister spoke, welcoming the dearly beloved.

I tried to scan the crowd, but my eyes stubbornly went right back to Chris. His eyes met mine, as if he'd been waiting for me. He winked at me, his eyes holding me there, unable to look away. Pleasure tingled up my spine, and I couldn't hold back a grin of my own.

A movement to my left caught my attention. Sarah was already handing her flowers to her sister and turning to face Ben for the vows. I'd nearly forgotten where I was. I forced myself to pay attention. In a few short minutes, Ben took Sarah in his arms, dipping her dramatically and kissing his bride as the recessional music swelled.

At last, my love has come along...

Everyone clapped and cheered for the new Mr. and Mrs. Ben Ford, drowning out the rest of the words. Ben pulled Sarah back up, laughing, and they stood together, looking around, taking in the moment, then it was time to go. Walking back up the aisle on the arm of Ben's brother Joel, I couldn't stop myself from seeking out Chris's sparkly brown eyes in the crowd one more time. He was still looking right at me. A flutter rose in my throat. Oh my. *Calm down, woman!*

There wasn't much time between the ceremony and the reception, so we all scattered pretty quickly. I grabbed my stuff and headed out to my car. I put my bag in the trunk then got in and turned the key in the ignition.

Click. I tried again. *Click.* I groaned. "No! Now? Are you kidding me?"

Car trouble is a little slice of Hell, especially for the single woman. It could cost a hundred bucks or five thousand. It could take an hour to fix it, or it could take a week. I immediately started doing the horrible math in my head, calculating in case I had to dip into my savings. *What if it needed to be towed? What if I had to get a rental car? Oh my gosh.*

I tried to breathe through the wave of existential dread. I truly didn't have time for this. Frustrated, I banged my fists on the steering wheel and let out a therapeutic yell, then I closed my eyes and tried to breathe some more.

A tap on the window startled me. I jumped and looked up into a very amused face. I hit the button for the window, but nothing happened. *Ugh.* Feeling sheepish, I opened my door. Chris took a step back to accommodate.

"What was *that*? I heard you clear across the parking lot," he drawled, grinning down at me.

I sighed, trying to keep my cool. "Just…letting out some frustration. My car won't start."

Chris made a sympathetic face. "That's bad timing. I'm sorry. Do you want to ride with me, and I can take a look at it after the reception?"

It took me a second to work my way out of my frenzy and actually process what he was saying.

"You know about cars?"

He shrugged. "Enough to jump a battery."

"You would do that?"

"Of course. It's no problem, but we'd better hurry."

I nodded and grabbed my purse.

On the drive, Chris tried to take my mind off my car, chatting about the wedding. We were laughing about Ryan's besotted error (or error of besottedness? We couldn't decide.) when Chris slowed and turned into the parking lot.

"Okay, there's only one rule at this reception." Chris turned to me, convinced of his hilarity.

I rolled my eyes dramatically and held up a hand. "Let me guess: Don't fall in love with your dance moves?"

He cracked up. "You know me too well."

I played along. "It's only fair to warn you I've got moves of my own. Better watch out, or you'll be the one falling for *me*." I pointed at myself.

He barked a lighthearted laugh. "I'll try to stay strong, but I'm just a man, Reed."

I looked into his eyes, invigorated by his outrageous flirting. "Bring it on, Calvert."

CHAPTER 30

After lots of pictures and instructions from the wedding coordinator, I walked over to our table where Chris sat with the guys and Emma. I looked around, confused at the drink and plate of hors d'oeuvres sitting in my spot on the table. Was I taking someone's seat? Chris gestured to me to sit down and leaned in closer until his shoulder touched mine.

"Gotta keep up your strength for the dance-off."

He'd gotten the plate for me?

"You didn't have to do that," I told him.

He shrugged. "I don't mind."

"Thank you."

It was just a plate of food, but apparently, that was all it took to turn me into a gooey mess. I considered holding back or trying to hide, but why? The man could read my mind. I leaned into him.

"If I forget to tell you later, I had a great time tonight."

His eyes sparkled at me. "Me too."

"Well, hello, everybody!" Pam Martin interrupted our little moment, and we both straightened in our seats. Pam swept around the table, squeezing hands and shoulders, her husband John at her side. John made his way over to chat with Mia and Ryan. Pam stopped between Chris and me, looking elated.

"Well, well, well, this looks fun!" she exclaimed. "I bet y'all are having a great time tonight!" I smiled, but the suggestion in Pam's voice made me tense up.

Pam leaned down to me and lowered her voice. "You look gorgeous, hon! I love that dress on you!"

My shoulders sagged with relief. I'd had a sudden flash of alarm that she was going to say something embarrassing. I should have known better.

"Thanks, Pam! It has pockets!"

I shifted to show her, but Pam didn't respond. She was busy giving Chris a pointed look. Chris licked his lips, then he looked me in the eye. "Pam's right. You look great, Maddie."

Yurgh. My soul shriveled like a raisin. I tried to gather my wits, smiling weakly at his forced compliment. I looked up at Pam, silently screaming. She winked at me and patted Chris's shoulder, then she and John moved to the next table to greet the people there. I sat back in my seat with a sigh and sipped my drink. Chris pressed his shoulder to mine. I leaned in, ready for him to level the playing field with a joke.

"Sorry I didn't tell you sooner. You look beautiful, Reed. I forgot how to breathe for a second when you walked down the aisle." He gave me a crooked smile and stole a carrot off my plate.

I blinked, whiplashed. *Wow.* That was...maybe the most thorough compliment I'd ever received. Heat crept up my chest, even as my shoulders relaxed. It went far outside the bounds of our normal conversation. Had something changed for him? Should I say something in return? Obviously. But what?

"Um." I cleared my throat. "Thanks. You look pretty dashing yourself."

"*Dashing?* You sound like Ms. Rosemary, but I'll take it," he quipped, steering us back to something more like our usual way. I exhaled, relieved to be headed back to normal footing.

Joking around and laughing with Chris was easy and comfortable. His sincerity had knocked me off-kilter, but I needed to get back to the right headspace, or it was going to be a long night. My stomach fluttered, insistent. *But what did it mean?*

Don't get me wrong, I was thrilled at his words. But I was fighting hard to keep my heart happy in the *friend zone* as it was. A few more compliments of that caliber, and I may never recover. Butterflies swooped through my stomach in fighter jet formation. *This is not the time,* I insisted to myself. *Calm down. Focus.*

"Okay, let's see this spray tan up close." Chris craned his head, looking around my shoulder. "It's doing a nice job covering your battle scars from New Year's. All better?"

I looked down, turning my arm so he could see. The scars were still pink, but everything was pretty much healed.

"I heal fast." I shrugged. When I looked up, my gaze got trapped in his. My heart rate kicked up again. This was getting out of hand.

"Hey, Maddie!" Chris and I both jumped, startled at the interruption across the table. "Are you going to eat your green beans?" Gage teased. *Huh?* I looked down. Sure enough, there was a plated meal sitting in front of me. I hadn't noticed the servers coming around. I opened my mouth to answer Gage, but I stopped. Every gaze at the table was trained on Chris and me, each person's smile bigger than the last. Blushing, I straightened my shoulders then picked up my fork.

"Definitely," I answered Gage, my voice uncharacteristically quiet. He winked at me and dug into his food. *Someone must have been sharing some stories with his accountability group.* Unfortunately, at the moment, Chris was turned away from me, talking to Emma and Luke. I couldn't ask him about it.

"So when are you thinking about taking this trip, Gage?" Ryan asked, mercifully changing the subject. *Thank goodness.* I could have hugged him then and there. "Maybe we could all go," he suggested.

Everyone started chatting at once, excited at the idea of a group trip to Florida. The idea of a beach vacation sounded fine to me, so I nodded along. But I couldn't focus very well on anything but the man next to me. His knee found mine underneath the table, and he bumped me playfully. My skin warmed, but my mind churned.

It had only been a couple of weeks since New Year's. Was it possible something new was actually happening? And so soon? I was so distracted by my own thoughts I didn't realize Sarah and Ben had taken their places for the first dance. I looked around, startled, when the music changed. That was our cue.

"Come on, *mi fuego*!" Gage hopped up enthusiastically from his chair and reached for Anna's hand. Everyone else followed suit.

I turned to Chris, feeling a little wobbly. "Ready?" I asked, breathless.

He nodded. We stood, and he took my hand, leading me out to the dance floor with the rest of the wedding party for a slow dance. He wrapped one hand around my waist and took my right hand with the other. I slid my left hand up to his shoulder, feeling clumsy. Suddenly, I'd lost all my coordination, but Chris expertly put us on the beat. He leaned down and spoke softly in my ear.

"Are you feeling okay?"

"Yes," I breathed. "I just got kind of…overwhelmed." That was a good word for it. *Overwhelmed that I'm feeling so much, and it's all for you.* I needed to lock this down. Knowing him, he would read my feelings on my face any minute. I danced awkwardly, feeling like a middle schooler at an eighth-grade dance. In contrast, Chris moved with confidence and poise, his arm solid under my hand.

"I've got you, Reed. I won't let you fall," he assured me, full of confidence. He tightened his grip around my waist, bringing me closer.

Too late, I thought, but I appreciated his reassurance. As if I wasn't already overloaded, feeling everything at once, now I was wrapped in his arms, dancing.

Oh my. At this point, overthinking was a waste of time. I needed a distraction.

"I guess all that cotillion training paid off," I joked, and he laughed. The sound jostled me out of my self-consciousness. I let myself take a second to marvel at this man, this friend, who meant so much to me. It felt positively decadent to be held close and dance with him. *Moments like this don't come around often,* I reasoned. *Would it be so wrong to let myself enjoy it?* I relaxed against him and gave myself to the moment.

The song lasted about sixty more seconds before it faded away, then everyone cheered as the familiar intro for "Yeah!" played. The rest of the wedding guests flooded the dance floor. Chris squeezed my waist then stepped back from me and moved with the beat, singing along with Usher. I felt like myself again. I sang the *yeahs* along with Chris and all my friends. This, I could handle.

To no one's surprise, Chris turned out to be the perfect choice for a wedding date. We danced and danced. He knew the lyrics to almost every song—even more than Ryan. I couldn't believe it when he sang through the entirety of "Wannabe" by The Spice Girls, but he did it flawlessly. When the deejay played a country song, Chris didn't hesitate. He twirled me once, set his hand on my waist, and we two-stepped around the whole dance floor. Every time our eyes met, he smiled. It was so easy to enjoy the moment with him.

By the time we passed out sparklers to the revelers so Sarah and Ben could leave in style, I had sweated through my dress, and my updo had completely fallen. My blonde hair fell messily to my shoulder blades, but I didn't care. We'd danced and laughed and had the best time all night. I stood between Mia and Chris as we cheered and waved to Sarah and Ben. They drove away in a flurry of sparkles and joy. I looked down at my burnt-out sparkler stick and then at Mia.

"A top night!" I exclaimed.

Mia nodded, leaning back against Ryan. "For sure. It's not over yet. Ryan and I are going to go to the diner for a late-night waffle. Want to join us?"

I shook my head. "I would love to, but I have to go deal with my car. And Chris has to work tomorrow." I hugged my friends goodbye. Chris shook hands with the guys, and we took off.

———

As tired as I was, I couldn't hold back a smile on the way back to the church. "I had so much fun! I haven't danced like that in years!" I told Chris.

He smiled in the darkness. "Me too."

"Oh, I don't believe that," I said. "I bet you dance all the time with Noah and Hannah."

He tilted his head, considering. "They enjoy a good dance party. But their style is a little less Usher and a lot more Kids' Praise Songs."

A yawn snuck up on me as I snuggled down in the seat, pleasantly warm. "That is a pretty big variation in genre," I conceded. "I love to dance."

We pulled into the church parking lot, and Chris parked nose to nose with my car. "I'll see if I can jump it, and we'll go from there. Sound good?"

I shrugged. "You're the boss."

Ten minutes later, we stood side by side in the dark parking lot, facing the open hood of my car. Chris had given me his suit jacket to ward off the chill of the January night, and I'd repeatedly lost the fight against the temptation to bury my nose in the collar and sniff. I aimed my phone flashlight toward the battery so he could see, and now he had the engine running nicely. I looked up at him in the dim glow.

"A great dancer, a fantastic date, and a car trouble hero, all in one? You're the total package, Calvert. Thank you!"

He smiled humbly, wiping his hands clean on a napkin I'd found in my glovebox. He'd rolled up the sleeves of his white shirt hours ago. He reached up, his forearm flexing as he released the lever and let the hood drop into place. I turned off the flashlight and put my phone in the pocket of my dress. All we had to see by was the moonlight and the distant streetlights.

"You're all set for now, but you'll need to get a new battery sooner rather than later." His face grew serious, and he tilted his chin down, looking me in the eye. "Like, *tomorrow*, Reed. Don't put it off. I can take you if you need a ride."

"It's kind of you to offer, thanks. Emma can probably take me, if my car won't start in the morning. But I'll keep you in mind as a back up."

He nodded. "Thank you for inviting me tonight I had a great time." Something about the way he said it made me catch my breath.

"Thank *you*. You made it really wonderful. I'm glad you said yes," I admitted.

His eyes softened. "I'll always say yes to you, Maddie."

Helplessly starry-eyed, I shifted a step closer to him and looked into his tired eyes. I held my breath. Chris licked his lips, about to speak.

A car turned into the parking lot, and we both turned to look. The police SUV spotlight turned on, blinding both of us. We straightened and stepped apart as the officer pulled up beside us and rolled his window down. My stomach leapt in a tiny kick of anxiety. I couldn't remember committing a crime in the last few minutes, but still.

"Everything okay here, kids?" The officer's grin spread from ear to ear. I recognized him from church but couldn't recall his name. Chris held up a hand and waved.

"Hey, Howie, it's been a while."

The cop got out of the car and walked over to us. He shook Chris's hand, a teasing look on his face. He clearly enjoyed ruining our little moment. He introduced himself and shook my hand. The men chatted for a little bit, and

Chris explained about my car. Eventually, Officer Howie said his goodbyes then climbed into his car and drove away.

I exhaled a slow sigh of relief. Chris opened his mouth to say something, but he paused, his eyes trained on the SUV. Officer Howie didn't pull out onto the road. He pulled across the lot, parked on the edge, and sat, his engine idling. Frustration flamed up my spine.

"I don't remember inviting him to stay." I joked, angling my head to look over at the black SUV.

Chris made a face and shook his head. "Howie likes to give people a hard time. He'll probably sit there until we leave," he said apologetically and shuffled his feet. "It's getting late anyway, and I have to be at church early tomorrow." He yawned. "Sorry. My thirty's showing."

Mildly crushed, I forced out a chuckle. I straightened my spine and took off his suit jacket, taking the moment to collect myself. I passed the jacket to his outstretched hand.

"I'm tired too. It's been a long day. I'll see you tomorrow?"

He nodded. "Yes, ma'am." He walked around to my driver's-side door and opened it for me then sent me on my way.

On the way home, I tried to curb my disappointment. We'd had an amazing night, dancing and laughing, then Chris had put me safely in the car and sent me home. What more could I ask? I should have no complaints.

Looking back over the evening, I considered the facts. We'd literally danced the night away. We'd laughed, sang along with song lyrics, and shared a piece of cake. It was a wonderful night, but that didn't necessarily mean Chris wanted more than friendship. Maybe he was about to say something before we got interrupted, but maybe he wasn't. Maybe I had underestimated the strength of this stupid crush.

I needed to get out of my own head, or I was going to drive myself nuts. I recited my verse from Philippians again. *I am sure of this, that he who started a good work in you will carry it on to completion until the day of Christ Jesus.* If that was true, then this must be part of the process. *God doesn't waste anything*, I reminded myself. The truth lifted my gaze and my spirits. *I trust you, Lord,* I prayed. *You're good and you do good. This whole thing is in your hands, and I believe that is best.*

CHAPTER 31

A couple of days later, I was at work, in the thick of another busy shift. I hurried from room to room, assessing patients and gathering the necessary items. As I left the supply room, a team of nurses and EMTs rolled a patient past me toward the elevator. Seeing the face of the person on the gurney stopped me in my tracks.

It was Heidi. She was extremely pale, her face streaked with tears. Her pregnant belly rose up underneath the blanket. Houston walked behind the gurney, tears rolling down his face. Heidi locked eyes with me.

"Maddie!" She held out her hand. Instinctively, I took it and walked alongside the gurney toward the elevator with the team. I assumed they were headed upstairs to L&D, but I didn't think Heidi was far enough along yet. Wasn't she due around Easter? *Oh, no.* Something was wrong.

At the realization, panic closed in on me, stealing my breath. Heidi squeezed my hand. I squeezed back, trying to focus, but my vision was gray. I looked into my old friend's terrified eyes. She cried as she explained, "I have placenta previa. It's been under control, but I started bleeding, and the doctor told me to call 911 and come here. I'm only thirty-one weeks!"

A breathless voice I didn't recognize said, "It's going to be okay."

The elevator doors opened, and we pushed the gurney inside. The nurses spoke calmly about Heidi's vitals.

This was a normal day for them; they didn't know this woman. Medical professionals didn't treat their friends or family members for a few reasons—the most obvious being this moment right here.

If I stayed here, I was going to be sick. *I can't do this. I shouldn't be here.* I released Heidi's hand, nodded reassuringly, and stepped away, off the elevator. Houston moved up to take her hand, but Heidi's eyes stayed glued to mine until the elevator doors slid closed.

My heart pounded in my ears, and my scrubs felt too tight. I couldn't stay there. I looked around until I found Cindy, the charge nurse, and told her I didn't feel well and needed to take a break. I held it together long enough to get outside, then tears filled my eyes as I turned to walk up the sidewalk. I roamed through the parking lot and ended up at my car.

My keys were in my locker, inside, so I sat on the ground in the cold. I cried and cried, begging God for I didn't know what, lost in all the feelings churning around inside me. Sadness, confusion, fear. It all mixed together in a jumbled mess of emotions. I took deep breaths and looked up at the cloudy sky, trying to get myself under control. *One thing at a time: Placenta previa is not deadly with treatment. She's going to be fine.* I repeated it over and over until my breathing regulated.

Finally, I calmed down enough to breathe normally, though it was accompanied by the steady rhythm of my chattering teeth. I needed to get back to work. Walking up the sidewalk to go inside, a familiar baseball cap-covered head caught my eye. It was Chris, walking toward the doorway of the ER.

Chris was *here?* What in the world? My chest immediately relaxed and warmed with relief. *Thank you, Lord!* Chris would understand. He was the perfect friend for a moment like this.

My stomach gave a little flip, and butterflies taunted me. *Friend?* I was already so tender that the truth permeated every cell of my body. Chris Calvert was more than a friend to me.

I swiped my fingers below my eyes to be sure there was no mascara trailing across my cheeks and took a breath to yell his name. But at the last second, I paused because Houston came through the doors and did something incomprehensible. He walked directly to Chris and held out his hand for a handshake. Time seemed to slow down, as I absorbed the scene in front of me. They hugged, Chris patting him on the back. Houston said something I couldn't hear. Chris smiled and nodded, and they walked inside together.

I stood rooted to the spot, mystified. *What did I just see?* That wasn't the awkward handshake of a minister coming to comfort a stranger. *Why would he...?* My stomach dropped as, all at once, the cobwebs cleared. They knew each other.

No, worse, my mind whispered. Chris was *friends* with Houston? The butterflies in my stomach fell, dead. My heart, having jumped all over the place in the last half hour, frosted over like glass. I turned away.

I tried to stay calm. *Chris is an adult. He can be friends with whomever he wants*, I reminded myself. *But Chris is my friend.* Shouldn't that count for something? It tore at my heart.

Chris understands what it feels like to have the person you love choose someone else. He knows how it feels to tell your family the wedding is off, all that money down the drain. He's experienced the hurt and the sadness and the anger. He knows how hard it is, how brave you have to be to go on a date after that, to try for love again. He's been through all of it, and he is friends. With. Houston.

The joy from seeing Chris only a moment ago gave way under the sickening weight of betrayal. A few weeks ago, we rode in the car together and talked about all of this. I thought back to everything I'd learned in East Texas and all our conversations up to this point. Maybe the wedding hadn't ended with us riding off into the sunset, but when I woke up this morning, I believed Chris was my friend. I assumed he would choose me. *I guess this is what assuming does,* I realized painfully.

Why does this keep happening? Why do the people who are important to me keep choosing stupid Houston? I wanted to scream. *I can't believe this!* Between seeing Heidi and this new development, it was all too much for one day.

I had patients. I needed to pull myself together to do my job. I took a breath, trying to push through. I looked around at the wall of hospital windows rising up in front of me. Heidi was up there, somewhere on the fourth floor.

Tears threatened again. *No.* There was no way I could stay there.

I walked in and found Cindy. I told her I felt sick, which was true. I distributed my charts to the other nurses, then I walked to the break room to get my bag from my locker.

I walked out the ER doors and headed toward my car. The cold wind cut straight to my bones. As soon as I hit fresh air, the tears flowed again. Halfway down the sidewalk, a hand touched my arm, and I instinctively turned to see who it was.

"Maddie! Hey! I thought I might see you here." It was Chris, a delighted grin creasing his handsome face. His brow furrowed when he noticed my tears. I wiped my eyes with the backs of my hands. "What's wrong?" he asked, concerned.

"I can't talk right now. I don't feel well," I muttered.

"Okay. Can I give you a ride or anything?" He pulled out a packet of tissues from his jacket pocket and held it out to me. I took it and teared up again. His soft smile was so endearing the last time I saw him. Now it just felt like loss.

"No, I need to go." I turned away, but something stopped me. *I might not get another chance.* I turned back to him. "Actually, I need to ask you something first." I looked into his eyes and squared my shoulders. "How long have you been friends with Houston?"

Chris looked back at the hospital and shrugged. "I wouldn't say we're friends."

I scowled. "The semantics game? Really?"

He looked confused, but he explained. "I went into the men's room before the Christmas play, and Houston was in there, crying. He was upset about their baby. They found out something was wrong with the placenta; it's in a bad place or something? Anyway, they don't have a church home yet, since they just moved here, so I gave him my card. It's what I do every time I find a man crying in the bathroom—which happens more often than you'd expect."

I can't believe this.

"So for weeks? The whole weekend at your mom's. The whole time we were sharing about Becca and Houston. All the fun we had, flirting and laughing…" I trailed off, catching my rapidly accelerating breath. "I trusted you, and you were friends with him the whole time?" I asked, accusation sharpening my voice.

He shook his head. "No. We don't hang out or anything. He's new in town, and they need community, so I set him up with some guys who play basketball in the mornings."

"The guys *you* play basketball with in the mornings?" I asked.

He nodded. "I used to. I haven't been able to since I moved in with Chelsea. It's too far. I figured he could take my spot."

It was so *him*. It almost broke me, because only Chris would be that secure, that generous, to give up his place of belonging for someone who was new in town. But I couldn't make myself give him the benefit of the doubt.

"And then I just saw him now. Today," Chris said, pointing his thumb toward the ER.

"Were you planning to tell me?" I asked.

He shook his head. "There's nothing to tell. I'm not supposed to talk about that stuff because of the confidentiality thing. I mean, you get that." He gestured to the hospital building.

I nodded. "I get it. You didn't think it would impact our friendship at all? I mean, why would it matter? I guess bros are gonna bro."

I stepped away from him, ready to walk away. But he moved forward, staying in my space.

"What? No. Maddie, please talk to me," he pleaded.

"I just… You didn't think I might have some reservations, or maybe I would want to avoid a repeat performance of losing *another* friend to Houston Rueland?"

Chris sighed. "First of all, you could never lose me. To him or anyone. I'll say it again, I'm not friends with Houston. I'm friends with *you.* You're important to me, Maddie. And I think you know that, when you're not feeling…however you're feeling right now. But I *am* a minister. My job is ministry. It's complicated sometimes! I'm not supposed to talk about care cases with anyone except for a spouse, and you're not my wife."

I nodded. "Thank you for that reminder. Of course I'm not your wife! You would *never*!"

He stepped back as if I'd slapped him. "Maddie!" Shock and hurt crossed his face. He shook his head. "That was…that was mean! And not true. You know I'm not that guy anymore. I'm sorry you're upset. I never want to hurt you. But this doesn't really seem fair. Can't you see I'm trying to do my job here? I'm trying really hard to balance two things that are very important to me."

I sniffed. "Well, never feeling like that again is important to *me*. Houston Rueland has already cost me one best friend, and now she's in there bleeding, and I—" My voice broke. At the thought of Heidi, panic rose up, choking me, and tears filled my eyes again. I took a breath. "I have to go." I looked away, about to run to my car.

"Maddie, please!" His fingers gently grasped my elbow. Looking up at him, I could feel everything overflowing at once. All my insecurity. Every doubt and fear. Everything I felt afraid to want. I took a breath and tried to speak.

"I—"

Unable to hold back the tears, I covered my face with my hands and sobbed. Chris stepped forward and wrapped his arms around me. I wanted to pull away from him, but he was so steady and warm I couldn't make myself. I leaned in and let him hold me while I cried. Before I knew it, my fingers gripped his shirt, clinging to him. He held me, rubbing my back, smoothing his hand over my hair and down my braid.

He spoke softly near my ear. "It's okay. She's going to be okay, Maddie. She's in the right place, with great care.

She's going to be okay. I wouldn't have left them if she wasn't."

His gentle reassurance broke through, and I finally hiccupped and took a deep breath, calming down. Chris wouldn't leave them alone if things were bad. A hiccup escaped, but I stayed melted against him, resting on his chest. I took another deep breath and breathed with him. It was heavenly, being in his arms, feeling understood and safe. I sighed. *Thank you, God, for Chris Calvert.*

I let myself stay there for a few seconds, savoring the peace. But it didn't last long. As relief settled in, guilt pricked at my conscience. I hadn't fought fair. In fact, I'd said some truly awful things to him. Yet, here he was, being wonderful. Again.

I wanted to wallow in his gentle embrace, but I couldn't outrun the crimson embarrassment biting at me, thinking of how I'd treated him. I pushed in closer, burying my head in Chris's chest. Clinging to him started out as a comfort, but now I wanted to hide.

He rubbed his hand along my arm. "Are you okay?"

I sniffed and stood back from him, putting a little space between us. I wiped my eyes. "I said horrible things to you. I'm sorry."

"You were scared. I understand." He said it so kindly that tears filled my eyes again. I wiped them away, and Chris went on. "Maddie, grief can make you feel like a crazy person. It's really hard, and it would be awful to be blindsided like that. Who wouldn't be upset?"

My breath shuddered.

"Thank you for telling me Heidi is okay," I told him. I wrapped my arms around myself. "When I saw her in the ER, I panicked. Then seeing you with Houston, I just…freaked out even more. I'm sorry I took it out on you."

Chris put his hands in his pockets. "I'm sorry too. I didn't mean to keep something important from you," he said. "I was trying to do my job and keep it separate from my personal life. Working for my church is complicated sometimes. I have to compartmentalize a lot."

I rubbed my arms in the chilly wind. "I can understand that." A black splotch on his shirt caught my attention. "Oh no, I got mascara on you."

Chris shook his head. "It'll wash. Are you okay, for real?"

"Yeah. I'm good now. Are *we* okay?" I asked, gesturing between the two of us as best I could. I shivered in the cold wind.

"Of course! I'm your friend. Nothing could change that." He looked up, distracted by the wind whistling around the corner of the building. A shiver went through him. "Gosh, that wind is freezing. Here, maybe we can try to work up some body heat." He stepped closer to me and pulled at the sides of his jacket, bringing them around me. I wrapped my arms around him and let him tuck the jacket in place. It helped.

I hummed with gratitude as I snuggled closer to his warmth. "How are you always so warm?" I asked, looking up at him. He shrugged and rubbed his hands along my back, warming me.

"I'm a hottie," he joked, and we both laughed. From this close, I could see tiny flecks of gold in his brown eyes. No wonder they sparkled. He was so close, so comforting, and he smelled really nice. I was still shivering, and my breath was shuddery from crying, but a different kind of warmth sparked to life in my chest.

I could feel his breath mingle with mine and how perfectly I fit against him. We grew quiet. Lost in his eyes and that smile, I didn't pause to think it through. I couldn't. It was the most natural thing in the world to lift up and draw closer to him. I tilted my head, closed my eyes, and pressed my lips to…his cheek? I opened my eyes, confused.

"Maddie," Chris spoke softly. Even in my muddled state, I heard it in his voice: he was saying no.

"You're upset and cold. You should get home," he said, looking away. I had wondered, hadn't I? Now it seemed I had my answer. Chris rubbed my arms briskly and stepped away from me. "Do you need a ride?"

It was a very gentle rejection—I had to give him that. But it didn't stop the boiling waterfall of humiliation from pouring right over my head, scalding my skin. Chris was right about one thing: I was upset. *Oh, Lord, take me now*, I begged, ready to die on the spot. But the Lord had a different plan. I remained there, alive, disgraced and trapped on the sidewalk. *Say something!* My embarrassment grew with every second of awkward silence.

The compassion on Chris's face made it worse. I covered my mouth with my hands as I stepped away from him. *What have I done?* He'd been good to me in a moment of need, and I'd...misread things entirely. I may as well have shoved our friendship over a cliff without a parachute.

Disappointment and loss mingled with the humiliation of rejection. *Oh no.* Tears blinded me. Again. I couldn't stay there and cry over him *in front of him!* I took off, running as fast as I could. Chris called my name, but I kept going. He didn't follow, thank goodness.

My lungs screamed for mercy from the cold January air by the time I reached my car. I sat down in the driver's seat, gulping air, and turned on the heater. My thoughts blew every which way in one big storm. *What was I thinking? It was an impulse! I can never look him in the eye again.* I pulled my phone from my purse and sent an emergency text. I needed my girls.

Me: Can y'all come over after work? I have a 911 situation.

CHAPTER 32

When I got home, Kevin was happy to see me. I picked him up and petted him hello. He went berserk, licking the salt from my face. Emma was still at work, so I had the apartment to myself. I grabbed the leash and walked Kevin then took a quick shower and went to bed.

I woke up a little later, when Emma opened the front door. Feeling groggy, I rolled over and found myself nose to nose with Kevin. He flapped his ears and rolled onto his back, his tongue lolling out the side of his mouth. I obliged him with a tummy rub, and his tail wagged furiously. Life was simple with Kevin. His doggy breath blew in my face, and I sighed, the events of the day rolling back over me.

"I wish people were as easy as dogs," I confided. Kevin licked my hand, as if to say, *I'm here for you, champ.* It would be so much easier to lie here and hide forever, but that wasn't reality. I reached over and checked my phone. One text message stood out among the rest:

Chris: I'm sorry. Can we talk about it? Please call me.

I wasn't ready to face that quite yet. I dropped the phone onto the fluffy comforter beside Kevin with a sigh before heaving myself out of bed and trudging down the hall. When I entered the living room, Emma rushed over to me and hugged me.

"What happened?" she asked.

I winced, the embarrassment still sharp. "It's a long story. Chris and I argued. Then I tried to kiss him, and he gave me the dodge."

Emma didn't need words; her face articulated her shock perfectly well.

I pressed my lips together and shrugged. "Your dreams of anything happening between Chris and me are officially dead."

Emma shook her head. "What? No! The others will be here soon, and we'll figure it out. Everything is fixable, Mads!"

I slid down onto the couch, wrapping my arms around one of the colorful throw pillows, and changed the subject. "How was your day?"

Emma sighed, but she allowed the change in topic. "It was good. The first couple of weeks back at school are always a little crazy after the holidays."

That reminded me, I should check in with Chelsea and see how she was doing. Oh man. Chelsea. She probably didn't like it when women made unwanted advances on her brother, so I had likely destroyed more than one friendship today. Great.

"What sounds good for dinner?" I asked. I wondered if we had any chocolate in the house.

Emma didn't hesitate. "Let's order pizza and eat your feelings."

I couldn't help but laugh. "Sounds good to me!"

"I'll order it," she said, picking up her phone.

A few minutes later, I was feeding Kevin when there was a knock on the door. Mia and Anna had arrived.

"Hey, Emma! Where's Maddie? Is this about Chris?"

"I will kill him! *¡Ay, este gringo menso!*" From there, Anna let loose a Spanish torrent I couldn't keep up with. All I could do was smile at her fiery support and love as I walked into the room to hug her.

Kevin bounded into the room ahead of me, looking around for Sarah. She was Kevin's favorite, and the feeling was mutual. Anna picked up Kevin and snuggled him, gleefully trading her Spanish tirade for babbling baby talk.

"Kevin! Who's a good boy? It's just us tonight, buddy. Sarah's on her honeymoon!"

I reached over to hug them both. "Thanks for coming, y'all."

Anna looked me over and shook her head. "Absolutely not. If we have to wallow over Youth Guy Chris, we will wallow in style. I'm getting you real clothes." She set Kevin down and headed toward my room, a woman on a mission.

I looked at my ancient sweatpants and shrugged helplessly. Mia walked over and wrapped her arms around me. I laid my head on her shoulder, and Emma joined in.

"It's going to be okay," Mia said gently. Tears filled my eyes.

"I haven't cried over a boy in a long time. I'm thirty-one years old!" I grumbled. They laughed. A knock sounded at the door, and we turned our heads.

"That'll be the pizza." Emma peeled away from our group hug to answer the door. Mia and I headed to the kitchen. Mia pulled a bottle of wine out of her bag, and I took plates and glasses out of the cabinet. Emma walked in carrying three pizza boxes. The smell of garlic and cheese filled the kitchen, and my stomach clenched. Anna's voice carried from the other side of the apartment, calling me.

"I'll be right back," I said.

Once I'd changed into Anna-approved jeans and a black sweater and my hair was brushed, I went back to the living room. The girls loaded up plates and poured wine in the kitchen. I stepped into the kitchen, next to Emma. She leaned in close, laying her head on my shoulder.

"I don't want to overstep, but I really want you to be sure and eat, okay?" she said quietly. Emma knew me too well.

"Good catch. Thank you." I reached for a plate, grateful for her care.

Eventually, the four of us sat down in the living room together, our plates and glasses in hand. I sat down next to Mia, picked up my pizza, and took a small bite. Anna took a sip of wine and set her glass down.

"Okay, let's hear it."

I sighed and settled in. I told them about seeing Heidi at the hospital. I explained what placenta previa meant and how Heidi would be on bedrest for the next several weeks.

"When I saw her on the gurney, I completely freaked out." My eyes filled all over again, but I blinked the tears away. Then I explained about seeing Chris. "It felt like, *Houston is stealing another person I love.* It isn't true; Chris isn't mine to steal. But all my insecurities sort of erupted. Everything overflowed. I didn't handle it well."

Emma reached out and grasped my hand. "That sounds awful."

I nodded. "It was. But it's no excuse. I acted horribly to Chris," I confessed. "I lashed out. I belittled all the work he's done, and how much he's grown. This tongue, y'all." I shook my head. "I did not hold back, and I should have. I hurt him."

Mia tilted her head, full of compassion. "Maddie, I am not an expert, but I don't think your freak-out was about Chris. It was grief! After seeing Heidi, you lashed out at the safest person in the vicinity. That's Grief 101. It had nothing to do with Chris. He will understand that—probably more than most."

I nodded. "He was really understanding. It was a big argument, but we apologized and made up right way. Then I made things so much worse."

The girls eyed me, curious. The humiliation rushed over me all over again. I closed my eyes and covered my face. "It was cold. We were hugging, and somehow my brain shut down." I took a breath. "I tried to kiss him."

There was a moment of silence, then Anna gestured, prodding me. "And?"

I sighed. "And he rejected me!"

A collective gasp.

"What is the matter with that man?" Anna huffed, indignant.

"That doesn't make any sense! Surely there's some explanation," Mia insisted, baffled.

I shook my head and lowered my hands. "I don't know. We've never kissed before. I don't know what I was thinking. It just happened! It's entirely possible he truly doesn't like me like that."

"That's not it." Mia adamantly shook her head. "Are you okay?"

I nodded. I really wanted to be okay. I still had my pride, after all. "I'm fine, mostly. But I'm so embarrassed." My resolve crumbled, and I started to cry. "And I'm disappointed. I like him so much."

Emma patted my shoulder. "That doesn't sound so bad. Maybe you should talk to him."

I blew my nose on a tissue before I looked at her, horrified. "You might be right. But talking to him feels impossible after a mistake of this magnitude. I don't think I can stand it." I shook my head. "How am I in a relationship with Youth Guy Chris, and *I'm* the immature one?" I asked. They all laughed.

"Sanctification," Anna declared and toasted me with her wine. "It's what makes you so perfect for each other, though!"

Mia nodded, smiling. "Anna is right. And you're not immature; you had a bad moment. Of all people, Chris will understand that. He gets you, and you get him, Maddie. Y'all are a great fit!"

"I agree. You don't need to avoid him. Y'all need to talk and work it out," Emma insisted. I could feel my insides shrivel at the very idea.

Mia reached for my hand. "Maddie, I will tear him limb from limb if you say the word. But is it possible there's more to the story? Maybe he didn't understand what was happening?"

I stared at her. "When I reached up to kiss him? What else would it be? I was right here!" I held up my palm in front of my face. "No, Mia. He definitely understood, and he gave me the dodge." I turned my head, demonstrating the move he'd used to avoid my lips. Everyone winced.

Mia nodded and crossed her arms. "Limb from limb it is, then."

Someone knocked on the door, making us all jump. Then everyone froze. A lead weight formed in my stomach. *No way.* I looked at Emma. She shook her head and held up her hands. I motioned for her to answer the door, but she dug in. No! She pointed at me. You!

Eyes wide, I looked around the room. Who was going to answer the door?

CHAPTER 33

Anna popped up from the couch. My first thought was *thank goodness*, followed quickly by *oh no*. Anna could be pretty spicy when she felt protective.

"Don't punch him if it's him!" I whispered. I picked up a throw pillow and held it in front of my face. I couldn't watch.

Anna opened the door. "Well, hello, Youth Guy Chris! What a surprise!" She sounded terrifyingly enthusiastic.

Chris's voice carried into the apartment. "Hey, Anna."

"What brings you here?" Anna asked pleasantly.

Chris hesitated, probably considering how to get out of the situation alive. "I'd like to talk to Maddie."

"Is that right?" Anna's voice was saccharine.

Chris sighed. "I can just go."

Yes. I released the breath I'd been holding.

"Actually, we were on the way out. Let's go, girls! I'm craving ice cream!" Anna ordered pleasantly.

What? I clutched the pillow for dear life. Why would she say that? I peeked around the pillow and watched my friends exchange looks around the room. Emma stood up from the loveseat and walked toward the door to get her purse, as if ice cream in January made perfect sense. Eyes wide, I peeked around the pillow at Mia.

She leaned toward me with a gentle smile and whispered, "You've got this, friend. I love you!" Then she hurried out of the apartment with the other girls.

The door shut, and the room fell silent. I stayed behind the pillow, trying to breathe. I jumped at the sound of his voice.

"Come on out, Reed. We need to talk."

The cushions shifted as he sat down on the other end of the sofa. Still hiding behind the pillow, I looked down at my outfit. In spite of having just been thrown under the bus, I took a second to thank God for Anna Jones. I wished I'd done something with my hair, but at least I wasn't wearing my hideous sweatpants anymore. I took a deep breath and lowered the pillow. Chris's eyes looked tired, but they sparkled at me, amused.

"You are very cute sometimes." He pulled a throw pillow from behind him and set it onto the cushion next to him before he settled deeper into the couch, his body angled toward me. Wasting no time, Kevin jumped up and laid down in Chris's lap. The traitor. Chris scratched behind Kevin's ears and looked at me.

"I'm sorry about earlier. And I'm sorry I didn't come over sooner. I had meetings the rest of the afternoon, then I tried to wait until you texted me back, but eventually I realized that wasn't going to happen. I decided to drive over and give it a shot, but I can leave if you really aren't ready to talk."

I appreciated him giving me the out; I considered it. He was already here, so we may as well get it over with.

Where to begin? My chin trembled as the embarrassment settled over me again. Honestly. How many tears could possibly be left before severe dehydration set in? I took a deep breath and let it out then risked looking at him. "I'm sorry."

Chris shook his head and shrugged. "It's okay. Happens all the time."

I laughed at his joke and threw the pillow at him. He chuckled as he caught it. His smile faded, his face full of understanding.

"Maddie, you were blindsided by grief. You were upset. You probably didn't even realize what you were doing. I wasn't trying to hurt your feelings; I was trying to protect you."

I sighed and nodded. The sooner this conversation ended, the better. "Thank you. I understand."

Chris waited until I finally lifted my eyes to his. "Are we good?"

I nodded. "Yes."

He read me in an instant, his shoulders falling. "No, we're not. What is it? What can I do?"

I shook my head, unable to look him in the eye. "Nothing! It's fine!"

He sighed. "I had to do the right thing, Maddie. It would have been wrong to kiss you when you were upset, and this conversation would be that much worse if I had."

He was right. The level of humiliation from a pity kiss would have actually killed me. I ran my hand across my face and tucked a stray hair behind my ear.

Before I could say anything, Chris drew a deep breath, tilted his head, and shifted in his seat. Sitting up straight, he looked me in the eye.

"For what it's worth, I would love to kiss you another time."

I blinked. Did I hear him correctly?

"But you…" I sat back, confused. Don't get me wrong, part of me wanted to leap across the cushions and throw myself into his arms. But the surprise of it held me back. I must have missed something.

He nodded. "I know. I'm sorry. I wasn't prepared. We were both emotional, and you were crying about Heidi, and I just… I didn't want you to regret it, or say it was an accident, or it didn't mean anything..." He trailed off. He was silent for a beat. "If I ever get the chance to kiss you, I want it to mean something. Something real." He blushed and turned his baseball cap around nervously.

A glimmer of hope sparkled to life. "Oh. Well. It's nice to know I'm not the only one overthinking the situation."

Chris released a short laugh, his eyes smiling at me. He shook his head, as if to say *you have no idea*. Hope lit up my chest like a lighthouse. It gave me courage to ask for clarification.

"But what does that mean? You said you like being friends with me. I thought it was too late for anything more."

He looked surprised. "When did I say that?"

A boulder settled onto my chest, stealing my breath. *Oh no. Now I've done it.* I sucked in a breath, trying to catch the words and drag them back into my mouth, but the damage was done. Chris looked thoroughly confused for a few seconds, then he stilled. His face pulled taut as his eyebrows lifted toward his hairline. I wanted to run screaming into the night, but I stayed put.

"I can explain," I said in a small voice.

Chris tilted his head, eyebrows still raised. "Okay."

I gulped and looked around the room for a good way to begin. It didn't appear. Would it be better to lie, just this once?

Chris read my mind again. He leveled a look at me. "Tell the truth, Reed. I promise I can handle it."

It was true—he could. It sunk in now, how safe I felt with him. I couldn't imagine talking with anyone else this way. The last few months had changed a lot of things between us, including this.

Even so, fear pushed on my chest. I didn't want to lose him. But what choice did I have? I swallowed my anxiety and took a deep breath. *Here goes nothing.*

"It was an accident," I explained, my voice barely louder than a whisper.

Chris sat quietly, listening. I looked down at the pillow in my lap and cleared my throat.

"At your mom's house, the night after the football game, I woke up and went to get some water. You and Rhonda were sitting out on the porch. I overheard her saying she liked me, and then I couldn't help myself. I promise, I meant to go back to bed after a minute. I didn't want to invade your privacy. But then Chelsea came down the hall, and I had to hide so I wouldn't get caught eavesdropping."

Chris smiled and softly interjected, "The irony."

I ran my hands through my hair and continued my confession.

"After she left, I tried to go back to bed again, but then Sushi came in, so I had to hide some more. I pretty much heard your whole conversation—accidentally. I'm so sorry."

I wrapped my arms around the pillow and buried my face in it, feeling a little sick. Several seconds went by in silence. Finally, I couldn't take it anymore. In a stunning act of bravery, I looked over at him. Now he was the one looking away, his face unreadable. He reached up and squeezed the back of his reddening neck, clearly embarrassed as he mentally flipped through everything they'd discussed. He took off his baseball cap then set it back down on his head.

Regret settled over me like a boulder. I scrubbed my hands over my face.

"It wasn't all on purpose," I told him. "But it was a huge violation of your trust, and I don't blame you if you hate me for it. I would be so angry if someone did that to me. Then I went and made things awkward between us today. It wasn't fair."

He finally made eye contact but still said nothing. He stared at me, processing.

I swallowed. "You were right. I was really emotional earlier, and I'm glad you…stopped it from happening. It was impulsive, and our friendship is not something to be impulsive about. I've been trying really hard to ignore my feelings and just not think about it. You're right. If we ever kiss, it *should* be because it's the real thing. I want that too, and whatever happens, I won't take you for granted again."

He nodded. "Thank you." His voice cracked. He cleared his throat. "So you're saying you want…what, exactly?"

I blanched. "You're going to make me say it *all*?"

"No! I mean…yes? I'm trying to understand," he insisted, his eyes imploring.

I sighed. I'd spent too long trying to quiet my own heart. It wasn't easy, but it felt good, untangling things and seeing what I wanted that much more clearly. I knew what I needed to say next, but there would be no going back. I gathered my courage.

"I'm saying I like you…romantically." Looking him in the eye, I said, "I have had so much fun with you over the last couple of months. I love hanging out with you and how you make me laugh. It's been good, getting to know you better. I see how hard you've worked to grow, to show up and love your people well. You are a really special person. Entirely lovable."

His eyes softened but remained on mine. I held up my hands before he could respond.

"I am saying all this as your friend. I love our friendship. Truly, I'm so grateful for it. If it is best for you for us to just be friends, then I respect that. But if you ever wanted to try to be more with each other, I would really love to have a chance to see how—"

He jumped up from the couch. Startled, I drew a breath, curious to see what he would do. He didn't leave. He reached for my hand and pulled me to stand in front of him. Holding both my hands in his, he looked into my eyes.

"Are you sure?" he asked intently. "I would understand if you weren't, 'cause I've been such an idiot."

I shook my head and smiled. "I'm sure."

He circled his arms around me and hugged me tight. I wound my arms around his waist and held on, burying my face against his neck. I could feel his heart racing against my own. Nothing was official, but whatever happened next, I knew we would be okay. Chris pulled back slightly, and looked down at me.

He brought his hand to my cheek and ran his thumb over my cheek-bone, his fingertips tucking my hair behind my ear.

"I feel the exact same way. You are one of my favorite people in the whole world, and I would love to have a chance to be with you," he said, his voice unwavering.

Every cell in my body expanded, weak with relief. But not for long. Joy flew through me like an arrow headed dead-center to a bullseye. *Finally.*

Chris leaned down, rested his forehead against mine, and closed his eyes. We stood there, savoring the moment. For the second time that day, I raised my chin toward him. His eyes opened. Half-smiling, he murmured my name, then he met me in the middle, his lips pressing to mine in a soft kiss. We lingered there until he pulled back. We smiled at each other, then we kissed again. I tightened my arms around him and held on. I'd waited my whole life for this kiss, and I didn't want it to end. I thought my heart might explode from the joy surging through my veins.

When he eased back, our eyes held. He took a breath and enveloped me in a hug, my name a whisper on his lips. We stood there, quietly holding onto each other. After a little bit, he tilted his mouth over mine again, kissing me slowly but so thoroughly my knees buckled. He caught me, laughing softly, holding me against his firm torso.

"Wow," I murmured.

At the same time, he said, "I really hope that wasn't a prank."

I giggled. "Not a prank for me," I assured him.

"Good, me either. I don't even have a frog in my pocket," he said.

I made a face. "No frogs! Well, I do like frog stickers. Was it you, leaving them around for me from time to time?"

He smiled sheepishly. "It was. I borrowed a page of them from the kids." I rested my hands on his chest.

"Mmm, confessions abound this evening," I joked, looking up at him. I reached up and ran a hand along his cheek, finally giving in to the impulse to feel his stubble.

He ran his thumb across my cheekbone and tucked my hair behind my ear. "One more for the road? I've wanted this for a long time. I just wasn't sure how to ask after so many false starts."

"Me too," I admitted. "It's been a winding road, but I kinda couldn't help myself."

"I know the feeling." He smirked. "I guess it's a good thing you put the moves on me, Reed."

I gasped and leaned away, scandalized. "It was an *accident*!" I insisted.

He laughed, pulling me back to him. I should have known I would fit perfectly in his arms. "Do you think I haven't wanted to put the moves on you?"

That sounded much better. "Like, lately?"

"Absolutely! My brothers have been razzing me like crazy since New Year's."

Smiling, I looked down then back up at him. I shrugged my shoulders. "Well, in that case, maybe it's a good thing I *misinterpreted* a moment and instinctively tried to kiss you."

Chris nodded emphatically. "A *very* good thing."

"Regardless of your brothers, are you sure you want to go for it now? Life has been pretty crazy for both of us," I admitted.

Chris shook his head. "Life is going to keep life-ing. I'd rather do it with you than without you."

The butterflies in my stomach multiplied by the dozens. I nodded. "Me too."

Chris ran his fingers along the hair around my face. "Thank you, Maddie," he murmured.

"Thank *you*," I replied. I lifted my chin, and he met me, kissing me gently.

Someone knocked on the door and slid a key into the lock. Emma. We broke apart, but Chris's hand lingered on mine, wrapping around it with an affectionate squeeze. Emma opened the door slowly, staying behind it.

"Hello? Is everyone decent?" she joked.

We laughed. "Yes!" I called.

Emma came in and bent down to pet Kevin hello. She stood and looked between the two of us. She sighed, relieved. "Thank goodness! I knew you could figure it out!"

Chris squeezed my hand again. We sure had. The rightness of his hand in mine made my whole body feel like a fireworks finale.

Emma put her purse on the hook by the door and grabbed the leash. "Come on, Kevin, let's walk and give these lovebirds a chance for a good night smooch."

I looked away, blushing. "Thank you for walking him," I told her.

"No problem! Make it a good one!" She wiggled her eyebrows at us as she and Kevin headed out the door.

Chris reached for me and pulled me close. "You heard the woman. Better make it a good one."

CHAPTER 34

On Tuesday, I woke up with butterflies throwing a celebration party in my stomach. The whole world seemed sparkly and new. I had the day off and nowhere specific to be, so I relished the slow morning and went to work out before I ran errands. While digging through my wallet at the grocery store check-out, I found some more receipts from the Christmas play costume props. I dropped off the groceries at home then drove over to the church to turn in the receipts.

Maybe I could sneak a peek of my man. I liked the idea of surprising him. Walking up to the church office door, I rang the doorbell. At the last second, I steeled myself for the loud crackle. It wasn't enough.

"Hello?" Ms. Rosemary's voice exploded through the speaker, louder than an airhorn. I jumped back, clutching my chest. How could anyone prepare for such a blast of sound?

"Hi, Ms. Ro—"

"Speak up! I can't hear you!" Ms. Rosemary's scolding echoed throughout the parking lot, startling me again. I looked around, frazzled and self-conscious, in spite of the fact that no one was nearby. I leaned forward and spoke directly into the speaker box.

"Hi, Ms. Rosemary! It's Maddie Reed. I'm here to turn in some receipts from the Christmas play!" I hollered, enunciating every syllable.

"Goodness! You don't have to shout! Come on in, dear," Ms. Rosemary's disembodied voice crackled through, loud enough to be heard from space. I huffed an annoyed breath. *Unbelievable.* When the buzzer sounded, I flung open the door and heaved myself through.

I stopped at the reception desk, fingers curling into the raised wooden counter as I willed my pulse to regulate. Ms. Rosemary stared owlishly up at me through her eyeglasses, the ghost of a mischievous smile on her face. She slid a glance to the glowing screen to her right and pursed her lips, holding back a smile. The screen was angled so I could not see it without craning my neck, but it was clear she'd gotten an eyeful on the camera feed. *Let her have her fun*, I decided, choosing to preserve the singular shred of dignity I had left after that fiasco.

"How can I help you, dear?" Ms. Rosemary tilted her head.

I dug in my purse and held up the wad of receipts. I fixed a pleasant smile on my face. "Hi there! I have receipts from the Christmas play to turn in."

Ms. Rosemary nodded, eyes wide. "Thank you for bringing them in. But I can't take receipts. I might get confused and lose them. You'll have to turn them in to your staff contact from the event."

My face fell. *Is she serious?* I couldn't tell. She certainly didn't seem confused to me. If anything, she seemed *diabolical*. I shook my head, looking helplessly around the empty office. This was supposed to be a quick errand, not a wild goose chase. "Okay. You mean Chris?"

Ms. Rosemary consulted a list on her desk, next to her phone. "Chris…Calvert?"

I nodded. "Yes. The only Chris on staff. Can you let him know I'm here?"

She shook her head. "I'm afraid he's in a meeting, dear. You'll have to wait. It shouldn't be long."

I drew in a breath. "Okay, sure. I can do that. Thank you." I backed away from her desk and sat down to wait in the small seating area. I checked my watch then looked up to find Ms. Rosemary watching me, a calculating look on her face. A feeling of mild alarm prickled across my skin. Did Ms. Rosemary act this strangely with everyone?

"How are you today?" I asked cheerfully.

Before she could answer, the phone rang, so she turned to pick up the handset. She talked quietly for a few minutes and set the phone down again. She craned her neck to look out the window then turned to me. Before she could say anything, someone said my name.

"Maddie! Hey! What brings you here?" Ryan emerged from a hallway. He smiled at me, a knowing smile on his face. Chris must have talked to him. Or maybe Mia. I'd texted the girls last night after Chris left.

I stood and hugged him. "Hey! I'm dropping off some receipts." I held them out for him to see.

Ryan looked at Ms. Rosemary, puzzled. She stared at him blankly then looked away. Shrugging, he reached out a hand. "I guess I can take those for you. Are they from the Christmas play? I'll put them on Chris's desk," he offered. "Chris isn't here. He had to run up to the hospital."

"Oh?" I looked over at Ms. Rosemary. She'd failed to mention Chris wasn't even in the *building*. How long would she have made me wait? Now she sat, utterly absorbed in typing on her computer. Something occurred to me: was *everyone* trying to set me up with Chris this whole time, and I'd been oblivious?

"Thanks, Ryan," I said as I turned to leave. "See you later." I looked over and cheerfully said, "Thank you, Ms. Rosemary!"

Ms. Rosemary looked out the window and huffed, frustrated. "Come back soon, dear!"

I waved and walked out into the mild winter day, shaking my head to clear it from the weirdness of the last ten minutes. I got in my car and drove toward the exit just as Chris's car turned into the parking lot. It seemed Ms. Rosemary would get her way after all. The butterflies had taken a break, but as soon as I saw him, they took flight again. Chris caught sight of me, and his face lit up, which of course drove the butterflies to greater fervor.

He pulled up alongside me, and we rolled down our windows.

"Hi!" I called, feeling suddenly a little shy. I should probably calm down.

"Hey! What are you up to all the way over here?" he asked.

I shrugged. "I'm out running errands. I found some more receipts I needed to turn in from the Christmas play. How's it going?"

He smiled. "Really good. *Now*."

I blushed, extremely happy to hear that. *Gosh. Pull yourself together, woman!*

Chris went on. "I was actually about to text you. Brooke needed to reschedule my appointment for tonight, so I have a free evening. Any chance you do too?"

I thought about it. "Yeah, I think so."

His face lit up. "Great!"

I looked at him expectantly, but he sat there beaming at me.

"Do you want to…" I prompted.

"Yes." He paused, staring at me, then frowned and shook himself. "Sorry. Can I take you to dinner?"

I nodded, holding in my desire to do a cartwheel and scream *yes!*

Chris looked pretty close to cartwheeling himself, but he held it together. "Pick you up at six?"

"Yup, I'll see you then."

He winked at me and rolled up his window. I drove away, holding in my squeal of excitement until I was safely on the road.

CHAPTER 35

That evening at six sharp, Kevin gave a suspicious growl and took off down the hallway from my room. I checked my pink sweater and jeans in the mirror one last time before I walked to the door. Kevin stood at attention, eagerly waiting to see who'd knocked. When I opened the door, Chris looked relaxed and handsome in jeans and a soft green button-down shirt.

"Hi," he said, smiling at me. "You look great!"

"Thanks. You do too," I told him. I was so antsy I could hardly stand still, but I paused. Something was different. It took me a second to see. "No baseball cap? Won't your head get confused?" I joked.

He smiled. "I have one in the car. I wanted to make a good impression for our first date."

I laughed. "Mission accomplished. Come on in. I'll get my purse."

Kevin rested his paws on Chris's knees, stretching up to sniff him.

"Hey, buddy!" Chris bent down and gave Kevin a thorough ear scratch.

"Ready to go?" I asked.

"Wait! I have to take a picture!" Emma called from the kitchen.

I laughed. "That is not necessary."

"It totally is, though!" She sauntered out to the living room, wielding her phone like a proud mom at Homecoming. "Hey, Chris! Okay, smile, you two!"

Chris wrapped his arm around my shoulders and looked at the camera. His smile was so genuinely excited I had to let myself take a moment and memorize the way he looked. His jaw was smooth; he must have shaved again.

Emma's phone camera flashed before I could turn to face her.

Chris looked down at me and gave my shoulders a squeeze. "Ready?"

All I could do was nod. I had no words. I was *so* ready.

Chris took me to Dan & Rusty's, a restaurant with an arcade for adults. We split an order of lettuce wraps and some wings and drank cold beer.

"So what did you do today?" Chris asked.

I wiped my hands on a napkin. "I had a lot of errands to run: store, Pilates, taking those receipts to the church, pet store. How about you?"

"I had meetings and went up to the hospital to see Ms. Alma. She had a hip replacement yesterday," he replied.

"Oh my goodness!" I exclaimed.

He nodded. "She's doing great, of course. Her daughters are taking turns staying with her, and she's got everyone at the hospital in line, doing her bidding." Chris huffed a laugh. "I don't know how she does it."

I shook my head. I certainly didn't either, but it was true. Ms. Alma was a tiny, winsome *force*. Between her and

Ms. Rosemary, they could literally get anyone to do anything.

Chris cleared his throat. "I also stopped in and saw the Ruelands. Heidi is doing well. The baby is good so far. They want to do a C-section in six weeks, if everything stays good."

I sighed and nodded, picking up my beer. I still felt a little embarrassed about my freakout the other day. "Thanks for telling me. I'm glad she's doing well. But I don't want you to feel like you have to keep me updated. It's none of my business."

"I actually have a little update about that: Ryan is going to oversee their pastoral care from now on," Chris said.

I looked at him. "What? That's not necessary. They're comfortable with you!"

He shrugged. "I talked with them, and they're fine with it. To be honest, I'd already decided to shift Houston over to Ryan, even before."

"Did you tell them the reason why?" I asked.

"That you've got the hots for me? Totally," he teased. I threw my napkin at him. He let out a laugh. "Nah. I told them I have a conflict of interest, and Ryan is able to be there for them instead of me. It wasn't a big deal."

I sighed. "I'm sorry."

"It's okay. It was an easy fix. Like I said, I'd already decided to switch them over to Ryan's care list anyway. I can't be unbiased about someone who hurt you, regardless of our relationship status. We're too close. I'm Team Maddie, all the way."

"Thank you," I told him.

"Well, you are way prettier than Houston."

I burst out laughing. "You are a mess."

"You have no idea." He smiled.

I got lost in his eyes for a second. I needed to come up for air. "These are pretty loaded topics for first-date conversation."

He chuckled. "I'm a little rusty. I've been too busy to date at all the last few months."

"Too busy *caring for your family*," I pointed out.

"Maybe now that I finally asked you out, Chelsea will stop extolling my virtues every time she sees you." He smacked his hand over his face. "I appreciate her heart, but it was a bit much."

I smiled. "I like your virtues."

He softened. "I like yours too. But I'm also interested in your vices." He looked slyly over at the games. "If memory serves, you and I are equally competitive."

I laughed and made a wry face. "Probably. I've been told I have big feelings. It wasn't a compliment."

Chris laughed. "Same here. But I'm not scared to go toe to toe with you, Reed." He smiled slyly. "We'll still be friends in the end, I promise."

I lifted an eyebrow, feeling saucy. "You should be a *little* scared. I'm very good at skee-ball."

He laughed aloud. "Bring it on. Let's go!"

We left the table and played every game in the house. We raced against each other, played skee-ball, and shot baskets. I beat him in the basketball shootout. It doesn't matter how. (*Don't listen to him when he says I cheated. To this day, I'm not sure how the ball got hit out of his hands. Personally, I believe the Lord sent an angel, and who am I to question it? God is good all the time.*)

Afterward, we had enough tickets to pick a prize, and there happened to be a small stuffed frog on the shelf. That was a no-brainer.

On the way to my apartment, Chris pointed toward the fluorescent lights of a miniature golf course right off the highway. "Want to keep the competition going? Or is it too cold?"

In spite of how frigid the weather had been two days before, it was a mild night. Typical Texas. I wasn't ready to go home yet. I nodded. "I'm in!"

Spontaneous mini-golf with Chris Calvert was a study in excellence. The man got a hole-in-one *twice*.

"How did you do that?" I asked after the second time, flabbergasted. I expected him to say something silly, like 'Holy practice,' or start in about math and angles.

But he winked at me and said, "I guess I found my good luck charm."

I blew a raspberry at him for being cheesy, but on the inside, my stomach flipped. In the end, he won the game, and I decided to be a good sport. "Congratulations," I told him, holding up my hand for a high five. He swatted my hand then held on and wrapped his fingers through mine as we walked to the car.

"Thanks for going out with me tonight." Chris parked in a space near my apartment a few minutes later, one hand on the wheel, the other still holding mine. The radio played softly.

I'd been on plenty of dates over the years, and it felt wonderful to not be worried about holding myself back on a first date. *Why try to play it cool and mysterious when he already knows me?*

"I had so much fun," I told him, brushing my thumb over his.

Chris looked over at me, his eyes sparkling. It was all I could do to stay in my seat. I wanted to leap across the console and kiss him senseless. I started to lean over to do just that, but my buckled seat belt stopped me with a jolt. I sat back, annoyed, but the seat belt had actually preserved my dignity. Chris brushed a thumb across my hand.

"I'll walk you to the door. A proper first date, to the end." He smiled. A giggle escaped me. *Calm down, woman!*

We walked up the stairs, my hand in his. At my door, he wrapped me in a huge hug and held on. "Thank you for a perfect night," he said softly.

"Thanks for taking me out. I had a great time," I told him, pulling back to bring my hands up to his shoulders and around his neck. I assumed he would finally kiss me, but he squeezed me tight and backed away. He put his hand to my cheek and ran his thumb across my cheekbone. Warmth fluttered through my chest. On the off-chance our mind-reading had kicked back in, I thought, *I like you so much.* I couldn't tell if he received it or not.

"Thank *you*. It was worth the wait. Can I call you tomorrow?" he asked, smiling.

"Yes, of course," I told him.

He nodded and looked away. "Stop looking at me like that, Reed. I want to do this right. I'm not going to kiss you on the first date."

"What? *Why?*" My protest sounded much more petulant than I meant for it to, and he laughed.

"I didn't realize you wanted me to so badly. I'm honored." He lifted a hand to his chest.

Embarrassment heated my cheeks. I was not accustomed to throwing myself at a man for a kiss. I stepped away from him and crossed my arms, indignant. "You don't have to do anything you don't want to do."

He reached out and gently unwound my arms, running his hands down my wrists to clasp my hands between his own. He waited for me to look at him.

"I absolutely want to. I just…" he trailed off. He looked away and back at me. Something shifted in him, and I could see his heart shining in his eyes. "I want to get this right. You're really important to me, Maddie."

I melted all over again. "You're really important to me too."

He winked at me and kissed my knuckles. "Next time, for sure. Good night. I'll see you later."

I nodded, my skin tingling, and took my keys from my purse. I stuck the key in the lock, and he started to walk away. I sighed.

"I'm sorry," I said, turning to him, resigned. He looked back at me, questioning. "I can't seem to help myself," I explained as I stepped over, reached for him, and pulled him to me.

His lips fit against mine perfectly. He made a sound and wrapped his arms around my waist, pulling me closer. My heart overflowed; how could it not? Kissing Chris Calvert was like coming home. It was sweet and fun, safe and tender. When the kiss ended, he wore a goofy smile and a dazed look in his eyes.

He nodded. "You're right. That was better."

I smirked then pressed my lips to his one more time for good measure. "'Night, Calvert."

He rubbed his hands over his face and nodded once. "Good night."

I smiled at him as he ambled away. At the bottom of the stairs, he turned and looked up at me. I blew him a little kiss.

"You're killing me, Reed. Go in the house!" he called, laughing.

I laughed and turned back to the door as the engine in his car turned over.

CHAPTER 36

I walked inside, and Kevin met me at the door. I picked him up and nuzzled him. "That was the best date of my entire life," I told him. He licked my nose and smiled his doggie smile at me.

"Glad to hear it," Emma said from the couch.

"You're up late," I observed.

"I got sucked into this documentary," she explained. "Kevin and I weren't spying, but it sounded like it ended well."

I spun around in a circle and flopped down on the couch. "Oh my gosh, Em, I can't believe this is happening! Eeee!" I squealed into a pillow. "I have *never* liked a guy this much!"

Emma laughed. "I knew it! He's perfect for you, Maddie. Did you see the picture I sent you?"

I shook my head. I hadn't checked my phone all night. I pulled it from my purse and saw I had text messages from Emma and Chelsea.

Chelsea: FINALLY! I hope you have the best date ever!

She sent a row of dancing ladies, alternating with celebration emojis. I laughed, but I was grateful for her encouragement. I sent her a quick response.

Me: Thank you! It was wonderful!

I added a spinning star emoji for good measure then opened the text from Emma and looked at the picture. Chris beamed at the camera, absolutely glowing, and I looked up at him like he was the best thing since sliced bread. It was a fantastic picture.

"See? It's perfect for your wedding!" Emma exclaimed. I laughed. Saying that on our first date seemed a little fast, but I couldn't stop the butterflies zooming around in my stomach. Emma stretched. "Okay, now I have to go to bed."

"Good night," I told her. She walked into her room and closed her door. I needed to walk Kevin then go to bed myself. I had work in the morning.

Before I went to bed, I pulled the stuffed frog out of my purse and set it on my nightstand. *Holy cow, I'm falling in love with Chris Calvert. Lord, what in the world?* I fell asleep thanking God for that man.

—

The following Sunday, after church ended, I stood in the foyer, chatting with my friends. I caught a glimpse of Chris out of the corner of my eye as he made his way through the room, interrupted by different groups of teenagers and adults. He smiled and stopped to chat with each one. He must have felt me looking at him, because his eyes found mine, and his eyes lit up, just for me. I could feel myself glowing at him in return.

Oh my goodness, we are either the cutest thing I've ever seen, or the cheesiest, I thought. Then he winked at me, and I didn't care which it was. I tried to focus on conversations, but my mind followed that dark head as he slowly made his way across the foyer to me. As soon as he moved past one group of people, another stopped him. Finally, after what seemed like five years, he reached me and lightly tickled my arm.

"Hey," he said softly, smiling at me.

I took his hand, and he wrapped his fingers around mine, holding on. I smiled up at him and squeezed his hand, stepping closer to him.

"Well, looky here, Stella, did we miss out on some news?" Pam Martin's voice broke into our little moment. She and Ryan's mom, Stella, had stopped walking to ogle our joined hands. Put on the spot, I blushed and started to pull away, but Chris grinned at me then at them.

"I finally won her over," he said proudly. Then he released me to give them each a hug.

"Well, it certainly took you long enough!" Pam exclaimed with a laugh, hugging him back.

Stella looked at me. "You are the perfect person to keep this sweet man in line, Maddie."

I laughed. "You could say the same thing about him," I told her.

She smiled and hugged me. "I'm happy for you!"

Stella reached out and hugged Chris, then the ladies moved on. John Martin waited for them by the door, visiting with some other men.

Chris turned to me. "I always go to lunch with the youth group kids, but could I see you tonight? Maybe we could go out, have dinner?"

I nodded, suddenly feeling shy. I had a feeling this was the first of many Sundays like this one. Butterflies swooped joyfully through my stomach all over again. "Sure, that sounds good."

"Great!" His eyes sparkled at me until everything else disappeared. Someone cackled loudly from across the foyer, and it brought both of us back to the present. He blinked. "Can I pick you up at six?"

I nodded, blushing. "Perfect."

—

Chris and I continued dating and spending time together whenever we could. We'd often hung out in the same friend group over the years, so we fit easily into each other's lives. I was grateful for that. Dating at church could sometimes feel as if you lived under a microscope, but somehow it wasn't awkward. It was just good.

We were out at a Thai place a few weeks later, talking about all manner of things. I finished telling him a story about work, and Chris shifted in his seat and put his glass down.

"Have you...gone upstairs at all?"

I sighed, understanding what he wasn't saying. "No." I looked down then back at him. "I've thought about it. A couple of times. But I haven't done anything. Technically, I can't, especially during work hours."

"Ryan told me they're planning to have the baby next week if everything continues the way it's been going."

He paused, as if he was unsure about his next words. "Do you feel like talking about it a little bit?"

I took a sip of water and considered it for a second. "Sure," I answered.

He looked at me, his thumb brushing over my knuckles. "Well, since grief is different for everybody, I don't want to overstep, but I wonder if it might help you to do a hospital visit at some point?"

I balked, my eyes widening. "What do you mean?"

He shrugged and took a sip of his beer. "Heidi was your best friend. Losing that would be a huge grief for anyone, maybe more than you even realized at the time. You were genuinely scared for her that day, and I want you to have space to do whatever you need to do." He released me and held up both hands. "I'm not asking you to do anything. But I wonder if it would be helpful. A hospital room is neutral ground. You could check on her, see her for yourself, maybe get some closure?"

I frowned. "That seems kind of weird."

He nodded. "It probably is. And it's fine if you don't want to. My feelings for you will not change either way," he assured me. "I want whatever you want. My point is, if you want to go up there and see her, I'll go with you."

"You would do that?" I asked.

He nodded. "I would. If there is a deeper healing and freedom available for you, I want you to have it. Like I said, I'm Team Maddie, all the way. But it's up to you."

This man. It was so freeing to feel understood and accepted, especially in such a complicated situation. Instead of bursting into tears, I tried to keep it light. "That's very ministerial of you."

He looked down at our hands clasped across the table. "Well, you're very important to me. Obviously, I can't *exactly* relate. That was a huge betrayal. It's not the same, but I don't know how I would feel if it was Trent sitting in the hospital. At this point, I'd probably still pound his stupid face into the ground. But my goal is to be here for *you*. All of my gifts are at your disposal: ministry, prayer, kissing. I could go on, but I won't." He smirked, so fully *Chris* I had to laugh.

"Thank you. I'll think about it," I told him. "Not to extol your virtues too much, but I love how passionate you are about ministry. You're good at it."

He shrugged and squeezed my hand, but he stayed quiet.

"Six months ago, you would have deflected that with a joke," I pointed out.

"I still can if you want," he offered, smiling softly.

—

Later on, at my door, he kissed me goodbye. We held each other until he finally lifted his mouth away from mine and looked down at me.

"Leaving you is *terrible*," he growled. He brought his forehead to mine, and we stood there, soaking up the moment. "Can I call you tomorrow?"

I nodded. "You can call me anytime you want."

"I like the sound of that."

"I'm all yours."

He made a noise of contentment. "I'm yours too."

CHAPTER 37

About a week later, I found myself walking down the fluorescent-lit hallway on the fourth floor of the hospital, holding onto Chris's hand for dear life. We paused outside the post-partum room. I took a breath and looked at him. The vase of pink tulips trembled in my hand, but we'd made it this far.

He nodded, fully confident. "You've got this, Reed." I knocked on the door, and we walked in together, Chris's hand on the small of my back.

Houston rose from the chair he'd been sitting in. Chris had texted him earlier, so he wasn't surprised to see us. Houston shuffled his feet awkwardly and reached over to shake Chris's hand. If he offered me a hand next, I didn't notice. I wasn't there for him. Chris stayed by my side, and we walked over to Heidi, sitting up in the bed. She held the baby—a tiny, healthy little girl. Heidi looked tired but happy, like many mothers the day after their baby was born.

Heidi shifted and angled the baby so we could see her better. "This is Natalie Paige."

I smiled when I saw her wrinkled face. "She looks like Carson," I observed. Heidi nodded, smiling fondly at her baby girl.

Chris congratulated the Ruelands, then squeezed my waist before he shifted his attention. "Houston, is there a place I can get a cup of coffee? Like a waiting room or something?" he asked.

Houston jumped up. "Sure. I can show you."

"Thanks." Chris smiled then winked at me. The men walked out the door, leaving Heidi, the baby, and me. I looked down at the tulips.

"These are for you," I told her.

"Thank you," Heidi said and pointed to a shelf. "You can set them down right over there."

I placed the vase on the shelf. The air grew thick with awkwardness, but I was okay. It felt right to be there.

"Would you like to hold her?" Heidi offered.

I shrugged. "Sure."

I quickly washed my hands then took the swaddled bundle. She stayed asleep, her eyelashes against her baby cheeks. "She's really beautiful," I said. "Natalie Paige is a pretty name."

Heidi lit up all over again, looking at her daughter. "Thank you. I'm really glad you came to visit. It's probably crazy, but I hoped you would."

I shrugged. "I wanted to. I wanted to see for myself that you're okay and meet little Natalie." I held my breath for a second and blew it out slowly. We started talking at the same time.

"I hope–"

"Maddie, I–"

We both stopped. I nodded for her to go ahead.

"It's been really good to see you these last couple months. Thank you for holding my hand in the ER that day. I was freaking out, and you helped me calm down. And I want to say I'm sorry again. For everything."

She started to cry. "I love my husband and my children, but I didn't understand all the ways I would feel the depth of the cost. I've never found another friend like you. You were a more important person in my life than I understood, and I have felt that void and missed you almost every day since. I'm sorry I let you go."

My eyes misted over. I rocked side to side instinctively, holding Natalie. The motion helped me stay grounded. "Thank you for that. I appreciate it. I missed you too. I didn't realize how much until I saw you in the ER, and I got really scared. I don't want anything bad to happen to you." I thought about what to say next. "I'm glad you love your husband and family. That's good. I forgave you all a long time ago. I don't want to carry that around, and I don't want you to either."

I could almost see the weight lift off of her. I was glad I'd come here. But I could hear Mia in my head: *Boundaries!*

"I'm not saying I want to be close friends, but we could get coffee sometime if you want. And..." I trailed off. This felt a little harder to say, but it was the right thing to do. "Dallas Christian is a wonderful church, full of really good people. Please don't let me keep you from going there."

Heidi wiped her eyes with a tissue. "Thank you. That's really kind. We haven't been back very long. We lived in Birmingham for five years for Houston's job. He finally transferred back here a few months ago, so we could be closer to our families. It's been harder than I expected, figuring out a place to belong."

I nodded. I could understand that. Before I could respond, the door opened, and the guys walked in. Chris's eyes met mine, his question clear: *You good?*

I nodded and smiled at him. "Do you want to hold Natalie Paige?"

He nodded. "Sure, if you're willing to share."

I passed her to him. She fussed at the jostling movement, and he expertly rocked and settled her in his arms. My ovaries perked up, laser-focused on Chris Calvert. Seeing Natalie fit perfectly in his arms, my pulse kicked up a notch. By now, I'd given up fighting it and accepted the fact: Chris made my heart (and my ovaries) explode. He always would.

"Are you a baby person, Chris?" Heidi asked, surprised.

"Definitely." He smiled. "I have twelve nieces and nephews. They started arriving when I was eleven, so I've had a lot of practice." He looked at Houston and Heidi. "Thanks for letting us visit. I'd love to pray for y'all before we go."

Houston walked over and took Heidi's hand, and Chris reached out and put his arm around me, cradling little Natalie in the crook of his other arm. My ovaries stayed in party mode, exploding like fireworks, while we all bowed our heads.

"Thank you, God, for this precious little girl. Thank you for protecting her life, and Heidi's life, and everything you have done to show us that you care for us and you are with us today. I pray for sweet Natalie, that you would keep her and protect her. That she would know you, and you would help her to feel how deeply she is loved by you for all her days. I pray you would fill her heart and the hearts of her family with faith, that they would all love you with everything they are. Give Houston and Heidi wisdom and joy as they parent Natalie and Carson and love one another well. Thank you, Father, that you are the giver of life, and that you give us every good and perfect gift in your perfect timing. In Jesus's name, amen."

He looked down at Natalie and smiled. Then he looked over at me. "You ready?"

I nodded, resisting the urge to scream, *In every way*! I still marveled at all that God had done and was doing in my heart and in Chris's. It had only been a few weeks. We hadn't talked specifically about the future yet, but we'd known each other for years, and I could feel it: what we had here was good. I wanted to be with Chris Calvert forever.

He handed the baby back to Heidi, and we said our goodbyes. He took my hand as soon as we stepped out into the hallway.

"Are you okay?" he asked as we headed toward the elevators.

I nodded. "I'm glad we came."

"I'm proud of you for going in there," he said.

I squeezed his hand. "Thank you for coming with me. You helped a lot. Your prayer was really sweet."

"Anytime you want a helpmate, I'm your guy." He winked at me and reached out to press the down button.

His words made my heart skip a beat. *Helpmate?*
As in *Genesis*? As in, *it is not good for the man to be alone?*
I gathered myself.

"Thank you. A helpmate is a good thing to have."
My voice sounded mostly normal. *Calm as a lake.*

"It is." He nodded as we stepped into the empty
elevator. Chris turned his ball cap backward then took me in
his arms as soon as the doors closed. He kissed me like he
was starving, holding me tight. When he lifted his mouth
away from mine, he stayed close, staring into my eyes. We
shared a hundred silent conversations in a single moment,
and I was practically seeing stars.

The elevator dinged, and he released me as the
doors opened. The silent conversations continued as we
walked out of the hospital with my hand in his. He pulled me
closer and bumped my shoulder. I looked up at him.

"I saw how you were looking at me when I held
that baby," he said, wiggling his eyebrows playfully. "You
want to swing by the JP on the way home?"

I laughed. My entire body screamed *yes* at the very
idea, but I could tell he was kidding. Probably. "That would
be a little too impulsive, even for us."

He gave me a sly smile. "That's not a no."

"You are a mess!" I exclaimed through our
laughter. He winked and held the car door while I sat down
in the seat. Once he got in and started the car, he turned to
me.

"Are you hungry? I'm starving."

After lunch, we took Kevin out for a walk. Several blocks away, Chris stopped walking. He turned to me, a serious look on his face.

"Will it freak you out if I tell you how I feel?" he asked, looking into my eyes.

I shook my head. "I don't think so. How do you feel?"

"We need to take our time, be wise. And we will. I'm not going to propose this minute. But I want to be really clear. I'm completely in love with you, Maddie. There's not a doubt in my mind that you are my future." He looked into my eyes, so sure, so solid. Everything in my rib cage did a quadruple flip. He continued, "It's a little funny. After all those years of being so scared, I want everything. Right now. With you."

Wow. His cards were on the table. A volcano of peaceful joy erupted in me. I tried hard to stay in one spot, fighting my instinct to leap into his arms in broad daylight, out here in front of God and everybody, and howl.

He eyed me. "Anything you'd like to say to me?"

I looked up at him and smiled as calmly as I could, though my heart tried to pound right through my rib cage. I laid my palm on his smooth cheek. "Thank you. That's quite a compliment."

He took hold of my hips, anchoring me in front of him. He searched my face, concerned. "Did I freak you out?

I'm sorry. I don't want to rush you. But I need you to know. I'm serious, Maddie. You're it for me."

"Thank you for that," I murmured, looping my hands around his neck. "But I already thought about it, and I'm all in. I love you too."

His face softened. He slumped with relief, and lowered his forehead to mine. "That is very good news," he murmured softly. He wrapped his arms around me and squeezed. "I wasn't going to say all that yet. I planned to hold it in for longer. But I couldn't help myself."

I shrugged, holding onto him too. "I know the feeling." Then I remembered who I was talking to. I leaned back in his arms. "Hang on. That wasn't a prank, was it?"

He laughed. "No. Was it for *you*?"

I shook my head. "Not a prank. I'm in love with you, Chris Calvert. You're my future, and I am very happy about that."

"Praise the Lord." He leaned in and kissed me.

EPILOGUE

Three years later

"Chris Calvert!" I yelled. "You come get this frog this *minute!*"

"Huh?" he answered, sounding genuinely shocked. The old wooden floors creaked as he hurried across the house from the kitchen to our bathroom. It didn't take long. Our little fixer-upper bungalow was small, the perfect size for the two of us. It was exactly halfway between the church and the hospital, and a few blocks from several of our friends. We loved it. Chris stopped in the doorway and looked at me.

"What's wrong?" he asked, confused.

I stood with my hands on my hips. "You heard me. There's a frog in the shower," I told him, pointing. I stepped aside and gestured for him to proceed.

Eyes wide, he shook his head and held up his hands. "Baby, I didn't put a frog in the shower."

I believed him. In our two and a half years of marriage, he'd only put a frog in the shower once, thank God. I told him if he did it again, he would have to sleep on the couch, and so far, the threat had kept frogs outside, where they belonged.

"Are you kidding me?" I asked. "Well, somehow or another, there's one in there! Can you get it please?"

He nodded, still befuddled, and moved past me. He pushed the shower curtain aside and froze. I clasped my hands and held my breath, waiting for his response. He reached out slowly to take hold of the tiny hanger hanging from the shower head. Frogs danced across the newborn-sized sleeper in the cutest print. As soon as I saw it in the store, I knew it was the perfect way to tell him the news. He turned around, holding it in his hands.

"Are you serious?" he asked softly, his eyes glassy with tears of joy. His face lit up with the smile I loved so much.

I nodded, stepping over to him, and laid my hands on his cheeks. "I am. We're going to have a baby!"

"Wow!" He wrapped his arms around me. He picked me up and spun me around, both of us laughing in the tiny confines of the bathroom. He kissed me and set me down, keeping a tight hold around me. "Oh my gosh, this is amazing! I love you, Reed. I love you so much." The look on his face was so joyful it brought tears to my eyes.

I reached up for one more kiss. "I love you too."

—

After dinner that night, we sat in Anna and Gage's living room, surrounded by our friends, chatting and laughing. Sarah and Ben had just returned from their most recent trip to Europe, and Emma and Luke sat on the loveseat. Luke held their infant daughter in one arm. She was fast asleep.

Chris and I considered waiting to tell everyone. It was still early; anything could happen. But he pointed out that if something bad happened, we would tell our friends about it and ask them to pray. Why not tell them now? So we agreed, tonight was the night. We hadn't all been together in a couple of months, so the timing was perfect.

Anna and Gage's two-year-old, Evelyn, played on the floor, bringing "Uncle Chris" (her favorite, in spite of Mia's persistent effort to gain the title) toy after toy. Next to Evelyn, baby Jamie pulled himself up to standing, using Ryan's leg. He took a cautious step and plopped down on his little diapered bottom. He had his daddy's eyes, and he was *precious*. Jamie rubbed his eyes sleepily and crawled over to his mama, lifting his arms. Mia picked him up, and he cuddled right in, rubbing his face on her shoulder.

"Looks like it's time for us to go," Ryan said gently, smiling at his wife and son.

Chris looked up at me. Wrapping his hand over my knee, he cleared his throat. "Before you go, we have a little announcement to make."

Everyone's eyes turned to us, an excited smile lighting every face. I could feel myself practically glowing. "We're having a baby!" I blurted. Saying it aloud was still surreal.

The joy was immediate. Sarah clasped her hands, her smile wide. Anna squealed, "Yes!" Then she burst into tears. So far, during her second pregnancy, everything made Anna cry. Everyone stood up and rushed over, hugging us and celebrating with us. In the middle of the group hug,

Chris wrapped his arms around me. I looked at him and had to laugh when I saw his eyes tearing up *again*. Who knew my goofy, fun-loving husband would be so tender-hearted? I loved it about him.

"I love you so much," he said softly.

I hugged him tight. "I love you too. I'm so happy," I murmured.

He brought his forehead to mine. "Praise the Lord."

I reached up to kiss him. "Amen." *Thank you, Lord.*

Acknowledgements

Writing this book was a lot of fun. Like most things in life, it was a more complicated process than I originally thought it would be. So many people were patient and loving with me, and I am grateful for each and every one.

Joe Dan, I love our life together. You have been supportive, encouraging, and so good to me. Thank you. I know it's been twenty years, but I still marvel that the Lord would see fit to give this crazy redhead such a steady, good, gentle man to love. I might never get over it. You are my favorite, and miraculous gift to me. I love you so much!

My sweet babies, you are so precious to me. I love getting to be your mama and watch you grow. Thank you for supporting me in a new career and in all things. You bring joy to my life, and I am so proud of both of you. To say I am grateful for you is a pathetic understatement. Praise the Lord for these precious gifts! Shine bright! I love you!

Ann, you are the best mANNager, ministry partner, and friend I could ever ask for. Thank you for cheering me on, pointing me in the right direction, and encouraging me at every turn. I love you, and I am grateful for you!

I am not a medical person. Aurlyn Wygle, nurse extraordinaire and future Nurse Practitioner, was so kind to answer all my questions to the finest detail, even to the point of making me want to puke. Aurlyn, you are an actual genius, and more than that, you are a great friend and encourager. I am so grateful for you. Thank you for always being willing to talk things through, answer questions, offer wisdom, and generally encourage me in life. I love you and I am grateful for you!

The sad stories of women resonate throughout the halls of churches and homes, in Bible study groups and classes, at Bunko nights, over coffee and lunch, and everywhere we go. Sweet sister, you are not alone. I am so grateful we have each other, and I am so sorry these struggles exist in this fallen world. Praise God, that He is always with us, and for the gift of Jesus—He will make all things new! In this book specifically, I wanted to handle Maddie's eating disorder with respect, honor, and wisdom. I couldn't have done that without the wonderful kindness of Jen Benich. Thank you so much for answering all my questions, guiding me on the best way to talk about this topic, and for all your feedback and expertise. You are such a gift to me, friend. I love you!

Sweet Mama, thank you for giving me a great example of someone who walked a hard road and stayed faithful. You always remind us, you had a lot of help. We had amazing support; I saw it, and I am so grateful. Writing Sushi, Rhonda, and Chelsea was precious to me, and yet also easy, because I had the best examples. Thank you for passing that gift on in your unflinching support for the three of us through our whole lives. Thank you for staying, for loving us so much and so well, and for all the grace you continue to give as we walk the road of life. You are the best, and I am so glad you are my mama. I love you so much!

Cindy Russo, thank you for your friendship and encouragement all these years. And thank you for helping me with the Spanish for Anna! I love and appreciate you!

Sarah Tudor, my sweet friend and alpha reader! Thank you! You are always so gracious to read my junky first draft and talk with me about it. There is no better cheerleader on the face of this earth. Thank you for your friendship, support, and contagious enthusiasm! I love you!

Lindsay Stadter, my critique partner! You ask the best questions. Thank you so much for reading early versions, helping me bring clarity, even helping me with the blurb! You have been a huge blessing to me in all this, and I am so grateful for you. Thank you x 1,000!

Jenn Lockwood, bless you. Thank you for doing whatever you did to know about editing, especially commas and the courageous use of em dashes, so that I don't have to. Ha! I love working with you—you are always so encouraging and easy to work with. You do great work, and I am so thankful for you!

To my beta readers: You are indispensable. Thank you, thank you, thank you! Martha, Ann, Joe Dan, Jen B., Bethany, Susan, Jen W., Angela, Aurlyn, Kristan, Aimee, Shanna, Jenn L., Brittni B., Lindsay…I hope I am not forgetting anyone! Your feedback and questions were incredibly helpful, and I really appreciate you taking the time. As an Indie author, it is a game-changer to have people interact with your work, help clarify what doesn't work and what does, and share honestly. That is not easy to do! I am so grateful for each of you. You are the best!

Also my ARC team! Brittni H., Tabitha, Faith, Jess, Courtney, Olga, Amy, Nicole, Lindsey, Jeannene, Alicia, Tricia, May, Melissa, Meagan, Abby, Natalie, Kristin, Katie, Dina, Courtney, Lin, Lynsey, and Rachel! Oh my goodness. What a blessing you are! Thank you for taking the time to read, and for all your support. I appreciate you, and I hope you love it!

Discussion Questions

1. Who in your own life do these characters remind you of? Can you relate to any of them yourself?

2. Do you have a favorite Christmas carol? Why is it your favorite?

3. As the author, one of my goals was to take Youth Guy Chris and grow him from someone we love to hate to someone we enjoy. Did you eventually find him enjoyable as a character? What was the turning point for you?

4. Family is a big part of this book. What is your family dynamic like? How has your role in your family grown and changed over the years?

5. Early on, Maddie admits to having written Chris off a long time ago. What do you think about that? Have you experienced some version of writing off, or have you been the one written off?

6. They say dating in one's thirties is a different ball game than earlier seasons in life. Who do you know who is experiencing this right now? How can you offer support and care for them? Maybe start by praying for wisdom for them. It's wild out there.

7. Maddie's eating disorder does not take center stage in this book, but it is a part of her past that shaped a lot of

things for her. How have you seen God redeem difficult seasons of your own life?

8.   It takes courage to ask for help, especially if we struggle with perfection. What is the root of this issue? How has perfection or other idolatry kept you from living life to the fullest? Who benefits from that? How can you turn from this and embrace the freedom God has for you?

9. Maddie often comes back to Philippians 1:6 *"I am sure of this, that he who started a good work in you will carry it on to completion until the day of Christ Jesus."* This verse seems to help her stay grounded. Is there a passage of scripture that helps you do the same? Where do you turn when you need wisdom or encouragement?

10. Chris's discipleship group was an encouragement and source of growth for him. How has community impacted your walk with the Lord? Do you have discipleship practices you share with people in your life? Some examples would be prayer, time in the Word of God, accountability, confession, honoring others, worship, fasting, and service. If you are looking for a resource to help you put these into practice, I recommend the book <u>Lord, Make My Life A Miracle</u>, by Ray Ortlund, Sr.